THE EXPENDABLE SPY

By Jack D. Hunter

THE BLUE MAX
THE EXPENDABLE SPY

THE EXPENDABLE SPY
Jack D. Hunter

E. P. Dutton & Co., Inc.　　　New York　　　1965

To Siegfried, Fritz, Anna-Marie, Frau Münzer,
and the others over there.
And to George, Tim, Don, Tenny, Scotty,
and the others over here.

They were the good guys.

PART 1 PENETRATION

File No. M-25AA7   1 Feb 45

To: Central Registry

Subject: Establishment of New Case

1. Please see attached decoded wireless messages exchanged with me by Bingo, an SI radio operator sending strategic-tactical info from Wiesbaden area, and Peppermint, one of my key agents in Operation *Appleseed* (see your file re same). Also attached is subsidiary correspondence with G-2, SHAEF, and Top Dog, Washington.

2. You will note that in working on their separate and unrelated missions Bingo and Peppermint have unearthed a third matter of potential significance.

3. Therefore, request attached material be copied and used to establish new and separate file under code name *Scab Case*.

Manley Smith

Manley Smith
Maj Inf
Case Officer

48 Attachments

SCAB CASE

Putzi:

On station. Activity here accelerating. Strong elements SS Panzer division supported by horse-drawn supplies, infantry, moved west below Wiesbaden this date, then turned north on Limburg Road. Airstrip being built Map A, Coordinates F27G32.1. Bad fires seen direction Rüsselsheim.

Bingo

ENCODE   27 Dec 44

Bingo:

Advise airstrip size soonest.

Putzi

DECODE   29 Dec 44

Putzi:

Airstrip small, now in use by Storch liaison plane. Possible it serves new corps hqs rumored established Wiesbaden environs. Heavy traffic still heading west toward Rhine. Seem now to be mainly Volksgrenadier units. Talk in town of New Year's Day offensive west side of river as part of Bulge continuation. Running low on funds. Most mine lost in parachute arrival. Can you drop more?

                                        Bingo

ENCODE   29 Dec 44

Bingo:

G-3 requests definite data on corps hqs you suspect. Send soonest. Expect funds Jan 2 0200 hours your time Map A, Coordinates F13G28.7.

                                        Putzi

DECODE   1 Jan 45

Putzi:

Urgent. Cannot meet fund drop you propose. Will advise better time and place. Cannot check corps hqs data. Am ill. Can friendly bring medicine?

                                        Bingo

ENCODE   1 Jan 45

Peppermint:

Take sulfa, aspirin, other drugs you can spare to house Map C, Coordinates M22Q17, soonest. Upstairs occupant is friendly. Your code name for him: Alex. Advise soonest.

                                        Putzi

DECODE   2 Jan 45

Putzi:

   Drugs delivered. Alex running fever but seems improving. Also left
him some funds but he will need more soon.

                                                      Peppermint

ENCODE   2 Jan 45

Bingo:

   Change location immediately. Do not want your recent druggist
to have further knowledge of you.

                                                      Putzi

DECODE   4 Jan 45

Putzi:

   Affirmative. Have new address, Map A, Coordinates L25D7.03. Illness
over.

                                                      Bingo

ENCODE   4 Jan 45

Bingo:

   Send data suspected corps.

                                                      Putzi

                        12

DECODE   5 Jan 45

Putzi:

Will do soonest. May have to curtail messages. New landlord seems suspicious. Rumors are that last fall's recruitment for Bulge and related offensives continues unabated. Factories at Höchst and Mainz now drained of skilled men. Still no apparent major enlistment of women in industry. New Flak battalion arrived from east last night, is setting up Map A, Coordinates 126E6.14. Infantry, company strength, moving to bivouac woods Map A, L30F2.08.

                                           Bingo

ENCODE   5 Jan 45

Peppermint:

Check rumor new corps hqs Wiesbaden vicinity. Airstrip for command plans said to be Map C, M27R1.06. Any word from Spike?

                                           Putzi

ENCODE   5 Jan 45

Bingo:

Keep advised of infantry disposition. Also armored movements.

                                           Putzi

DECODE   6 Jan 45

Putzi:

On station. No report.

Bingo

DECODE   7 Jan 45

Putzi:

No new corps hqs. Airstrip for ambulance planes, officer wounded.
Still await word from Spike.

Peppermint

DECODE   7 Jan 45

Putzi:

Corps hqs suspicion unfounded. Planes bring critical wound cases
to base hospital here. More armor moving direction Mainz. Company
strength only, Panther tanks, all in bad condition. Funds low. Landlord
is pirate.

Bingo

ENCODE   7 Jan 45

Peppermint:

Send cutout to Map C, M26S11.2 with 10,000 RM. Cutout to deliver
funds to man reading Faust on bench by kiosk at 1530 hours 8 Jan.

Putzi

ENCODE   7 Jan 45

Bingo:

Be reading your Faust on bench by kiosk at 1530 hours 8 Jan. Map A, L25D8.19.

                                          Putzi

DECODE   8 Jan 45

Putzi:

Shortages acute here. Small riot by foodstore yesterday. Civilian police very active. Good source says trainload of coal and food caught by our planes Frankfurt-Wiesbaden trunkline. Destroyed. Volksturm units drilling on Casino grounds. Looked to be 2–3 companies. Two tank destroyers toward Limburg at 2145 hours 7 Jan. Appeared to be Pz. Jäg. Tiger with 12.8 cm PJK 44 (1/55 less muzzle brake). Funds received. Thanks.

                                          Bingo

DECODE   8 Jan 45

Putzi:

Funds delivered. Will meet Spike in Berlin 3 March 45.

                                          Peppermint

ENCODE   9 Jan 45

Bingo:

   G-2, G-3 need all possible info re pioneer and demolitions movements toward Rhine.

                                                    Putzi

DECODE   9 Jan 45

Putzi:

   Roger. On station. No report.

                                                    Bingo

ENCODE   9 Jan 45

Peppermint:

   Need all possible info re pioneer and demolitions movements toward
Rhine. See if Spike can help with this.

                                                    Putzi

DECODE   9 Jan 45

Putzi:

   Negative. To contact Spike on mere tactical matters is out of the
question. His position is too delicate to permit our nagging him with
trivialities. Must reemphasize that I myself am supplying tactical info
only as good will gesture.

                                                    Peppermint

DECODE   10 Jan 45

Putzi:

   On station. No report.

                                                Bingo

DECODE   11 Jan 45

Putzi:

   On station. No report.

                                                Bingo

DECODE   12 Jan 45

Putzi:

   On station. No report.

                                                Bingo

ENCODE   12 Jan 45

Bingo:

   You all right? Need pioneer, demolitions data soonest.

                                                Putzi

DECODE   13 Jan 45

Putzi:

   Roger. On station. No report.

                                                    Bingo

ENCODE   13 Jan 45

Bingo:

   What did Groucho say when his lady friend told him it cost her ten
dollars for his ticket to the opera?

                                                    Putzi

DECODE   13 Jan 45

Putzi:

   Ten dollars? For ten dollars I can get a phonograph record of Minnie
the Moocher. For five I can get Minnie.

                                                    Bingo

ENCODE   13 Jan 45

Peppermint:

   Urgent. Send cutout to dwelling Map C, M23S19.21. Ask for Herr
Eduard Zimmermann. Report soonest on Zimmermann's serenity.

                                                    Putzi

DECODE   14 Jan 45

Putzi:

Sent cutout to address M23S19.21. Cutout arrested.

                                    Peppermint

DECODE   14 Jan 45

Putzi:

Most urgent. Am sending under supervision. Custodian is paramilitary personality of very high rank. Repeat: very high. He has extraordinary offer to make you but cannot risk protracted discussion via
my wireless. Requests that responsible US officer be sent to road junction Wehrmacht Map F, Coordinates B18N42.02 on 24 March 1945,
0300 hours Greenwich civil time. Our man to contact occupant of black
Opel sedan parked at junction. Details given then.

                                    Bingo

ENCODE   14 Jan 45

Bingo:

Urgent. Must know identity of your custodian. Also why 24 March,
why Bavaria.

                                    Putzi

DECODE   14 Jan 45

Putzi:

   Negative. Can say only that custodian offers to help us thwart Nazi
plot of great danger to Allied plans for military government of German
national territories as they fall under our control. He says although
our code unbroken by unfriendlies as of 13 Jan 45, break expected
momentarily. Therefore cannot risk details via this medium at this time.
Urge you comply with custodian's proposal. This looks big all the way.

                                                    Bingo

ENCODE   14 Jan 45

Bingo:

   Roger. Wilco.

                                                    Putzi

ENCODE   14 Jan 45

Peppermint:

   Most urgent. Change to Code 4. Most urgent. Change to Code 4.

                                                    Putzi

To: Kingpin, London   14 Jan 45
Memorandum to Officer in Charge

See attached flimsies of messages received by this desk from agent, Code name Bingo, this date, also my answers. Request you follow up as indicated.

Putzi

TO: Putzi   15 Jan 45
FROM: Kingpin

Do you think Bingo message authentic?

Allen

To: Kingpin, London   16 Jan 45
Memorandum to Officer in Charge

Bingo is experienced agent to be trusted in severest difficulties, and all messages from him were in his wireless fist. Must assume that by "under supervision" he meant custodian was present during sendings. Urge that lead be followed up by having man at road junction on date and time given. If Bingo says it's big, it's big.

Putzi

TO: Putzi   17 Jan 45
FROM: Kingpin

   Will follow up as you urge. Our code name for Bingo's custodian:
Scab.

                                                   Allen

DECODE   17 Jan 45

Putzi:

   Urgent. Alex should be removed from your book. Saw him this pm
hanging from telephone pole, Map C, J7K3.08. Sign on chest: "Death
to Spies."

                                                   Peppermint

ENCODE   17 Jan 45

Kingpin:

   Bingo executed.

                                                   Putzi

TOP SECRET

TO: Putzi   17 Jan 45
FROM: Kingpin

   Think Bingo execution has material effect on rendezvous scheduled
with Scab? Opinions please.

                                                   Allen

To: Kingpin, London   **18 Jan 45**
Memorandum to Officer in Charge

Re your query of 17 Jan 45, undersigned sees Bingo execution as having no material effect on Scab rendezvous. Reasons follow:

Estimate of the Situation:

1. Bingo was obviously under surveillance by German security services and more than likely was scheduled for arrest.
2. Surveillance party presumably included Scab, a ranking officer anxious to turncoat.
3. It is assumed that Scab approached Bingo prior to arrest and induced him to send proposal messages. It seems clear that Bingo—and it must be stressed that he was an agent of exceptional capability and dedication—was thoroughly impressed with Scab, his proposal and motives.
4. Scab, if sincere, is concerned over his own security. Thus he has been compelled to take two steps:
   a. execute Bingo to eliminate possibility of Bingo's talking of Scab's intent under subsequent interrogation by those unaware of Scab's intent.
   b. to give us details of his proposal in the safest possible manner at the best possible place and time—and these seem to be at site in Bavaria on 24 March.
5. Scab, if not sincere and making a phony offer through Bingo for reasons impossible to guess at this time, would in any event have had to execute Bingo to lend credibility to his pose as incipient turncoat.
6. Bingo was experienced enough to know his execution was inevitable. If he had sensed a phony, he would have alerted us by means agreed upon prior to his mission.

Recommendations:

1. That a German-speaking US Officer, trained in intelligence work and currently engaged in an auxiliary, noncritical intelligence specialty, be sent to rendezvous. (It is preferable that officer be untainted body.)
2. That the officer be required to take Scab's message and return

at once so proposal can be evaluated and acted upon if necessary.

Conclusions:

If Bingo was right, we have much to gain. If Bingo was wrong, we have only a courier to lose.

Putzi

TOP SECRET

19 Jan 45

To: Supreme Headquarters Allied Expeditionary Forces
   Attn: AC of S, G-2
From: OSS Liaison
   1. See attached communications.
   2. Request assignment of US officer qualified as indicated. Urgent. Note rendezvous date.

Allen

1st Endorsement: Top Dog, Washington, from SHAEF, AC of S, G-2, 19 Jan 45
   1. See attached, also above.
   2. Request card-file search for officer (Military Occupational Specialty: Intelligence, general), preferably German-speaking untainted body from ZI.
   3. When found, assign officer to espionage paradrop training Ft. Benning, Ga., then transfer to Kingpin, London, under cover orders reading assignment to IPW pool this hqs.

For the AC of S, G-2
H. E. Davis
Major, Inf

2nd Endorsement: SHAEF, AC of S, G-2, Attn Maj Davis, from Top Dog, Washington, 29 Jan 45

1. Officer assigned: Peter Klaussen, 1st Lt, ORC, ASN O-545169; MOS Counter Intelligence Corps, special agent; currently on det asmt WD Intelligence Training Center, Camp Ritchie, Md.
2. Officer will proceed Kingpin, London, upon completion special two-week paradrop course, Ft. Benning, Ga.

Simmons

TOP SECRET

TO: Putzi   2 Feb 45
FROM: Kingpin, London

Since *Scab Case* is offshoot of your work on *Appleseed,* you are therefore assigned as case officer in charge of both. Please supervise Klaussen upon his arrival.

Allen

ONE

Funny how you can't hear anything when you spin out the hatch of a plane. Something happens to the ears, they say. Several of the paratroop instructors at Benning had admitted to deafness on their first jumps, but on others (so they claimed, anyhow) they'd been completely at ease and aware of everything, even in night drops. But for me it was like stepping into a vacuum. Except for a multicolored whirling behind my tight-shut eyes, there was an instantaneous paralysis of sensation. More than anything, a huge silence. Only after what seemed to be a prolonged half sleep did the silence end. And then a peculiar shift in the numbness let in the Liberator's diminishing hum, the nervous sighing of wind, the creaking of harness.

I glanced aloft. The canopy was an indigo smudge against the filmy quarter-moon sky. Already I could smell the earth rising from below—thawing snow and pines and steeping manure—and somewhere, far off toward the pale blue wall of the Alps, there was the faint call of a night bird. I had a crazy notion that if I exhaled heavily I could become less buoyant and so hurry the end of this interminable drifting.

The parachute's hissing gained in volume—the echo of ground at hand. I flexed my knees the way they'd taught me and, clutching the risers, prepared to chin myself just before contact to ease the shock. Even so, I hit sooner and harder than I'd expected and had no chance to pivot and roll. A stinging exploded in my boots and sped up my spine to rattle in my teeth. Then I was tumbling, hands to helmet, eyes clamped shut, and lips compressed against the spattering slush and winter-stiffened stubble. Hunched against the jarrings and tearings, I tried to roll onto my back, but it was a

27

very long time before I could get enough purchase on my forearms to accomplish the turn and hit the harness release. I managed it finally and scrabbled downwind to snatch the tail of shroud lines and webbing that slithered along behind the deflating canopy.

I sprawled to the prone and scooped the silk into a bundle. Then I shot a glance across the field to where a fir forest brooded black against the night. Flipping the steel helmet from chest to shoulder and forcing the kit bag and gas mask to the small of my back, I towed the bundle along a chain of dark ground patches that laced through the snow.

When I reached the tree line I paused for breath, but I gave it only a second or two. I broke out the folding shovel and dug into the taffy-like earth behind the bole of a yew, wondering which made more noise—the digging or my heart. Luckily the soggy drifts were still fairly high where the trees were the closest together, and after I'd covered over the jump suit, leather helmet, chute, harness, knife, and shovel, I used a branch to spread a mixture of pine needles and snow over the area so that the coming day's warmth would blend an innocent mulch. Leaning against the tree then, I took inventory: all treacherous jump gear buried; all honest German gear—from the mountain trooper's uniform with green piping to the square Wehrmacht flashlight and carefully forged paybook—in place. I had decided to jump without a rifle or an overcoat, despite the consternation of the supervising dresser at Home Plate. If anyone chanced to question the lack of a coat, I'd simply claim that it had been stolen from me the morning I'd left the sappers' school at Murnau. The missing rifle had been noted in the paybook as having been returned to salvage.

But my job was to avoid any explanations—even the absence of a coat.

At the wood's rim I consulted my compass. While the needle decided where to settle, there was the grinding of a truck in the distance and, straining, I could make out the arc of a road beyond the spur of a hill.

I felt the nudge of panic.

That road shouldn't be to the west, as the compass showed, but to the north.

My pinpoint was to have been the open field nearest the precise crossing of 11 degrees east, 48 degrees north, at a spot on a direct line between Hegenheim and Utting. The Liberator's navigator, obviously impressed by the American brand of English coming from a spook (most spooks were natives of the areas they jumped into and so usually were pretty skimpy on their English), had enthused over what he'd termed ideal drop conditions. With a wedge of moon behind a film of cirrus and the twin lakes of the Ammersee and the Starnbergersee for reference, how could we miss? Being a relatively new hand at dropping spooks into Bavaria, the navigator had offended me with a cliché, saying, "I'll pop you out the door and plumb bob you on the third cabbage in the fourth row from the left."

Maybe so, but no one had figured on a faulty jump signal light that would cost precious seconds in my leap clear of the aircraft. This, coupled with a freshened wind that had shifted to come out of the east, could place me now only God knew where.

But maybe not. Maybe the compass had been damaged in the landing. I shook it, and the needle wobbled, then settled primly on the north indicator. The truck noise faded beyond the ridge, continuing its labors, and its unslackened pitch was a tiny reassurance. If it had been a search patrol, the vehicle's sounds would have died away abruptly while the crew dropped off and fanned out. I tried to forget the truck.

I decided to trust the compass and to head out indicated full east, ignoring the misplaced highway and keeping the Alps to my right. Walking along the tree line, hugging the shadows and holding my hands to the gear to keep it from rattling, I skirted the snows and made for the rise ahead. But my worry began to take bigger bites. The charts had shown no rise here. I should have been on high ground at touchdown. I tried to calm myself by remembering the sloppy drop and the shifty wind and giving myself a silent lecture: charts are fine, except that they don't show the wandering wind or the look of a hill in the night or the sound of a truck beyond a ridge where a highway makes misleading twists through the trees; you're probably off a kilometer or two, maybe, so what's a little hike?

But the dryness wouldn't leave my mouth, and my mind, with

a queer independence of its own, went to another time when I'd been with the Mason brothers and had shagged some apples from an orchard out near Ellicott Creek. The farmer had come at us with rock salt and weird, yipping cries of outrage, and I'd run, panicky, all the way to Colvin Avenue. My mouth had been dry then, too.

A wandering mind is a disease in this business, they told me, and I recognized the Mason brothers as a symptom. I took the only antidote available—the rosary-like recitation of my mission —and tried to keep this mental disciplining free of Smith's superciliously indifferent voice. I didn't like Smith. There was a phoniness there, a suggestion of the poseur. Even the name, Smith, rang out of true. But Smith was my case officer, and I had to take it for granted that if I did what he'd told me to do I'd have a chance to stay alive.

"Your mission is relatively simple, as missions go," Smith had said through his faint sneer. "You are a messenger, nothing more. On Saturday, March 24, 1945, at 0300 hours Greenwich civil, you will arrive at the road junction just outside the Bavarian village of Obermühlhausen. A black Opel sedan will be waiting there, and its occupant will give you a message, presumably oral. After you've understood the message and determined the contact's identity, you will give him our instructions. Then you will leave the car and, as an itinerant German soldier, make your way to the Rhine, where, with help from another agent, you will cross to friendly country. Simple, hm?"

I walked—my eyes wide, my breath shallow—filling in the chinks:

I, Peter Klaussen, first lieutenant, ORC, US Bigod Army, Serial Number 0-545169, am now and hopefully not forever Ludwig Schaue, former machine-gunner of the 96th Mountain Regiment. I am en route from the sappers' school at Murnau in the Allgäu to Karlsruhe, where I'll join the Pioneer pool charged with the removal of Rhineland bridges. My paybook shows a history of Scandinavian duty, a hitch on the Eastern Front, and the proper posting to the 96th. My demolitions assignment (validated by a gorgeous forgery of the Murnau commandant's signature), my travel orders, and my ration tickets are sufficient to cover me to

Karlsruhe. As for travel orders, I'm carrying a set of alternates to be used only if emergency makes me break trail. Once I've left the Opel I will follow the road northwest to Hegenheim and on to Landsberg, where there's a Red Cross canteen near the Bayer Tor, a high gate tower. I'll go to the latrine there. The toilets have doors, even in the enlisted men's section, so I can shut myself off as I mix sympathetic ink—seven parts water to one part urine. With a toothpick dipped in the solution I'll transcribe the contact's identity and the gist of his message on the back of the envelope in which I carry my papers. From there I go to the roadside crucifix, coordinates M25F17, Special Map A. While seated beside the road, resting and eating my bread and cheese, I'll wrap the envelope in the waxpaper cover and slide it into the knothole in the north side of the crucifix's base so that rain can't get at it.

(Smith's smirk again: "This, you see, is to cover us in the event you are, ah, canceled before you return to our lines. We'll pick up the envelope when the territory's overrun, then heat it with a flatiron to see what you've written. The message may be a long time getting to us, but there's no sense in our losing it altogether, is there? Mm?")

After I've stashed the envelope I head straight west to Buchloe and on to Memmingen. At Memmingen I turn almost due north on the main highway that runs beside the railroad all the way into Ulm. From Ulm I parallel the Autobahn to Stuttgart. There I go to Bopserstrasse 15, where I tell the woman with the eye patch that I bring word of her son, Tomas, a fellow student at Murnau. She'll take me to a contact who will, in turn, show me how to cross the Rhine at Karlsruhe. Once across, I surrender myself to the nearest American tactical commander and ask him to relay my code name, Mairzy Doats, to Home Plate. I wait until you, Smith, arrange my release from the PW cage. Then you debrief me.

(Smith: "You have a delightful voice, Herr Schaue. You've missed your calling. You should be one of those disk jockeys on the Armed Forces Network. Now let's hear your instructions to Scab, our man of the Opel. What will you tell him? Hm?")

I tell him this: As a messenger, I've been given three days to return from Obermühlhausen to the U.S. forces along the Rhine's west bank. Allowing two days more for my debriefing and a command decision, Scab is to tune in the BBC at 2300 hours, Greenwich civil, on March 29 and 30. At that time each of those nights the announcer will signal our approval of Scab's proposal by saying, "Schnitzel is good." On April 1, at exactly 0200 hours Greenwich civil, he is to be on station on the Holy Hill of the Andechs, three miles south of Herrsching on the Ammersee. There's a Benedictine monastery there—elevation 2,335. At that time he will hear a plane approaching from the northeast. The plane will fire three machine-gun bursts into the steamboat landing at Herrsching as if casually strafing on the way home. As this plane passes over the Andechs, Scab will confirm receipt of the BBC message by showing three Z's with a hooded flashlight.

(Smith again: "Ah, but what if you, the messenger, fail to return to hearth and home? What then, Herr Schaue? What will Scab do then?")

I am a messenger only, and I'll not trade speculations with Scab. If he hears no confirmation on the BBC, all signals are off.

("You mean you won't tell him of the message in the crucifix?")

I tell Scab nothing. He hears no BBC, he has no deal.

("That's an unkind way to treat a high-horsepower Nazi, isn't it? After all, he's taking quite a risk—offering to collaborate. Shouldn't he have some sort of encouragement?")

Screw his encouragement. No BBC, no deal.

Involuntarily, I remembered Smith leaning against the wood stove, looking across the desk at me out of pale eyes and smiling his dusty smile at my aimless arguments.

"If OSS knows so damned much," I could hear myself grumbling, "why don't they handle the job? Why a CIC man?"

Smith had shrugged—Pontius Pilate calling for the bowl. "The OSS *is* handling the job, Herr Schaue. I'm in the OSS. You are now in the OSS. You and I are handling the job."

"But why an American officer? This mission is nothing but an exchange of messages, and any Kraut turncoat from any PW cage could be used as a messenger boy."

"Scab has specified that he be contacted by what he terms a 'responsible American officer.' You are, a card-file search shows us, a reasonably responsible American officer. You speak faultless

German. You are sound of wind and limb. But, jolly of jollies, you are also an untainted body. You have never been used on a mission before, so there's little likelihood that the Opposition"—the capital could be heard—"has attached any OSS secret intelligence significance to your transfer to European duty."

"Well, just who the hell is this Scab creep, anyhow?"

"I wouldn't tell you even if I knew. Your parachute might drop you into a Gestapo class reunion, and they'd make you guest speaker. Sufficient to say that Scab, an as-yet-unidentified participant in a Kraut operation of great danger to Allied political plans for postwar Germany, is amenable to subversion. Less elegantly put, he's offered to turn stoolie. Since we've learned this from an unimpeachable source, we can't fluff it off. That's where you come in. Find out who Scab is, what kind of plot he's in on, and what he proposes to help us do about it. Then sneak back to whisper in my nobly shaped ear."

I cleared the rise and descended through a grove of ghostly birches into the gloom of another fir forest when I saw the trail—a pale wash of clay winding off through a saddle in the hills. I tapped my compass and took another reading and had to work hard to stifle a shriek. The trail ran roughly southeast, while the charts had shown it to course almost due south, then a hair to the southwest. I gave myself another lecture: it's the night, and trails wind and twist; the path's going generally in the direction you've expected, so follow it. And take it easy, Buster. If it is the trail—and it more than likely is—you've got a whole hour and four minutes to cover no more than four kilometers, or some two to three miles.

Huddling against the chill, I took off down the lane. My greatest risk right now, I knew, lay in the chance that some air-raid warden or insomniac forester might catch me on this path. If, as my papers read, I were headed for Karlsruhe, it would be tough to explain why I was moving in the opposite direction on a trail that no sane man would consider with an improved highway only some two kilometers off to the right. But to have gone directly to the road would have been riskier. The enemy knew that Ober-bayern was becoming the increasingly favored drop zone now that the Rhine had been breached at Remagen and the war was due to collapse southward. So when a solitary plane dawdled through the Bavarian skies these nights, soldiers, old men, women, children, and dogs automatically peered aloft for the drift of a parachute. To have walked directly to the road and headed off on the long, wrong way to Obermühlhausen would more than possibly have placed me in the hands of patrollers. This way, if the lane was unpatrolled, I had only to walk to Scab, who, no doubt, had long since selected the rendezvous site for its safety. But I was plenty nervous, and more than once I froze, evaluating a shadow or interpreting a sound. There was even one time, when a small animal skittered off somewhere to the left, I felt for the Walther pistol snuggled under my tunic.

My tongue was tacky.

Again the trail led up a rise, the knee of a hill this time, and across the small dale another hill lay cold and still in the faint moonlight. Then I was easing downward once more and there, beside a highway running east and west, the roofs of a hamlet showed surrealistic slabs to the sky. I sought out the other road, which should have entered the village from the south.

There was another road, all right. But it came in from the north, directly over my left shoulder.

Panic surged again, insistent now, and under the mittens I could feel the icy slick of sweat.

Whatever this town was it wasn't Obermühlhausen.

I moved off down the lane, not too quickly, and drifted sideways into the shadow of an uneasy oak. Closing my eyes for a moment I tried to reconstruct the charts. What other town? What other hamlet had trails running down from the northwest, a road running east and west, another arcing in from the north? Which place, for Christ's sake, could this be?

Thaining?

Could it be Thaining?

Of course.

I was at Thaining—about three kilometers too far west.

I'd have to take the main road now. I'd have to skirt the village, cross the ankle of the branching north road, cut through the fields and trees to the east-west road, then strike out east by northeast to Obermühlhausen. Three kilometers in the wrong direction on an open road. I couldn't be coy now, since I had no way of knowing how long the Opel would wait. Three o'clock, Smith had said; not three to three-thirty, not threeish. Three o'clock. I held my watch to the moon and saw how close it would be.

I moved away from the tree and had just regained the path when, involuntarily, I sucked in my breath.

Somewhere—close by—a dog had growled.

Only once.

But, unmistakably, a dog had growled.

My hand clawed for the Walther. But then three figures, silhouetted against the soft gleam of rooftops, arose from behind a clump of bushes. The moonlight glinted dully on the sheen of what could be nothing but a double-barreled shotgun.

"Good morning," a voice said triumphantly. "Welcome to beautiful Bavaria, Herr Spy."

TWO

"Spy? I'm afraid I don't understand. I'm Ludwig Schaue, a trooper of the 96th Mountaineers in the Allgäu, now en route to a demolitions assignment in Karlsruhe. I—"

"Stand in the middle of the road. And put your hands on your head."

I did what the man said to do, carefully, the way he'd want it. I died a little when hands patted over me, paused, then sought out and seized the Walther. I felt one of the dogs snuffle at my legs where the trousers furled into the jackboots. Looking down, I had a mad impulse to laugh. What had my father said? When a dog wags his tail at a man you've found a man you can trust?

"Karlsruhe?" another voice asked in an easy Bavarian drawl. "Don't you know Karlsruhe is in the other direction?"

"I was—"

"Let's save the questions until we get him where we can see him," the nasty voice broke in.

"As you wish." I could hear the shrug in the drawl.

"Now, Herr Spy, keep your hands where they are and move down the lane toward that house that stands apart from the others. Gunter, you take the lead and we'll follow with the dogs."

The drawler, whose face was shadowed by a Tyrolean hat, shrugged a shrug I could see this time and turned toward the village. At a prod from the fowling piece, I followed, stiff-legged and stumbling, and I found I had unaccountably become hyperaware of sounds and smells and sights—as if this moment had endowed me with a special perception. The high haze dimming the slice of moon; the astringency in the air that announced the dawn; the creaking of the trees, trembling naked in the cold; the crunching of pebbles underfoot; the panting of the hounds; the ancient house, its shutters and bargeboards showing the faded scrolls of once-gay designs, its window boxes empty and stark— all these came through with a special clarity. As we waited at the darkened door for an answer to the drawler's soft tap, I wondered: Is fear a kind of dimension or something?

The door grated open, and the man in the Tyrolean hat muttered something to someone in the black vestibule. A woman's voice sounded frightened agreement; then, at a sign from the man, I went in, followed closely by the others and their dogs. A curtain parted, and there was the gleam of a lamp and the red of a banked fire showing through the smoked glass of a tiled corner stove. I caught a glimpse of an old woman hurrying off through an arch and into the gloom beyond.

"Stand there. Against the wall," the nasty-voiced one ordered. "And face me."

I went to the wall, stopped under a neatly hung trio of deer antlers, then turned, blinking. "May I lower my hands? My arms ache."

"Pity," the man with the gun sneered. "Your neck would ache even more right now if I could have my way about it. Hold your hands right where they are. Gunter, search him again, and bring his papers here."

The three were standing at the far side of a long family table, their backs to the stove. They clustered around the gun, and, with a nutty kind of irrelevance, I decided that their highlights and shadows suggested a Rembrandt. All three men had seen more than sixty Christmases, but the one with the gun was wiry and still well set up, and his eyes were mean. On his left was an Andersen type, round and apple-cheeked and fur-capped, while the other, the man with the hat, was squat and mustached, and gazed calmly through old-fashioned spectacles. This one came around the table in an easy stroll, a hint of a smile deepening the sun creases at the corners of his eyes.

"I don't want to spoil your fun, Karl," he said, "but this lad hardly looks like a spy to me. He has a nice face. And the hounds like him."

"You're an old fool, Gunter," the one called Karl rapped. "What did you expect a spy to look like? Satan in evening clothes? Now search him."

There was fire forming in my shoulders and a trickle of sweat sneaked along my spine, but I felt a vague hope. These men were mere farmers; their wind-burned faces and beat-up hands told me as much. And with only one gun—

The man called Gunter stood before me and again patted my chest and hips, stooping finally to probe at the folds of my trousers. Rising with a quiet sigh, he felt in my tunic, found the paybook and travel orders, and placed them in the side pocket of his worn woodsman's jacket. On what seemed to be impulse he opened the lid of the gas-mask canister and peered in. Then he poked at the kit bag, removed the chunk of bread and wedge of cheese in their waxpaper wrapping, sighed again, and returned the lot to its place atop the cache containing the tiny folder of false stamps and the alternate travel orders.

This was another little relief.

As a mountain trooper I still had a slim chance. As a mountain trooper with two sets of conflicting orders and check-off stamps dated three days ahead, I'd be done. I had to keep these farmers from searching further. What had the texts said—those brown-faced manuals that formed the spine of the CIC school in Chicago? What was it? When boxed in, take the offensive?

"If you don't let me drop my hands, you stupid old bastard," I

37

said, trying to look angry, "you'll have to explain how it was you let an otherwise healthy soldier die of gangrene of the arms."

The hard-eyed one waited until Gunter had placed my things on the table. Then he said, peevishly: "All right. Put them down. But place your palms against the wall, out where I can see your fingers spread."

The discomfort was really something, but as blood renewed its acquaintance with my arms I knew I had made my first step into the offensive. I felt my fright shift into a kind of excitement.

"Hold the gun on him while I look at all this, Heinrich."

The red-cheeked man took the piece gingerly. He was as nervous as a cat, and this, too, was an infinitesimal encouragement. My heart pumped loud enough to be heard in Paris. The sweat between my hands and the plaster wall was ice cold. My cheeks were hot.

The sharp-faced one spread out the documents and began to read, his features taking on that smug expression a German assumes when he considers a formal paper, be it a call to the colors or a laundry ticket. The only sounds in the room came from the guttering stove and the panting hounds curled before it.

After a time the man called Karl snorted. "I can't make head nor tail of all this military mumbo-jumbo." He glanced at the Tyrolean hat. "Gunter, go down and wake up Siegfried. Have him telephone the Hipo office at Diessen and ask them to send somebody over here. Somebody from the Wehrmacht or something who knows how to translate these hen-scratchings."

The fat one with the gun said, "There've been a lot of patrols through here tonight. Perhaps—"

"We haven't the time to go poking about the hills for those nuts. The police at Diessen will know what to do. Meanwhile, we can just sit here and keep our eyes on this Yankee gangster."

"Well, I don't know," the round man argued. "If this fellow isn't a Yankee gangster we could end up looking very foolish."

Karl sneered. "What else could he be? We see a flying machine in the night. We see a parachute leave the flying machine. An hour later this soldier comes tiptoeing down a back country trail at a time of morning any self-respecting soldier would be begging rides on the highway or tossing away in a feather bed with some grunting, damp-crotched farm wench. He's a spy, I tell you.

Now assemble all that suet of yours and make for Siegfried's."

"He's right, though," the one called Gunter put in. "We could look very foolish."

"You be quiet. Honestly, a man would think you two were apologizing for this cowardly sneak."

"Let's take another look at his papers."

"You don't know any more about those things than I do, goddamn it!"

"I know one thing, though: I certainly don't want the rest of the village pointing me out as one of the great spy-catchers after the police tell us this youngster is actually one of our war heroes. No, sir, not I."

Karl opened his mouth to answer, but there was the sound of engines from the village and somewhere a dog barked. The hounds by the stove raised their heads, ears cocked with curiosity. A motorcycle pounded up the cobbles, tearing the dawn with its flatulence, and there was the whine of a decelerating truck. I heard the squeal of brakes, a slamming of doors, and the crash of a tailgate. Before I could comprehend this as the decisive catastrophe it was, the vestibule was filled with men in Wehrmacht gray. One of the dogs growled testily. The soldiers knotted beneath the curtain, blinking into the room, moving aside when a large man wearing the pips of an Unteroffizier came in with self-important jabs of his elbows.

"All right, now," the noncom said irritably, "it's late, or early, or whatever, and I've been up the whole frigging night. I'm cold and hungry and in no mood for any crap. The observation tower on the Piessenberg Hill says a parachute may have come down north of here. The Wachtmeister at the corner says there's been some bustle around this house. Now tell me somebody, are the two events in any way related?" He squinted at me, and I attempted a grin that must have looked like a gas-pain leer. "Well, who are you, trooper? And why are you standing there like that?"

Karl, in the manner of an actor who senses he's being upstaged, snorted. "Trooper? This *trooper* is a Yankee spy. We saw his parachute." He paused, glowering at his pals for support. "Didn't we?"

The Unteroffizier paced across the room and stood before me, hands behind his back, rocking on his heels in pompous speculation. As he seemed about to make another speech, the curtain stirred and two men in trench coats and fedoras pushed through the cluster of uniforms. The noncom turned a fawning smile at them. Then he intoned like a housewife passing along privileged information, "These gentlemen are from the Gestapo."

Again I felt the weird levity disaster can generate. Here, poised at the door, casually surveying the bucolic kitchen as if they were real-estate men setting a price, were representatives of the Gestapo. And yet, faced with this enormity, I wanted to laugh. The thought: *Jesus. Trench coats and fedoras. Just like in the spy thrillers.*

The shorter of the two cocked his head toward me and asked with a kind of hoarse softness, "Who's he?"

The Unteroffizier started to say something, but Karl cut him off self-righteously: "As near as we can make out, he's a mountain trooper who calls himself Schaue. Ludwig Schaue. But he's a Yankee spy. We saw his parachute."

There was a flicker of interest in the short man's ice-blue eyes. With the vaguest of nods he sent the taller one into action. Swift, expert hands ran over me.

"Here—" the man said finally. With no change of expression he handed the alternate orders and stamps to his friend.

Karl puffed importantly, "All his other stuff is here on the table. We took it from him."

Ignoring him, the short one murmured, "Put the cuffs on."

I felt myself spun around, and there was the clasp of metal at my wrists behind my back. In the numbness I could hear a cuckoo clock clack open and sound the hour somewhere in the depths of the house. Moving on its own now, my mind converted the musical hoots: 3:00 A.M., Greenwich.

I was very depressed.

The shorter man went to the table, scooped my things into a pile, thumped them against the oak like a dealer readying a deck, then placed them in his trench-coat pocket. He drew a flat case from a breast pocket, flicked it open, and selected a cigarette. Regarding the farmers thoughtfully, he produced a tubular lighter, snapped it aflame and drew deeply, so that the cigarette's end glowed brightly and made small cracklings in the silence.

Then he said through a mat of smoke, "All right, Herr Schaue, you can go to the car now."

As I straightened and made for the door I heard the drawl. "Go with God, trooper," it said.

I paused, considered the little man in the Tyrolean hat and, moved somehow, said, "Thank you."

There was a rap on my shoulder. "Come on. Get going."

Day was already a rosiness over the hills, and below the village, where a patch of mist hung motionless over the meadows, there was the tinkling of a cow bell. The air was sharp and clean with the bittersweet of ancient manure and hay. I nearly stumbled when a hand pushed me into the car's back seat, but I caught myself and sank into the far corner. The short one took his place beside the driver's seat, where the other one got busy with the starter. The Unteroffizier came up to the car, his hobnails grating on the paving stones. "Well now. All packed in?"

"Yes," the short one said. "Thanks for your help."

"Glad to do it. Got ourselves a spy, eh?"

"We'll see."

"Off to Garmisch? I have to make a report, you know."

"Just tell the district security office that a suspect has been picked up. And get some sleep. You look fagged."

Self-pity fed by this little human touch from a Gestapo man, the large noncom pursed his lips and phewed. "I'm certainly that, all right. Well, nice working with you."

"You did a good job."

"Thanks. Any time at all." Collecting himself, he bawled over the car roof: "Abteilung! Ho! Assemble at the truck. Come on, you lard-asses—back to the truck!"

The short man said, "Headquarters, Heinz."

The car heaved into motion, its tires making a drubbing sound on the cobbles, its motor whining to be in a higher gear. As we drove off my eyes registered Gunter, who stood, shrunken somehow, in the doorway of the old house.

Beyond the village the highway wound about considerably, and I closed my eyes against the motion and the heat of fatigue.

"The moon's beautiful in winter, isn't it?" the hoarse voice said through a yawn.

Strange, went the maudlin thought, how kindness can be

41

found anywhere. The old man. He had been trying to make something right for himself in his own special way. An enemy of his country at hand, and he had wished the enemy God's aid.

"I said the moon is beautiful in winter."

Each man has his own story of private guilts and unhappy secrets, his own ledger of dismal inadequacies. What could a man like Gunter have been carrying in his heart that would enable him to comfort a spy?

"Yes," I heard myself saying far away, "but one man's beauty is another's despair."

My eyes snapped open. Insanely, the hoarse-voiced Gestapo man and I had exchanged a once-vital password.

The short man was turned in his seat and smiling thinly.

"What kind of car is this?" I croaked.

"It's an Opel," the man said. "And it's quite black."

THREE

Where had it been said?

Hamlet?

For this relief, much thanks; 'tis bitter cold, and I am sick at heart. . . .

Staring into that face, with its strange pale eyes, the slightly off-center nose, the seams at the mouth, the faint sparkle of gray stubble at the jawline—all of it magnifying glass clear—I heard the ancient lines echoing in some minute cell of recollection. Once, in a somber Center County afternoon when swirling leaves had rustled at the casements of the Sparks Building, I'd peevishly accused a frosty economics professor of jamming my mind with useless trivia. The fellow—I'd long since forgotten his name—had flared at my stupidity, snapping that in the human mind there is no such thing, that any jot of information once received can have its ultimate worth; that however seemingly unrelated to the press of any given moment, a nugget of thought—perhaps in itself the quintessence of some philosopher's lifetime of introspection—could emerge, dramatically auspicious, to play a significant role in the life of its current host. Who in hell could be so smug as to predetermine the value of a fact, of a slice of human experience—be it ever so modest as present coin?

Now, confronting reprieve, my memory had snagged a vagrant line of Shakespeare for the meaning of reprieve.

"You're my contact, then?"

"Yes. My name's Klottner."

"You had me worried," I said, still worried.

"No more than you had us for a while there, my friend. We thought we'd lost you."

"I had a bad landing."

"Yes. We saw your descent through the night glasses. When the soldiers began racing one another for the village, we knew somebody else had spotted you, too. So we left the rendezvous to tag along."

I eyed him very carefully. "Pretty nervy: bursting in, posing as Gestapo men."

The man showed that thin smile again. "Not so nervy. Because, you see, we are Gestapo men."

"Oh?" I hesitated, trying to think about this. Then I asked, "Where does this leave me?"

"Plenty of time for that. Turn around and I'll remove the cuffs."

I hunched over, face to knees, and heard the clack of a key and felt the manacles fall away, jingling. My heart was booming again and my mouth felt like cardboard. The man handed a flask over the back of his seat, and the bite of brandy was in the air. "You probably need this."

The brandy was icy, but once down, it felt great.

"You have my cigarettes," I said.

"Oh. Sorry. Here."

Noting with abstract satisfaction that my hand did not show the shakiness inside me, I selected a Zephyr from the man's flat case and winked at him over his lighter's flame. "My brand, I see."

The Gestapo man's eyes did not respond to the mild joke. "When you see your intelligence people again, tell them not to issue cigarettes of any description to their agents. On drops like this, at any rate. Cigarettes are becoming as scarce as intact hymens in Germany these days. A soldier carrying a full pack of even Wehrmacht-issue cigarettes is automatically suspect, since anyone in his right mind would split up the pack. Like a few bills in a pocket and the real cash in a money belt, so to speak. Tell your OSS that today's logic is tomorrow's insanity."

"I hope I'll get the chance."

"I do, too," Klottner said noncommitally.

There was a pause as we all watched the road ahead. Finally I asked, "Where to?"

"You'll see."

I felt my anxiety alloy with annoyance. "Look," I said (God, if I could only stop shaking!), "I was told to meet somebody at Obermühlhausen, take his message, give him some instructions, then get the hell back."

"That's not the way we see it. Your people got an invitation to send a man to Obermühlhausen; that's all."

I leaned forward. "I'm on a time limit. Also a well-planned itinerary. I can't go dawdling around Bavaria on a motor tour."

The cod-like eyes turned to regard me again.

"It seems obvious," Klottner said, "that you really have no choice, Herr Schaue. You wouldn't get from one kilometer stone to another now that our busybody Unteroffizier friend is reporting your name and description to the district security office."

"I have alternate travel orders."

"Correction: I have your alternate travel orders. But even if I were to return them to you they'd be made out to the same name. Such papers are good only for breaking trail, not for assuming a whole new identity."

"Well, then, just how in hell am I supposed to get back? Do you have any plans for that?"

The man smiled. "We have plans."

"Who are you? Klottner, you say. But who are you?"

"All in good time, Herr Schaue. Meanwhile, why don't you simply relax and enjoy our beautiful scenery? I'll wager you don't have any to equal it in the States."

"We manage."

I rested back against the seat, the cold already displacing the brandy. My hands and feet were slabs, and the fluttering in my stomach went on and on. The hours of tension had been the genesis of a resentment which, full blown now, I focused on these characters who found it so easy to be nasty-nice indifferent.

But I knew how dependent I was on these two. Without them I was no more than a mountain trooper whose name was already on its way to the weekly blacklist provided all security detachments in the German interior. It was the total dependence that rankled.

I despised being dependent on anyone or anything.

By the time my cigarette had burned low, the Opel slowed for a hill, where a tree of hastily nailed-up military signs overwhelmed the boundary mark for Diessen. The market town, with its baroque abbey sulking in the drifting ground haze, was peaceful enough. I half expected the car to turn north along the lake's west bank, but Heinz, or whatever his name was, chose the road for Weilheim. The high ground fell behind and, arcing southeast, we crossed the two-mile-wide flats of Bauern Moos, the sweep of peat bog where the Ammer River begins to feed the great bowl, two hundred and seventy feet deep, that serves as its rationale for the winding descent from its Alpine rise. Then, where the village of Vorderfischen marks the toe of the eastern flank, we made our northern turn at the command of an arrow labeled Erling-Starnberg. The Ammersee, deep green and placid in the early light, fell out of sight behind the choke of trees.

When we came to the road junction at Erling, a cluster of houses that formed an asterisk on the Kienbach about a mile below the Andechs, there was considerable activity. A huge Waffen SS man, his face square and brutish under a steel helmet, his greatcoat an expanse of crisp gray above the glisten of his jackboots, waved us to a halt with an impatient jab of a gloved hand. My tenseness sharpened when I saw an armored car parked beside the main road and a trio of VW Type 82's huddled at a roadblock. Farther on, lurching into a side lane, was a halftrack personnel carrier, the helmets of the men in it swinging back and forth in ludicrous unison like gray-green apples on a wind-blown limb.

The tenseness became depression. This very spot had been integral to my plans: a tranquil, wood-covered hill topped by an onion-towered monastery from which Scab was to send a flicker of code toward a strafing plane. But it was now a beehive, and if the bustling were any sign, it would remain that way for some time to come. If Scab was to signal an airplane, I knew with a dull sinking, it wouldn't be from here at the Andechs.

Was there anything else that could go wrong?

The big SS man stood aside to make way for an Obersturmführer who approached the car with an orange-bound booklet under his arm. His uniform, with its black SS tabs, was elegantly pressed, and the leather of his belt, pistol holster, and boots gave off a polished glow. His face was narrow, and his pale eyes—like penny marbles, they were—were veined from a heavy night.

"Morning," Klottner said through his rolled-open window.

The officer held out the booklet with a parade-ground flourish, ran a thumb along its edge, and flipped open the cover. His eyes, the color of white grapes, considered us deliberately, each in turn. His voice was like creaking wood. "Your papers, please?"

I wasn't scared. I was terrified. The booklet held by the SS lieutenant was the current blacklist. Smith had briefed me on this, and I knew my name couldn't possibly be on the list until next week. But just the same, I couldn't help staring at it in about the same way I'd stared at the VD films in basic training.

"You won't find any Gestapo men on your list, Lieutenant," Klottner wheezed placidly.

"Perhaps."

"Odd, isn't it, to have a spot check at a godforsaken place like this?"

"Nothing is odd these days, friend," the SS officer rasped. "Your papers?"

"Since when does the Waffen SS hold up the Gestapo?" Heinz put in nastily, and I was mildly surprised to discover that the man could use more than monosyllables. The Obersturmführer's glassy gaze flickered over the driver. He said between his teeth: "With the orders I have I could hold up Jesus, buddy. Now, are you people going to show me your papers or am I going to have to run you in? I don't care one way or the other."

46

Klottner reached into a breast pocket, drew out what I recognized as a green Gestapo credentials folder, and handed it to the officer. His words purred sarcasm. "Run in Jesus, pal. Meanwhile, let us pass."

The Obersturmführer glanced at the marbled paper, looked up once at Klottner, then read again, his lips slightly puckered. Eventually he closed the folder with a snapping sound, returned it, and stepped back to give the stiff-armed Deutscher Grüss. "Heil Hitler. You may pass."

Heinz threw the car in low and the wheels spun, kicking back an arrogant spatter of gravel. When the gears were humming their cruising tune again, I forced my tone to be casual: "What was all that back there?"

The man in front shrugged. "Many things are brewing in these Bavarian hills, Herr Schaue."

"You mean the Werewolves, the Last Stronghold—that stuff?"

"Perhaps."

"You're certainly a talkative bastard, aren't you?"

"Men in my business are rarely orators."

"I hope you'll drop me a note sometime, then, and let me know what I'm doing here. It would be interesting academically." It called for maximum effort to control the flash of anger.

"I'm not trying to play coy, Herr Schaue. It's simply that when we talk over all this there must be another person present. So please relax. We'll be at our destination by and by, and then we'll answer all your questions." In the manner of one who searches for a neutral pleasantry, he added, "That's a decent brand of German you speak."

"I come from a decent brand of Germans."

I regretted this as soon as it was out, because to irritate these people was only to clam them up more. But I'd already flubbed it: the short man hunched a shoulder indifferently and faced forward, signaling the end of the conversation.

Partly because circumstances compelled it, partly because the exercise of memory had a way of calming me down, I reviewed what little I knew of the Gestapo.

As a specialist in German paramilitary organizations, I had been lecturing at length on the subject only eight week ago (God!

Only eight weeks?) as a faculty member of the War Department Intelligence Training Center at Camp Ritchie, outside Washington. But I had always admitted to myself in rare moments of honest self-criticism that, for all my glibness, I'd been no more than padding the skeletal information already bound into the manuals. No one, really, knew much about the Gestapo; even the strange, withdrawn men who had tasted the Gestapo broth and miraculously survived could report precious little. (After all, I'd told my classes, the ant being crushed under a shoe is too busy with dying to ponder the nature of leather.) But beyond the lack of hard information, the murkiness of the organization and its operations seemed to be an intrinsic factor, much like one of those mirror mazes to be found in amusement parks. So, pacing before my blackboard, I'd been like the virgin who discusses copulation: nomenclature, modus operandi, and goal were shopworn hearsay, but of the thing itself I'd known nothing at all.

Riding along now, my face being warmed by the climbing sun, I wondered about Klottner and his gloomy buddy, Heinz. What memories lay behind those vacant, codfish eyes? What subsection of the Gestapo did they belong to? What peculiar specialties had these men developed under the tutelage of Heinrich Mueller, the elusive one who, as chief of the Gestapo, cast his nets from the big old house on Berlin's Prinz Albrechtstrasse? Sabotage? Parachutists? Frontier control? Catholicism? Protestantism? Jews? Concentration camps? Or were they more than specialists—administrators, say, of the whole crappy ball of yarn?

And, of course, the biggest question of all: Why, whoever they were, had they decided to throw in with the Americans?

I puzzled over this for a long time.

Clearing Starnberg, we cut northeast on a broad band of concrete highway which, after spanning the diminishing hills, stretched ahead like a white tape through the black-green fir forests. The day was full-blown now, and above the slight ground haze the skies were a faultless blue. Spring was in the breeze, and the gentle panorama could have been transplanted in upstate New York with nary an inconsistency to show. But after a while

48

war again began to flex its muscles. First there was another check-point, this one commanded by an obsequious Luftwaffe captain who waved us on with no more than an embarrassed glance at Klottner's Gestapo credentials. Then off to the right, barely discernible in the church-like gloom of the pines, a battery of Flak 88's pointed skyward from a clearing, and on the left, farther on, a self-propelled Vierling 38—the quartet of rapid-fire antiaircraft guns—squatted at the roadside, its crew sprawled in the sun and munching black bread. The VW's, like squarish beetles, hurried along the grid of foresters' lanes, and groups of men, most of them in Luftwaffe blue, lined up with mess kits ready at field kitchens that sent wisps of smoke curling up through the trees. Then, on the reverse side of a mild slope, there was a cluster of partially dismantled FW 190 fighter planes parked in slyly netted clearings at the edge of the highway, which apparently doubled as an airstrip.

A motorcycle pulled alongside, its driver waving a black-gloved hand, his face grotesque under glasses and padded helmet. Heinz drove to the side of the road and opened his window. Jockeying his bike to a halt, the cyclist dismounted and raised his goggles.

"Well?" Heinz grated.

"You'll have to get your car off the road," the trooper said officiously. "We're expecting a visit from the Yankees."

"Air raid?"

"Yes. And it looks like a big one. More than a hundred planes, they say."

"We've got to be in Munich. Urgent state business."

"Sorry," the man said, shaking his head.

"We'll take the chance. It's no skin off your ass."

"Orders. No traffic moves along this road during an alert. We have too much petrol and hardware hidden in these trees to let moving cars attract attention this way."

"You're arguing with the Gestapo?"

Klottner stirred. "All right, Heinz," he said reasonably, "do as the man says. We'd only run into more like him farther on."

"Now that's the ticket." The cyclist smiled, adjusting the lapels of his jacket. "Just pull over there under the trees, gentlemen, and, ha-ha, commune with nature for a spell. The Yankees will probably concentrate on the city proper, so you shouldn't be too uncomfortable. I'll come personally to let you know when everything's clear again. All right?"

"Don't keep us a moment too long, you hear?" Heinz grumbled.

"Not one moment. Ha-ha. Well, until then—"

He lowered his goggles and gunned the cycle to careen off in a blattering razzberry.

"Over there will be fine," Klottner said, pointing into the woods.

It was, too. Climbing out of the Opel, I saw that although we'd be hidden from sight ourselves we would have a first-rate view of the plains and the oatmeal-hued stretch of horizon that marked the outskirts of the city. The three of us sat in the pine needles on the cap of the ridge and lit cigarettes, silently studying the landscape and listening to the far-off wail of sirens.

Somewhere in the forest an 88 began to fire, its crack a pluperfect pain in the ears. Then, as a full battery opened up, there was the feel of a high humming in the air, a droning that persisted above the ensuing orchestration of thuds, bangs, and cracklings that went up from the plains. Somewhere a klaxon bleated, and a whistle warbled.

"There they are," Klottner said, staring aloft through the trees.

I strained a bit and finally caught the slow-moving silvery wedges that crossed wraith-like at the rim of the haze. They were B-24's, probably from the 15th Air Force, and the blue around them was speckled with tiny smears of smoke. One of the planes flared bright with flame and, falling, traced a dirty S down the sky.

There was a thunder, and even here the ground vibrated.

Great bubbles of smoke bloomed, bursting and rolling fretfully across the skyline like enormous, obscene cauliflowers. Then, as the shower built, clouds compounded upon clouds, and the visible expanses of suburbs fell under an evil red twilight. The shocks of concussion were continuous now, and the rapid pounding of the flak had begun to racket like a gigantic, insanely tuned engine. Another B-24, its tail gone, toppled end over end in weird slow motion, and I watched it whirl into a meadow. The ground splashed like water, and the airplane's corpse disintegrated in a wild flailing.

Nearby a Vierling opened up, a series of wheezing snaps.

Heinz shot a look over his shoulder, his eyes widening. "One of them's coming in low—" he shrilled, and somehow, in a microsecond of crystal insight, I sensed the emergency above that would make the words Heinz's last.

I could hear them coming—turning slowly in the sun, whistling softly, drably sleek—and I knew the jettisoned bombs were one of those things the texts call haphazards unique to war. And, as they drubbed along the ridge, shredding trees, boiling earth—draining the universe with a monstrous vacuum, then filling the void with sound so intense it was soundless—I could almost smile at this conclusive irony.

Spiraling out of the silence, hauntingly sweet in the black, the warbling of a bird.

A subtle shifting in the numbness.

A mote of intellect receiving, weighing, then passing on the meaning of the delicate music.

My father's voice, chanting one of the old Lieder, rising and falling with the gentle nodding that had set the meter:

> O sprich, woher
> Über Land und Meer
> hast du die Kunde vernommen,
> dass im Heimatland
> der Winter schwand,
> und der Frühling, der Frühling gekommen?

I had not been wounded.

I discovered this finally when I staggered to my feet and, leaning against the sap-sticky splinter of a tree, examined myself with stinging eyes and stiff, dirt-caked fingers.

Klottner, I saw, was beyond help. The short man was suspended just clear of the ground from a branch that entered his back at the vertical seam of his trench coat and emerged where the third button would have been. In idiotic contradiction, his face was burned and pitted with blast scorch, but the fedora still rested on his head at a jaunty slant, making him a barbecued boulevardier.

Turning, hurting all over, I looked for Heinz. After a time I saw him. He was laid out like a store dummy, his shoes toed in at a crazy angle, his hand reaching a chalky greeting through the broken timber and drifting dust.

The Opel—another haphazard—stood in the sun, miraculously on its wheels, and aloof.

The quiet was all the more palpable for the trilling of the bird.

I understood finally how very alone I was.

FOUR

The house could have been a pleasant place, but in a dusk painted orange by the inferno across the river it huddled dark, brooding, and withdrawn. It sat behind an ivied wall, its gables and upper tier of window boxes peering out at the world like worried, heavily bagged eyes. But a pair of lindens that already showed decision to produce leaves, an entrance gate with amiable farm-type hinges, and a carefully trimmed border bed of azaleas collaborated in a wan effort to conjure up a silver lining. Houses have personalities—a triteness, maybe, but one I'd long been fond of—and I decided in a momentary fit of sentimentality that this one was waiting in patient melancholy for some kind of good old days to come back again.

I guess it was the alley that did it.

I'd driven around the block twice. The second time I noted an alley coursing down the center, a rutted lane that separated the back gardens of the houses, which faced east and west. With the garages and their links of picket fences and gooseberry bushes, my memory had gone back to another alley where Roger and Bruddie and Sax and Wally and I had ridden our bikes and sneaked cornsilk cigarettes and bragged and traded baseball cards and told lies about girls we'd seen without their clothes on. When I'd pulled the Opel into this lane and parked it in the shadow of a halfhearted spruce, I'd had a really spectacular case of homesickness and loneliness.

It had taken me most of the day to get to the alley. Munich's southern perimeter had been a cobweb of refugees, roadblocks, emergency vehicles, fires, and wreckage, so just getting the car through all that had been a sweaty business. Funny, though: the roadblocks had given me the least trouble. The people manning them had been helmeted kids or diffident old men, mostly, and the SS and Orpo types in charge had been too busy arguing on field phones and chewing each other out to check my papers themselves. I suppose the car, the flash of the green Gestapo folder, and my hard-nosed grumbling had cooled any curiosity that might have developed among the professionals. At any rate, they'd let me alone.

The biggest problem had been my indecision. The house was where Klottner had lived—or at least it was the house Klottner had listed on the Housing Authority registration card I'd found in his wallet. It was on a tree-lined side street in the suburb of Bogenhausen on the city's east side, and after I'd located it I drove on to a place where the streets thinned out, and pulled into a grove of trees and sat for a couple of hours trying to make up my mind whether to go back and ring the doorbell.

My first move had been, of course, to get rid of the mountain trooper's uniform. Still fuzzy with shock, I'd clawed away the limbs and turf and found that Heinz had apparently died of concussion—his clothes were smeared with clay but were free of obvious bloodstains. I'd stripped him of the tweed suit, the faded cotton shirt, necktie and shoes, then dressed in these. The suit was too small, and the shoes, with their run-over heels and ersatz soles, pinched badly. But anything was better than the uniform.

Next I'd pushed and pulled and bullied the uniform onto the corpse, trying not to look at the face. Then I'd torn open the breast pocket, ripped the photo page from the paybook, and, crumpling the remainder of this together with the incriminating travel orders, crammed the wad into the pocket and set it afire with the lighter I'd found in the tweeds. After making sure the char was a reasonable simulation of blast scorch, I'd rolled the body into a crater, covered it with debris, and whispered a nervous good-bye to the late Ludwig Schaue, mountain trooper. My own picture I slipped into my new pants pocket. Finally I thumb-smeared dirt across the photo inside the Gestapo credentials and repeated half aloud the name typed on the marbled flyleaf: *Heinz Jaeger, Heinz Jaeger, Heinz Jaeger.*

I also took the credentials and wallet from Klottner before pulling him down from the tree and burying him. Once I'd almost thrown up. The sight of blood always made me want to throw up.

As bad as I'd felt, I'd worked like a stevedore to get all this done because the motorcycle trooper might have returned at any minute. If the trooper had found the car and a single survivor, embarrassing interrogations would have followed. With no car and no trace of its occupants, though, he'd assume we had all left undamaged, and so the new Heinz Jaeger would have another tick of time to work with. At least that's the way I'd figured it.

The Opel had not started easily, but finally—when I was on the near side of hysteria—the motor blared and the wheels had spun me off the smoky ridge and onto the highway.

I'd not seen the trooper.

Sitting in the darkening cold of the alley, I tried to make peace with the hopelessness of my situation. I had missed the rendezvous with Scab; I was irreparably off my itinerary, both primary and alternate; my cover had been broken and I was now, as Ludwig Schaue, about to be added to the blacklist. I'd left a trail, too. I was known by name and sight as Ludwig Schaue, mountain trooper, to three Bavarian farmers, a Wehrmacht Unteroffizier, and a squad of sleepy soldiers. I was known by face and uniform to an SS Obersturmführer at Erling, to a Luftwaffe captain at the Forstenrieder roadblock, and to a motorcycle trooper. For any one of them my appearance in civilian clothing would be a matter of considerable interest.

Against these liabilities I weighed my assets. They were nothing to rave about: two sets of credentials whose vital statistics in no way resembled my own; a car, a pistol, and other tools of the trade; a borrowed suit that didn't fit; a house address whose significance was anybody's guess.

It was a mountain of negatives against an anthill of positives.

Survival demanded that I work my way as quickly as possible to Bopserstrasse 15 in Stuttgart, where a friendly spook might help me to the Rhine and beyond. Or, at worst, where I could hole up until the good old U.S. Bigod Army overran the city.

I reached for the ignition, but changed my mind for the thousandth time.

The curiosity was just too much.

The mystery behind Scab could not be solved by working my way into a hole-up in Stuttgart.

When I walked around front I found that it wanted very much to be a friendly house; only a small hook latch held the gate against its stops. Lifting this quietly, I let myself in. Then I took a moment to brush down the tweeds with my hands and to rub the uppers of the curled shoes against the backs of my trouser legs —remembering a parental mandate: "When you ring a doorbell, Peter, always look your best. It shows the one who answers that you value his time and attention." The irony of this under present circumstances gave me a moment of wry amusement.

I went up the path, climbed the three steps, and pulled the bell knob.

I waited, listening for a movement inside, but the keening of fire sirens and the distant rumble of the hell that still swept the city made it a silly thing to do.

I rang again.

This time I heard the clack of heels hurrying over hardwood floors, woman-fashion, and I had already removed the fedora when the door eased open. There was no light, of course, and so I couldn't see her.

"Yes? What is it? Do we have a light showing?"

"No, miss, I'm not the warden. I—"

"What is it then?" Her voice was taut.

"Does Herr Klottner live here?" I tried.

She paused, a ghost in the gloom, and the familiar panic began

55

to build. Just as I decided the try had failed and I'd somehow alerted this woman to some secret danger, she answered hesitantly: "Yes, he does. But he's not here right now."

Again I parried, my breath in low gear. "I know. He asked me to wait here for him. Until he returns."

"Oh? Did he say when that would be?"

"Not exactly. This evening some time."

"Have I met you before?"

"Oh—I'm sorry, miss. I'm Jaeger. Heinz Jaeger. I don't believe we've met. . . ."

"Well then. Won't you come in, Herr Jaeger?"

The relief was almost a faintness. She had not known Heinz Jaeger. Nobody was that good an actress.

I followed her through the murky vestibule, down a plank-floored hall toward the back of the house where, beyond an arch, a lamp with a red shade glowed. The place smelled of polish, books, and clean wood, and a collection of pewter pieces in an alcove behind the lamp glistened like a jeweler's display. The room itself apparently served double duty as solarium and library; heavy maroon blackout drapes covered the line of French doors facing the garden, while most of the remaining wall space was dominated by bookshelves from floor to ceiling. A divan upholstered in burnished red leather and fronted by a low mahogany coffee table was in one corner; a reading table, from which a radio gabbled softly, an elegant desk, easy chair, and pyramid of potted plants filled another. It was a pleasant room, and I could sense it was her favorite.

She turned off the radio. "I was just listening to the news. It's terrible, isn't it?"

"Yes, it is."

I was aware of her scrutiny, and right away felt awkward because of my stubbled face, clay-stained suit, and scuffed shoes.

"Won't you sit down, Herr Jaeger?"

"Thank you, but no, Fräulein—"

"Frau. Frau Werner. This is my home, but Herr Klottner keeps the rooms upstairs," she explained carefully.

"I'm a bit of a mess, and I wouldn't want to soil this nice furniture."

"Nonsense. Sit down. Please." The invitation was devoid of cordiality.

"I had a time of it in the raid. I don't make a practice of paying visits in this condition."

"It was a fearful thing, this raid. Horrible. Like the others. We've had more than sixty of them by now. Are you from Munich, Herr Jaeger?"

My German was free of the identifying taint of locality, so I held essentially to the truth: "No, I'm a Hessian—" (Father had grown up in Frankfurt) "—but my parents traveled widely. So I'm afraid I have no real home town to speak of."

"I see," she said, her tone stilted. After a moment she sat tentatively on the edge of the divan. She motioned toward the easy chair. "Please."

I sank into the cushions, proud that I was able to hold in the groan of pleasure. "This is good," I managed. "I'm very tired."

"I wish I could offer you some refreshment, but the electricity came on only a moment ago. The gas is still—"

I waved a hand and shook my head in what I hoped was polite refusal. "Thanks, no. I've already imposed on you—"

She gave me a diffident glance, then lowered her eyes to examine the sheen of the coffee table. She was a straight, well-formed woman, young still, and smooth-skinned. Her brown checked skirt was neat to perfection, and she wore a tan cardigan over a crisp white blouse. Her dark hair, even in this light, shone with auburn. But her manner was that of one who wonders what to do with a stray dog that has entered the house.

I got edgy. The woman had given me nothing to go on so far, and I knew I couldn't continue this charade forever. And if I didn't soon get out of this chair I'd collapse in sleep, and sleep under any circumstances was something I couldn't afford.

"Would you mind if I were to use your bathroom while I wait? This dirt—"

She seemed relieved that I'd suggested the means by which to break the stalemate. Standing somewhat too quickly, she said: "Please do. I'm afraid there's no soap, of course, but the towels are fresh and the water is running again and—"

"That will be fine. Sure it's no trouble?"

"No trouble at all."

As we climbed the winding stairs that led up from the foyer, I was pleased with myself for this idea. Not only would I be freed of some of the grime (thank God for little favors) but also, if I could avoid too much fuss about it, I might be able to look around Klottner's rooms. The second floor—first floor in Europe, I reminded myself—featured a large rectangular hall with an ornate railing surrounding the central stairwell. Doors led off from the hall's circumference, but there was no clue as to what might lie behind them. Only the bathroom was visible, and this, too, I could see, was diamond clean. Frau Werner was a fine campaigner; her house, steeped in war, was as shining as one of those sample houses Father and I used to inspect when there was no money for better entertainment.

"This is a lovely home you have," I said, pausing at the top of the stairs.

"Thank you. I'm very fond of it."

"I can tell. It's kept so well . . ."

She gave me a quick glance, her green eyes level and cool, and I could feel that she was taking my measure again. "One tries. But it's difficult these days. And the place is large for one person to take care of."

"You're alone, then?"

"Yes. My husband—he was a physician—fell at Stalingrad."

"I'm sorry."

She shrugged, a tiny motion of one shoulder. "Everyone in Germany has had such a loss. Death is now a way of life, as the saying goes."

Question: Why had she said "in Germany"? Had there been the barest emphasis on the phrase? If so, why? Why would she have used the term as if interpreting Germany for someone slightly less familiar with Germany than she was? Did she suspect?

I rubbed my eyes, sick with worry.

"You're weary, Herr Jaeger. Why don't you freshen up and then rest a bit? There's a chaise in Herr Klottner's study, and I'm sure he wouldn't mind if you were to stretch out on it while you're waiting for him—" Her voice seemed to take on a touch of assurance; she was now in an area prized by women, which was the supervision of the faltering male.

"You're very kind. You really are, you know."

Her fine skin reddening slightly, she said, "You've obviously had a trying time, and, after all, Herr Klottner rents these rooms and frequently has guests and—"

"You don't even know who I am. I might even be a criminal or something."

Her expression remained unchanged by my little joke. "Perhaps."

"Well, I certainly appreciate all this."

"Nonsense. If you need anything, just call."

She turned and went lightly down the carpeted stairs. I heard her steps fading toward the library.

There had been a razor in the medicine closet, and I used it as well as the lukewarm water would permit. The blade, even though performing with halfhearted authority, had removed most of the stubble and so now my face felt a little less like burlap. The mirror reported that although there was a puffiness around my eyes I seemed to have weathered the storm with passably few dents. Morale thus patched, I went into Klottner's rooms, eyes roaming over the low bookshelves, the carefully correct desk and easy chair, the chaise and table radio, the hulking wardrobe and, finally, the alcove occupied by a massive cherry bed with feather quilt. It was a man's room, free of frills, and I wondered about the late lamented Herr Doktor Werner. What measure of passion had linked the luckless doctor and the impassive, mannequin-stiff woman downstairs? Thinking of the woman again, I decided that passion had played little role in this house.

I forced my mind to the job at hand.

Systematically I went at Klottner's things. The wardrobe held three suits of colorless cut, an Alpine jacket, a set of climbing boots, and a pair of brown oxfords. Four neckties, three shirts, and a sweater were in the bottom drawer, and two sets of underwear were folded neatly beside the rolled socks that took up a corner of the drawer in the side table supporting the radio. The bookshelves were given over mainly to medical tomes, a set of encyclopedia, a French-German dictionary, a collection of phonograph records whose pinkish hue dated them from the twenties, a copy of *Mein Kampf*, and several stamp albums. The suit pockets revealed nothing, nor did the books—each of which I removed from the shelves and riffled through, pages down. Klottner obviously had been a clean-desk man, too; the desk's drawers held nothing but stationery and the usual office supplies, and its top displayed a fountain pen set, stapler, telephone, two clean ashtrays, a paperweight, and a lamp.

I stood in the center of the study for a time, wallowing in loneliness and frustration.

To regain control, I sat at the desk and piled the contents of the two wallets on the plate-glass top—Klottner's to the left, Jaeger's to the right. I dispensed with Jaeger's first: driver's permit, credentials, a War-Important Work pass, three hundred Marks, some change, a battered photo of two women in lascivious play with a man clad solely in shoes and socks, a shoemaker's bill for the ersatz soles, two theater stubs, a small wad of ration tickets, and a special RSHA-Sipo card authorizing unlimited gasoline allotments in the interest of the State. I replaced all these and returned the wallet to my breast pocket, because as the new Heinz Jaeger I'd need them all. Klottner's wallet revealed nothing significant or useful. There were a thousand Marks there, though, and I placed these in Jaeger's—my—wallet.

Next I carefully removed Jaeger's photo from the credentials, my own from the leaf of the now-buried paybook. After stapling my picture to the Gestapo folder, I used the pen to write Jaeger's name across the signature I'd affixed to the paybook portrait back at Home Plate. Then, while the ink was still damp, I smeared it with a blotter so that the mud and ink blended to further confuse the scrawl. The alterations would never stand up under scrutiny, but at least my face was now in Jaeger's ID folder.

Anxiety pressing pretty hard, I went through the room again, drawer by drawer, pocket by pocket, book by book. Only one new item turned up in this second search—a business card for the firm of Kaufmann Kompanie, produce and fuel haulers. It had been slipped under the telephone as if a reminder Klottner might have made to himself. I considered this for a moment and was about to replace it when my eye caught a roughly penciled note on the reverse side. There were three words and a parenthetical question mark:

Job for Despair (?)

It was only after lighting one of my three remaining cigarettes and sinking onto the chaise that I could accept the merit of my intuition.

There could really be no doubt.

Klottner had not known the identity of the man the Americans would send. "Despair" had been the key word in the countersign the American was to give Klottner's challenge, "The moon is beautiful in winter, isn't it?" What would be more logical than for Klottner to use the word Despair as his code name for the Yankee he'd expected to drop from the night sky? Lacking the name Schaue, Klottner had used Despair. It had to be. But—

Job?

Was Despair promised a job at Kaufmann Kompanie?

Or was Despair to seek a job there?

What kind of job?

Job?

I dragged a lot on the cigarette, compelling my mind to stay with this question and all the others.

Somebody, presumably in the Gestapo, had turned traitor and wanted truck with the Americans. Why? No answer. Klottner and Jaeger had been the traitor's henchmen. But had they? Where was the proof of this? No answers. The woman: Did she know Klottner had been a Gestapo man? No answer. If she did, was she also a Gestapo agent? No answer. Job for Despair—promised or hoped for? No answer.

Long after I'd stubbed out the cigarette, the same questions revolved in the same senseless whirling.

Somewhere in the pattern, sleep came.

Somewhere in the sleep, there was a faint and shifting image, ethereal and imprecise, important but unheeded.

It was as if the woman had stood over me.

And behind her, a man.

✠ ✠ ✠

To: Central Registry
From: Smith
Instructions: Add all to *Scab* File

URGENT: File ZF22-9438. 25 March 45. Receiver: Zombie Radio
TO: Smith (Code name Putzi). For note, action, file.
Wireless as follows:

Putzi:
Jaeger dead in air raid 24 March 45. Parachutist named Ludwig
Schaue has assumed Jaeger identity. Is Schaue yours?

Peppermint

To Zombie Radio: Please send as follows, Code M. From: Smith.
URGENT, 25 March 45

Peppermint:
Repeat your transmission. Suspect garble.

Putzi

Incoming via Zombie. To Smith (Putzi). For note, action, file.
URGENT, 25 March 45

Putzi:
Jaeger dead in air raid 24 March 45. Parachutist named Ludwig
Schaue has assumed Jaeger identity. Is Schaue yours?

Peppermint

To Zombie Radio: Please send as follows, Code M. From: Smith.
URGENT, 25 March 45

Peppermint:
Did you say Schaue? S-C-H-A-U-E?

Putzi

Incoming via Zombie. To Smith (Putzi). for note, action, file.
URGENT, 25 March 45

Putzi:
S-C-H-A-U-E. Landed vicinity Thaining, Oberbayern, 24 March
45, about 0200 Greenwich. Klottner, Jaeger took custody. En
route to Munich, Klottner and Jaeger killed in raid. Later I checked
Klottner residence, found Schaue, pretending to be Jaeger, asleep
in Klottner's room. If Schaue is yours, please advise. If not, I'll
destroy.

Peppermint

To Zombie Radio: Please send as follows, Code M. From: Smith.
URGENT, 25 March 45

Peppermint:
Schaue is ours but is not related to your work. He is courier on
another matter and must have stumbled into picture. Presumably
he assumed Jaeger identity after his own cover was blown somehow and plans to hole up. Suggest you keep him under surveillance.

Putzi

Incoming via Zombie. To Smith (Putzi). For note, action, file.
URGENT, 25 March 45

Putzi:

Spike is furious. He thinks Schaue has been sent by you to double-check his and my reports.

Peppermint

To Zombie Radio: Please send as follows, Code M. From: Smith.
URGENT, 25 March 45

Peppermint:
Spike is wrong. To reassure him, destroy Schaue at once.

Putzi

Incoming via Zombie. To Smith (Putzi). For note, action, file.
URGENT, 25 March 45

Putzi:

Spike reassured by your willingness to destroy Schaue. However, we prefer not to destroy Schaue yet since he might be useful in repenetration via Klottner's landlady, Christl Werner.

Peppermint

To Zombie Radio: Please send as follows, Code M. From: Smith.
URGENT, 25 March 45

Peppermint:
How do you propose to exploit landlady?

Putzi

Incoming via Zombie. To Smith (Putzi). For note, action, file.
URGENT, 25 March 45

Putzi:
Landlady is Kolb's daughter. She has inherited father's moral peculiarities.

Peppermint

To Zombie Radio: Please send as follows, Code M. From: Smith.
URGENT, 25 March 45

Peppermint:
Roger. Keep me advised. But destroy Schaue the moment he gets in the way. We must not—under any circumstances—alienate Spike.

Putzi

TOP SECRET

To: Kingpin, London   25 March 45
Memorandum to the Officer in Charge

1. US officer serving as courier in the *Scab* affair has missed contact as planned and faces imminent execution. Expect confirmation of his death via agents working on *Appleseed* matter.
2. Request you retire your file on *Scab* case.

Smith

FIVE

My eyes eventually fought free of the glue. I lay there a long time, sunk in the awakening process, half aware of the rustling of branches in the wind outside. Somewhere along the line I discovered I could move, so I brought around my wristwatch and, once it was in reading position, waited for something to translate the message.

I sat up fast, wincing. Comparing the watch with the bright band of daylight showing below the blackout drapes, it had to be noon.

I'd slept at least fourteen hours.

There was a flurry of that same old sickish realization of how vulnerable I was: How in God's name could I hope to continue this farce when I couldn't even guard myself against simple sleep?

I sat listening.

Somewhere below, a radio, muted, sent out the moan of "C'est Fini," and once I thought I caught the clatter of dishes. Again the questions began (What was this house? Who was the reticent woman downstairs?), but now I sort of welcomed them, because although there were still no answers the effort of reviewing the list had a calming effect. And again I lectured myself from the book: *The difference between rout and strategic withdrawal is knowledge of the enemy's own weaknesses.*

Walk, don't run, to the nearest exit. . . .

I lit a cigarette, the second to the last, and made a deliberate business of it so as to consolidate my slowly returning composure. Then I went to the window and drew aside the curtains. Blinking against the glare, I opened the casement and sniffed the spring that rode in on the breeze, taking care to stand out of full view of the garden and street below. On the back of the wardrobe door was a full-length mirror, and I went to it for an examination of the wreckage. The face was even more puffed than it had been the night before; the suit was even more disreputable; the shoulders were even more stooped. I knew I had to take some action, and soon, but what it was to be was something else again. No matter what, I decided in a sudden fit of disgust, a bath, a shave, and fresh clothes headed the list.

Speculatively, I took one of Klottner's suits and held it to me in the reflection. I was standing there like that when there was a knock and she entered, carrying a tray. A thick napkin covered it, and I smelled ersatz coffee.

"Grüss Gott," she said evenly in the Bavarian manner. "I heard you stirring and thought you might want this—"

Awkwardly, like a boy caught at the cookies, I replaced the suit. "Good morning, Frau Werner."

She went to the desk, her skirt swinging. She placed the tray on the glass top, removed the napkin, and motioned to the chair. "Please, Herr Jaeger. It will get cold if you don't take it at once."

I considered her in the glare of day. Her hair (it was undeniably auburn in this light) was braided and rolled in the Oberbayern style, and there was a satin-like patina to her quite remarkable skin. She wore a white turtleneck sweater that clung to her shoulders and curled, precisely casual, at her waist. Below the red wool skirt her legs were bare. Her wedge-shaped sandals, made of wood and strapped at the ankles, were sad discord in her otherwise tidy appearance. The sandals, as much as anything I'd seen in this country, spoke of the creeping shoddiness war brought to all things. As she stood there watching me, absorbed and solemn, I felt the elusive guilt the victor feels when regarding the vanquished. (Oh, boy. Some victor . . .)

"I appreciate this, Frau Werner. I'm hungry."

"Well then . . ."

I sat and found out how hungry I was. Besides the chicory coffee, there were two slices of brown bread, a tiny cup of marmalade, a slice of tired-looking cheese, and an apple that showed signs of having been in the fruit cellar too long. It wasn't until I'd finished it all in a frenzied gobbling that I remembered she was there. She was at the door, leaning against the jamb, studying me. I felt my face grow warm. Despite the common sense that told me I should be grateful, annoyance flared. I didn't like to be watched, and I remembered the dream.

"I suppose, Frau Werner," I said not too amiably, "now that I've imposed on you so thoroughly you feel due some explanation. Who I am, and so on—"

There was no mobility in her face. "You wouldn't have come here unless you had a reason."

"I was sent here by Herr Klottner. He said to meet him here."

"Reason enough," she said obliquely.

"Tell me," I pressed, "are you a good friend of Klottner's?"

She blushed slightly, and I sensed something elusive in her eyes. "He has lived here only a month. I've talked to him twice, only twice, in that whole time."

"Oh?"

"Yes," she added with the barest hint of defensiveness, "he comes and goes. He has friends in. He stays away for days at a time. Then he returns. Then he leaves. I know nothing of him."

"How is it he took rooms here?"

"The refugee problem is growing very serious. The government is making many families double up. I was told by friends that Herr Klottner, who is some kind of official, was looking for quarters, and I offered my rooms. It's better to have one than many—" Again there was something in her eyes, and I thought I could define it. Frau Werner was frightened. Moreover, I had the distinct impression that I was the one who frightened her.

"You didn't expect me last night?"

"No."

"I didn't upset you? Arriving unannounced?"

"Not really. Herr Klottner's ways are his own."

"But I do worry you."

She looked at me directly now, her lips compressed. "No."

"You're afraid of me, aren't you? Why?"

She came to the desk and picked up the tray, high color in her cheeks. "I'm not afraid of you, Herr Jaeger," she said crisply, a dark look in her eyes.

I wanted to ask her if she had actually come into my room during the night, as the dream had told me. But the question would be the grossest kind of presumptuousness, and I wasn't ready to alienate Frau Werner altogether. I needed all the help I could get, and to valve off this one potential well of information —no matter how shallow it might be—would be nothing but stupid.

"I hope not," I said, trying to get warmth into my voice. "I'm really not such a bad type."

She turned to leave without comment, her face a mask again.

"Please, Frau Werner, don't be afraid of me. And don't be angry. You've been very kind, and I really appreciate it. I'm still jumpy from my bad experience yesterday, I guess."

She considered me coolly. "Who are you, Herr Jaeger? Why have you come here?"

I'd expected this question all along, of course, but time and sleep had ruined my plans to prepare a careful answer. So here it was and improvise I must: "I was wounded in the fighting in France. No more soldiering for me, you see. Klottner is an old friend, and with his connections in the government he thinks he can help me find a job suited to me." Then, as a quick after-thought: "He said you might permit me to share his rooms while I look for work—"

"Well, I don't know—" Her tone was dubious.

I stood up and leaned across the desk toward her, forming a smile. "I won't be any trouble. I may look like one, but I assure you I'm not an oaf."

"You're a bit rumpled, to be sure," Frau Werner said over the tray, "but it's nothing a hot bath and fresh clothing can't fix."

"Fresh clothing? That will take some doing."

She nodded at the wardrobe. "Herr Klottner may be a good friend of yours and may even willingly lend you his clothes. But one as well set up as you would look rather silly in them, I think."

"So I've found."

She hesitated, her attitude pensive again. After a moment she seemed to make a decision. "You're going job hunting, you say?"

"Yes."

"Then you'll need to look as prosperous as possible. It's a para-dox of our preposterous world that employers want only em-ployees who appear as if they don't need employment."

"I thought I'd try to find a shop. I have money and ration tickets and—"

"There's nothing in the shops these days—those still standing. My husband left a full wardrobe. He was roughly your size."

I tried to keep the surprise from showing, but I knew I'd failed. Women would never cease to amaze me. I was distinctly aware now, as I had been from the beginning, that Frau Werner viewed me with cold distrust, and I'd been willing to settle for a mere truce and a room. But now, with an almost instantaneous shift from hostility to magnanimity, she was offering me a wardrobe over which she had probably shed many a tear.

"You'd let me wear your husband's clothes?"

"Why not?"

"Well—it's a very decent thing to do for a total stranger. . . ."

She shrugged a shoulder in that way of hers. "Mere things don't build memories, Herr Jaeger. I don't need a few suits of clothing to remember my husband."

"You're a baffling woman," I said, meaning it.

When she had left I lit my last cigarette and sat on a corner of the desk, a leg swinging, thinking about this gesture of hers.

It had been a gross contradiction. It was almost as if I held a special ambivalence for Frau Werner: I worried her sick, but she could not ignore me.

Frau Werner was shooting an angle.

Frau Werner was as phony as an eight-dollar bill.

The Opel was where I'd left it, and started without a wheeze. I backed it out of the alley, turned quickly, and headed through Bogenhausen for the Prinzregentenbrücke which, Frau Werner had told me, the Blockleiter reported as still open to civilian traffic. Bogenhausen was a high-class residential district with carefully-laid-out streets, wide lawns, old shade, and big houses. It was a place where much of Munich's higher-echelon bourgeoisie had elected to cluster, and the war had been relatively easy on it, leaving only a roof missing here and there, a crater or two, occasional shrapnel splashes on scattered façades. As I came to the Maria Theresa Strasse, the wide boulevard that parallels

the Isar, I was mildly surprised to see a gaggle of children skittering after a soccer ball. But then I remembered it was Sunday, and
why shouldn't children be skittering after a soccer ball? The
suburban atmosphere and the kids' laughing gave me a severe
jab of depression, though, and for a time I brooded about war
and the way it mixed shock and tranquillity.

I worked to counter the forming melancholy by reviewing my
growing list of assets.

The brown tweeds were in excellent condition and quiet good
taste; the oxfords, only slightly turned at the heels, were com-
fortable; the white shirt and brown tie and hat were a touch of
real elegance; even the socks—soft wool that matched the tie—
were my size. Combined with a long cold-water soak in Frau
Werner's glistening tub and a careful shave, my new duds brought
me a sense of tentative confidence. When I'd come downstairs I
had seen a startled look in Frau Werner's eyes which she had
tried unsuccessfully to hide. I was not insensitive enough to miss
the meaning of this reaction: the sight of a strange man swinging
down the stairs in the familiar old getup would be something to
give any female a bad time. I had done her the favor of avoiding
the subject and instead got off a lot of questions on directions and
locations. But mostly about streetcars. I did not want her to know
about the Opel. It was Klottner's, and therefore a notable inconsistency. She had responded as best she could—had even produced a Baedeker city map which she assured me I could keep—
but the shadow had never quite left her face.

I thought of her now, and despite my suspicions about her, felt
a tiny wave of sympathy. Women catch hell in a war, and she was
a woman.

As for new liabilities, I felt I might have one. I wasn't sure,
but when I'd left the house on Freudestrasse and headed for the
Maximilians Anlage a charcoal-hued Mercedes took up station
behind me by a block or so. It had hung there all the way to the
bridge and beyond. As I inched through the thickening traffic, I
kept a thoughtful eye on the other car, not at all convinced of
coincidence.

The center of Munich wasn't totally destroyed, maybe, but it
might as well have been. As soon as I'd crossed the Isar and had

skirted the Englischer Garten's boundary, it began: the great caverns torn in the blocks of buildings; the mountains of shattered masonry, timbers and steel; the still-smoking pocks in the boulevards; the broken-toy jumble of burned-out streetcars; the sagging lampposts; the high-hanging indecencies of bathtubs and toilet bowls that still clung to walls laid bare by gigantic collapse. Over it all hung the stench of violated sewers and seeping gas and undiscovered dead from previous raids, and everywhere the smoke was like a malignant fog. Emergency crews still played streams of water in the side-street labyrinths, and the gongs and whistles were a wild counterpoint to the Opel's low-gear whine.

Actually, the ruin was so great it left me curiously unmoved.

Kids playing in a shrapnel-spattered suburb, the sweep of pain in a widow's eyes—these could pick at a man. But acres of rubble were a glut that came off only as unreal.

I followed the signals of soot-blackened fire police and Schupo men because I had no choice, and it was a long time before I could clear the Hofgarten's wasteland and get beyond the Königsplatz and its damaged Propylaen. Four times I had to flash my Orphan Annie Gestapo credentials to penetrate the cordons manned by sullen-faced Orpos. At the first of these the blackish Mercedes had been turned away. If the car had represented a tail, its occupants were carrying lightweight credentials, that was sure. My Adam's apple returned to its customary post.

By the time I reached Dachauerstrasse and found the offices of Kaufmann Kompanie I'd changed my mind. My original plan had been merely to locate the place and size it up, but now, to make the hellish trip in some measure worthwhile, I decided to park the car and reconnoiter a bit.

As I sauntered down the splintered sidewalk I felt my warning system go on the alert. The Mercedes went by, its tires sizzling. I tried to catch a glimpse of the driver, but the car passed at too fast a clip for me to see anything but a dark fedora and a leather topcoat.

Add to the liability column: one more anxiety, for use as needed. . . .

To my surprise, the front door opened when I tried it, and somewhere inside I could hear the tacking of a typewriter. I went in, closed the door gently, and followed the sound down a dim hallway whose paint hung in gritty blisters. At the end of the hall there were double doors of frosted glass. Beside these a wall plaque announced in dignified script that here were the offices of Kaufmann Kompanie G.m.b.H., Eilbestellung der Lebensmittel, and, parenthetically, that those who wanted to see the transport chief should call at the garage at Number 20, one block to the rear.

As a corporation specializing in the express delivery of foodstuffs, I decided, Kaufmann and Company would seem to be almost on its uppers, from the looks of things around the main office.

I pushed through the doors and entered a reception room that featured a scattering of yellowed oak chairs, a weary table with an assortment of even wearier magazines, and two dust-colored potted palms, both fake. At a desk behind a low railing a platinum blonde in a fire-engine-red dress and black-rimmed eyeglasses drubbed a creaky typewriter that had probably been used by Goethe. She finished a burst of words, added an emphatic period, then looked at me over the tops of her glasses.

"We're closed today," she said in a tone that precluded appeal.

I gave her a grin and glanced at the nameplate on her desk. "I imagined as much, Fräulein Meier. But I was in the neighborhood and, since I plan to stop in tomorrow, I thought I'd make a little reconnaissance. I hope I'm not intruding."

The grin had helped, but not much. She took off her glasses and studied me with slightly narrowed eyes. They were very pretty eyes—cornflower blue, as they say in novels.

"We open at nine, Herr—"

"Jaeger. Heinz Jaeger."

Her gaze traveled over me, deliberate and slow. "Do you have an appointment with someone?"

"As a matter of fact, I'm looking for a job, and a friend of mine tells me there may be an opening here."

"Oh?" One of her carefully drawn eyebrows raised delicately. "Who is your friend?"

When going for big money, roll your whole wad. I did so,

throwing in another shot of grin. "Klottner's his name. An old pal of mine from Berlin. Know him?"

Whether it had been the name or the grin I couldn't be sure, but there were immediate results. She stood, placed her glasses on the desk, smoothed her skirt with a practiced sweep of an immaculate hand, showed her even white teeth in a smile, and nodded toward an inner door.

"Herr Behncke is in, Herr Jaeger," she purred. "Come in, won't you, please?"

"Thank you, Fräulein Meier," I said, giving her a wink to hide my astonishment. We went through the gate, and as she rapped at the door, whose gilt letters spelled Otto Behncke, I realized that I was now leaving the effective range of grins and was entering no-man's land. I was not ready for a meeting such as this, of course. But luck had gilded my lily with a final favor and pushed me without benefit of rehearsal into what I sensed was the featured act.

"Come in," a voice called from inside.

Fräulein Meier opened the door and, leaning her handsome back against it, breathed: "Herr Jaeger to see you, Herr Behncke. You know: Herr Klottner's friend from Berlin?"

SIX

Otto Behncke was a round man in his heavily cologned fifties. He sat on the far side of a large flat desk of pickled ash, not unlike the island of an aircraft carrier on which someone had painted horn-rim spectacles and a Menjou mustache. A saucy boutonniere snapped whitely against the lapel of his blue serge, and his wine-colored tie sported a pearl stickpin. His carefully trimmed hair was gray at the temples; his hands—pudgy and incredibly pale

and garnished with a huge cameo ring—were faultlessly mani-
cured and made a steeple that pressed against his pursed lips; his
eyes were like plums behind the thick lenses of his glasses and
were already appraising the cut of my coat. He did not stand up.

Instinctively and immediately I knew I would not like Otto
Behncke.

But that was not the problem of the moment. It had been
extraordinary luck to find that Heinz Jaeger had not been known
to Frau Werner or to the blonde outside. But to Behncke? *Dear
God, don't let it be that Jaeger and Behncke grew up together. . . .*

Behncke's enormous eyes blinked. "So. You're Jaeger, eh?"

"That's right." I nodded, dying one of those little deaths.

"You're young. I had no idea you'd be so young."

(*Dear God in Heaven, thank you, thank you, thank you.*)

"And I had no idea you'd be so young, Herr Behncke," I said
tentatively, wondering if I'd ever breathe again.

"You're only a boy. They must be out of their minds, picking
you. You're only a boy."

"Tall for my age, too, don't you think?"

"Don't get smart with me," Behncke said around the tip of his
steeple.

"Then stop complaining about me."

"You seem to forget I'm in charge."

"You're not in charge of me."

"So?" Behncke said with a faint sneer. "Then why are you
here? Tell me that, Herr Smart Aleck."

"Because Klottner told me to come here. He didn't tell me I
had to be fat, fifty, and fawning to do so." I kept my tone reasonable. It was quite a job, what with the raw heart I was chewing.

Behncke's natural pout deepened and he signaled to the blonde
with his eyebrow. She went out, and the door clicked shut with a
substantial sound. The fat man lowered his hands, picked up a
pen, and slid it between his fingers as if working a slide rule.

"You've inconvenienced me a great deal," he huffed. "I've been
waiting here for most of the weekend." His manner, for all its
irritability, was made of the stuff that enables a relieved father to
spank a missing child he's found safe at home.

"Sorry. I didn't plan it that way."

75

"Where's Klottner?"

"Klottner is indisposed."

"What's that supposed to mean?"

"He's down with a bad case of death."

Until this moment I'd really not known what to do about Klottner (as if I'd known what to do about anything). But when I saw Behncke's suppressed annoyance fade to discernible confusion, I knew the trump had been high enough to take the trick. I waited, concentrating on my effort to appear indifferent, while Behncke sank back in his chair and struggled to swallow what seemed to be a roll of barbed wire.

After a time Behncke managed: "Klottner's dead?"

"Yes."

"What happened?"

"Yesterday's raid. Direct hit."

"Where?"

"On the Starnberg road, near the airstrip."

Behncke ran the tip of his tongue along his cupid's lips. Then he sighed and shook his head, eyes to the ceiling in resignation. "We're in trouble."

"How so?"

The plum-like eyes came back to me, a flicker of something new passing through them. "Don't you know?"

"You forget. I'm a new man around the shop."

"You mean Klottner didn't brief you?"

"How could he? I arrived only yesterday morning, and we were on our way here when the raid hit. He said he didn't want to talk about things until we could go over it from scratch with you."

"I thought you were flying down Friday, not Saturday."

"Business. I was held up by business."

"There's no more important business than this."

"Think so?" I winked mysteriously.

Behncke pursed his lips again, preoccupied. Rubbing the cameo against a sleeve, he said finally: "You surprise me, Herr Jaeger."

"When dealing with the Gestapo one must learn to expect little surprises."

"Here I am, beginning one of the most delicate operations of the whole regime—in all of German history, possibly—and you keep me waiting for a whole day because business held you up." He gave the word "business" a nasty emphasis.

I shrugged. "Well, as my dear Uncle Aesop once said: 'Be content with your lot; one cannot be first in everything.'"

"You're a real smart aleck, aren't you, Jaeger?"

"I'm at my best at parties. I wear ladies' hats and things."

Behncke's eyes narrowed. Leaning forward slightly, he said, lips barely moving: "Say something in English."

I tried to keep my eyes level, every sense testing every eddy in the atmosphere. *Did Behncke know? Why would he ask a crazy thing like that?*

"English?"

"Yes, English."

"Why?"

"Well, you're supposed to be the redhot English-speaking black-market specialist, aren't you? Or is that something else Klottner thought to be unimportant? Like your obvious immaturity. And like your obvious disrespect for superiors."

"I speak English, if that's what you mean."

"Well then, say something in English."

"The quick brown fox jumped over the lazy dog's back."

"Go on. Anybody can memorize a phrase. Let's hear some more."

"Very well: You, my friend, are without a doubt the silliest son of a bitch I ever did lay my eyes on. And if I ever get a chance, just a teensy-weensy chance, buster, I'm going to kick your ass so hard your eyeballs will light up with tilt."

I watched Behncke closely. The fat man sank back in his chair again, expression unchanged. "You certainly rattle it off," he said.

Behncke either was a better actor than he'd indicated up to now or did not in fact handle English himself. I filed this latter as a strong possibility. No, probability.

"I have many talents that will delight you, Herr Behncke."

"I hope so. With Klottner gone we'll need all the talent we can get."

Vaguely I sensed a thread of reassurance insinuating itself into the lump of anxiety pressing against my ribs. The little linguistic demonstration seemed somehow to have satisfied something in

Behncke, as if with the unhesitating flow of Yankee vulgarities Behncke had set aside a hesitation of his own. I felt compelled to say something at this point and, with curiosity naturally outweighing prudence, said what was on my mind. "What do you want of me, Herr Behncke? How come Klottner sent me here?"

Behncke lowered his eyes and, finding a mote of lint on his blue serge sleeve, removed this blasphemy with a dainty flick of the cameo finger. Studying his nails then, he said: "Sit down, Jaeger."

I did, crossing my legs and wishing I had a cigarette. "Well?"

The plums raised and regarded me thoughtfully. "You had me worried for a moment, Jaeger."

"How so?"

"I thought you might be a Mueller plant."

My brain accepted this, weighed it for meaning, then set it aside for a moment, not daring to concede the enormous significance that suggested itself. "Not likely," I parried.

"Why not? You could have picked off Klottner and the real Jaeger, then inserted yourself as Jaeger, explaining Klottner's absence as a bad case of death, as you put it, I believe."

Still struggling to adapt, I decided through the confusion to risk another attack. "Do you want to see my credentials?"

Behncke's lips formed a dim smile. "You know as well as I, Jaeger, that papers are meaningless. As a matter of fact, it has never ceased to amaze me—the preoccupation we Germans seem to have with papers. I've often said that Germans would pass up an orgasm to shuffle papers. Even false papers."

I manfactured a chuckle to mask my relief. "That's funny."

"Yes. I think so."

"You mean you're accepting me at face value, Herr Behncke?"

"Let's put it this way: I feel better about you."

"Because I speak English?"

"Because you speak English."

"A lot of people speak English. Englishmen. Americans. Even Mueller plants."

"True, Jaeger, true. But only Klottner and I knew of the need for English in this case."

"I could have squeezed Klottner for that knowledge."

"Not enough time," Behncke purred.

"Klottner could have ratted on you."

Behncke made another steeple, and his huge belly heaved with a grunt of laughter. "You didn't know Klottner very well, did you? Even though you were old buddies, as he said."

"Who can ever say he really knows another man?"

"Well, maybe so. But you didn't know Klottner very well if you think he'd turncoat. Nor could you have known what he was up to."

I registered annoyance, and I found it easy to do. "All right, so what was he up to? You're beginning to irritate me."

Behncke looked annoyed himself. "Don't get pushy, young fellow. You're under my orders."

I sensed this was the time to let my real anger show. "Look, Fatso, I don't know you or anything about you. But I do know this: if you think I'm going to work for a pompous dandy like you just because you say so you're out of your mind."

"Klottner told you to come here, didn't he?" Behncke snapped.

"Yes. But you seem to forget that I'm a Gestapo man. And as a Gestapo man I say you're acting very frigging suspicious. And so was Klottner, for that matter."

Behncke's suet reddened. "All right then, smart aleck, what *did* Klottner tell you? How *did* he induce you to come down from Berlin? Eh? How about that?"

I'd been afraid of this one. The question sliced into the most vulnerable area of my broad spread of vulnerabilities. Unwittingly, though, Otto Behncke himself had provided a key to an answer. *You might be a Mueller plant,* he'd said. Instinct told me that in this game there could be only one Mueller: Mueller the Gestapo chief. Two members of the Gestapo—Klottner and Jaeger—had been in on some kind of plot involving cooperation with the American enemy, and Behncke, ostensibly a businessman, was also engaged in that plot. But Behncke obviously feared Mueller. Therefore Mueller, although head of the Gestapo, apparently was not among the schemers. Whatever the plot, then, there seemed to be two camps: Behncke, Klottner, Jaeger, and X number of Gestapo or other colleagues in one; in the other, Mueller and perhaps X number of Gestapo people who, if not actively working against the conspirators, at least posed a threat to them.

So Mueller was Otto Behncke's major vulnerability. I knew I'd have to play that weakness for all it was worth.

"Klottner didn't induce me to come to Munich. I was transferred," I said.

Behncke's color faded. "Transferred?"

"Correct."

"How?" The question had a constricted sound.

"How should I know? All I do know is that I got orders to report to Klottner for an indeterminate period."

Eyes narrowing again, Behncke put in: "Verbal orders?"

"Written. Want to see them?"

"You know how I feel about papers."

"As you wish. But orders I have."

"Who signed them?"

"My bureau chief. Who else?"

Behncke blinked three times, slowly. His voice dubious, he said, "Well, I hadn't figured on this. I don't like it. Not at all . . ."

"Well, after all, the Gestapo is an organization, and when it moves people around there have to be orders."

"Yes. But so many people getting involved . . . Bureau chiefs signing orders and all . . ."

"Relax, Herr Behncke. Bureau chiefs sign a carload of papers a day. What's one more transfer?"

Behncke sat quietly, staring into my eyes with a gaze which, despite its directness, had something of the oblique about it. "Frankly," he said finally, "I don't know what to do about you. You may look all right, you may talk all right. But I can't feel right about you, somehow."

"Why don't you check Berlin? They'll confirm my orders."

"Fah. How can I trust anybody up there? How do I really know who I'm talking to up there? Eh? How do I know that?"

I permitted myself a smile. "You don't, of course."

Behncke studied the far wall, his pudgy fingers drumming softly against the pickled ash. I felt I could wait no longer to tie the bag. I said: "Let's look at it all calmly and objectively, shall we? You are engaged in some kind of business, obviously of a highly delicate, confidential nature. You require the help of an English-speaking Gestapo man who specializes in the black market. Klottner, one of your aides, has arranged my transfer here in that capacity. But you can't thoroughly accept me without Klottner's being here to vouch for me. Nor can you, for reasons as yet unclear to me, check Berlin to establish my authenticity. Correct?"

Behncke's silence was confirmation.

"Correct," I answered myself. "So it seems to me, Herr Behncke, you have no choice but to accept me. On one hand, I seem on a prima facie basis to satisfy both your expectations and needs; on the other, you can't afford to send me packing back to Berlin because then I'd have to explain why I didn't follow my transfer orders and there'd be a lot of attention sent this way. So you may think I'm a too young smart aleck, Herr Behncke, but it would appear to me that this is one too young smart aleck you're going to have to live with for a while. Eh?"

Once again Behncke gave me that long, thoughtful look. After a time his pouting lips thinned into a wet smile. "You're quite a fellow, aren't you, Jaeger?"

"There's no one like me, really."

"I think you might be worth the gamble after all."

"One thing about good old Otto Behncke: he's a real thinker."

"If you can control that boorishness, you could become an asset around here."

"Not boorishness. Youthful exuberance for hard work."

"Boorishness. All of you Gestapo and SS characters are full of it. You'll learn some day, my friend, that arrogance defeats more purposes than it helps."

"A philosopher, eh?"

"On the contrary. A hardened materialist." Behncke shot out his left arm and consulted the expensive-looking watch that peeped from under the French cuff. He was now all studied briskness. "I shall," he said, winding the watch with a rolling action of his thick forefinger and thumb, "accept your armed truce. Because I need one, and because it will afford me maximum opportunity to keep my eye on you, you will serve as my chauffeur. Since you are already drawing your Gestapo pay, I'll not be lavish with wages.

In all truth, I really shouldn't pay you anything, but that would look very odd indeed if there were to be an unfriendly audit of my books. Nobody works for nothing, eh?"

"You're the boss," I said, trying to sound indifferent.

Behncke showed that pouting smile again. "Three hundred and fifty a month. Then, if business improves and your performance warrants it, there may be more. I'm not the one to overlook good performance, Herr Jaeger, and I'm certainly not the one to let it go inadequately rewarded."

"All heart, hm?"

"I'll not need you until Tuesday, Jaeger. I'll be here all day tomorrow, preparing for a meeting of our district managers. Schultzi, our garage chief, will pick me up and take me home. I suggest you take the day to familiarize yourself with the city and seeing to the car. Which reminds me: where is Klottner's car? He had an Opel drawn from Berlin, didn't he?"

"Blown to bits in the raid. A bomb landed right on it."

"Pity. We could have used that car."

"C'est la guerre."

"How did you get here today?"

"Begged rides."

"I see." Behncke stared at the desk top for a moment, then pressed a buzzer beside the phone. The heavy door clicked, and Fräulein Meier looked in. Even from here I could smell the scent she wore.

"Yes, Herr Behncke?" she breathed, studiously keeping her eyes averted from me.

"Put Herr Jaeger on the payroll at three-fifty, will you? He'll be my chauffeur."

The girl glanced at me then, but I failed to read her expression. "Very well," she said.

"And make it retroactive to the first of the month." Behncke's spectacles glinted. "You see, Jaeger? I want you to have money in your pocket. It keeps your mind on your work. Expenses incurred in duty will be reimbursed upon submittal of the proper voucher."

"I appreciate your generosity," I said.

"Do you have a place to stay?"

"I've arranged quarters at Klottner's place in Bogenhausen."

Behncke nodded. "Good. I live on Maria Theresa Strasse just beyond Consulate Row. You'll be handy should I need you." He turned his gaze to Fräulein Meier. "Since Schultzi is picking us up at five, give the keys and War-Important registration of my car to Jaeger when he leaves. He can take it home with him tonight."

"Yes, sir."

"The car—it's a Mercedes phaeton—is parked in the alley to the rear, Jaeger. I believe it's fueled and so on, but you can check." Behncke thought for a moment, then asked, "You have a cover story, I suppose."

"Not yet."

"Well, we have one prepared for you that should do. You'll keep your own name but use the biography we've worked up. Fräulein Meier will take your picture and make out the personnel forms to suit—also war worker's identification card, War-Important chauffeur's license, those kinds of things. Check in with the Housing Authority right away. We don't want to get snagged on some silly oversight."

As I turned to go I asked, "Anything else?"

Behncke gave me a speculative look and that sly smile. "Only a question. Two questions, really."

"Well?"

"First: you're not going to report Klottner's death to Berlin, are you?"

"I follow my boss's orders. You're now my boss. If you don't want me to, I won't. And your second question?"

"How is it," Behncke murmured, "that for a young man who has survived a bombing that killed his companion and wrecked his car, who had to beg rides to Munich and his new job—how is it you've managed to look so crisp and natty?"

I did not return the smile. "In the same way, Herr Behncke, I've managed to find a girl friend who has given me raiding privileges in her soldier-husband's civilian wardrobe."

"Fast worker, eh?"

"That's the way it is with us young, handsome types."

"Mm. Well, au revoir, as the Frenchies say."

"Screw you, as the Yankees say."

I waited in the office outside while Fräulein Meier typed my new cards. She handed them to me eventually, then, dangling a set of car keys from her elegant fingertips, appraised me with a slow sweep of her remarkably blue eyes. "Is it true? That you've already found a girl friend in Munich?"

I gave her the same business, lowering my eyes deliberately from hers to take in the set of her shoulders, the flare of her hips, and the curve of her ankles. Raising my eyes again and taking the keys, I said, trying to look like George Raft, "Sort of."

"Lucky girl."

"You flatter me."

"Young men are a rarity these days. Young civilian men."

"Then you don't flatter me."

"No, I don't flatter you. I appreciate you."

"My heart is thumping with joy."

"I mean it."

"So do I."

"But you've got a girl friend."

"She's just been fired."

"And I have a gentleman friend."

"And he's just been fired."

"He won't like that. He can get quite jealous."

"I'm terrified."

"He's been altogether fatherly. He's very possessive."

"All the more reason to fire him."

"My address is among those papers. The phones never work."

"For what I have in mind a phone would be in the way."

"Don't drop in unannounced. It could be awkward."

"Don't keep me waiting too long."

"Not likely. As I say: young men are a rarity."

"Especially young men like this."

"I'm anxious for you to prove that."

"Tired of fatherly types?"

"You'll see."

Kaufmann Kompanie
G.m.b.H
Eilbestellung der Lebensmittel
München

25/III/45

Most Secret
Via Courier to the Reichs Chancellory, Berlin

Attention: Martin Bormann

Most Honorable Deputy Führer:
   Please send at your earliest convenience a photograph of Heinz Jaeger, Amt IV operative. Cannot overemphasize the urgency of this request.

Heil Hitler!
Behncke

Otto Behncke

SEVEN

The electricity was off again and the room was in clammy dusk. Frau Werner, in another wooden attempt at small talk, had offered me a stub of candle when I'd come in, pointing out that it was always this way after a raid—the electricity and telephones were invariably the first to go and the last to stabilize; water pressure would fail next and gas last in the chronology of collapse. However, there always seemed to be some gas, she'd said, even in the worst of things. As she understood it, the gas lines were deeper underground and, even if they were ruptured, some gas would manage to get through. In all the raids she'd never been without gas, but there had been many times when the flame had been no more than a soft glow above the burners.

I was glad to get the candle. I had to transcribe a message and would need the light.

The day's tension had hit me with full force when I'd parked Behncke's Mercedes in the alley next to the Opel and had removed the distributor cap. This had been no more than a gesture, really. Automobiles, Smith had told me, were jewels in very short supply in the Reich. Cars were allotted only to certain military commanders, high party functionaries, security forces, and police, and, of course, civilians engaged in so-called War-Important work. Everyone else in the German interior—soldiers in transit included —rode in public transportation (when it ran). Smith had warned me: Only big shots ride around in automobiles, so stay out of cars unless you can wangle the necessary permits; if you can't drive safely, walk; if you must hitch a ride, for God's sake don't use your thumb, like a Yankee does, but point with your forefinger, like a German does.

It had taken me nearly four hours to leapfrog the Opel back

to Frau Werner's. After leaving the Kaufmann offices I'd driven the Mercedes several blocks beyond the side street where I'd parked the smaller car, then pulled to the curb to study the city map Frau Werner had given me. First I'd plotted a rough course that would bypass the police checkpoints I'd penetrated en route to the crazy meeting with Behncke. With reasonable luck I could retrace the same route in the Opel; the bypass route was for ferrying the Mercedes. So I'd driven the Opel to an alley near the Odeonsplatz and, leaving it there minus ignition connections, had walked all the way back to the Stiglmeierplatz, where I turned south on the Hasenstrasse to the waiting Mercedes. I'd taken this car north almost to the Siegestor. Here I'd found a section of trolley line operating and, clinging somehow to the outer fringe of the humanity that nearly smothered the car, had ridden south on the Ludwigstrasse to a point only a few blocks from the Odeonsplatz. Alternately driving, riding, and walking, I'd worked the Mercedes back to the Englischer Garten, around Kleinhesselohe and over the Isar into Bogenhausen. I used the same kind of routine to return the Opel to its parking place under Frau Werner's spruce tree.

Now, in a nation in which autos were precious tools to be doled out only to those working in the national defense, I—an enemy alien—was the proud possessor of two: a Mercedes I could use openly, an Opel to be held in secret reserve for the emergencies I knew, with a smoldering depression, would sure as hell arise in this insane effort to go it alone.

Sitting at the desk in the dark, I evaluated the status of this effort.

The interview with Otto Behncke had not gone well, that was certain. But it could have been much worse, and although my association with the fat man was little more than impasse it was at least association and not total divorce.

I tried to sort out the possibilities, telling myself that I mustn't reject something simply because it might seem too farfetched or grandiose. Someone had gone to a lot of trouble to get me here, and whatever the plot it would have to be very meaningful indeed to make treason worthwhile. Moreover, with names like Mueller involved, no plot could be too outlandish.

Other questions: Why had Klottner and Jaeger expected an American officer and why had Behncke seemingly not? And why did Behncke need someone who spoke English? Why a black-market specialist? How did all this tie together? Or did it?

Ultimately I made some basic decisions. I would maintain my pose as a Gestapo man as long as practical; I'd consider Gestapo chief Mueller the over-all theoretical enemy until facts might prove otherwise; I would play Behncke's lackey to the hilt; I would exploit Fräulein Meier's overly active libido; and, above all, I would wait for Klottner's anonymous pals—the ones who had called in the Yankees—to reveal themselves.

After all, I had no choice.

Lighting the candle finally, I went to the bathroom and, with the aid of a vase and the cap of Klottner's fountain pen, mixed my repugnant sympathetic ink. I'd just finished transcribing the pitifully few things I knew—Frau Werner's address, Kaufmann, Otto Behncke, Klottner, Jaeger—on a piece of Klottner's stationery when I heard her sandals click along the hall and stop at my door. She tapped softly, three times.

"Come in."

Her face, half aglow in the candlelight and half in deep shadow, was as impassive as usual. "I've prepared a supper, and it occurred to me that you might like to join me, Herr Jaeger," she offered stiltedly.

"That's very good of you. But I've already abused your hospitality, and I'll be going out later, anyhow. Thanks, though."

"I have to eat in any event, and there's enough for two. Please."

"Are you sure?" I asked, sensing her loneliness.

"I'm sure."

After folding the napkin and crossing the knife and fork on my plate in the European manner, I sat back and looked at her. She had placed the candle on the table beside the centerpiece, which featured a bouquet of rather cleverly wrought artificial flowers, and the pale light caught her fully, so that her features contrasted pleasantly with the black-brown paneling behind her. She'd made a first-rate meal of potatoes, turnips, and onions, and I felt fine.

For want of anything better to say, I asked: "How is the food situation, Frau Werner? I mean how are you making out with the rationing and all?"

She made that small motion with a shoulder. "It's atrocious, of course. I have sufficient stamps for myself, but there's simply nothing to be bought. Nothing to make a real meal, that is. Frankly, I don't know what I'd do without potatoes and turnips."

"How do you get to the store?"

"Walk, mostly. Take a trolley when they're operating. One makes do."

I studied the tablecloth. After a moment I said, without fully intending the protectiveness that crept into the words: "No more of that. I have a car."

She looked at me with barely concealed astonishment. "A car?"

"Yes. I am now the chauffeur for a fat capitalist engaged in War-Important work."

"Oh? Then your job hunting has already been successful?"

"Mm. I happened to find the man doing some weekend work in his office."

"Why, that's fine. I'm glad—" Her voice hinted guarded pleasure, and for some reason I was gratified by this. I supposed it was a continuation of the general Gemütlichkeit I'd felt during the meal. Frau Werner's small talk, the coziness of the room, the blessed absence of tension presumably had contributed to the notion that I'd found sanctuary in a cocoon spun in a corner of a frenzied factory. The picture sort of amused me, and I felt myself smiling.

"You seem pleased, too, Herr Jaeger," she suggested.

I nodded and gave her a little wink. "A man needs something to do."

"I'm glad you made a connection so soon."

"And I'm glad I can put the old buzzard's car to some good use."

We sat for a time, trading small smiles. Then, again not knowing exactly why, I was moved to put out a feeler. "Where did you and your husband meet?"

She ran the flat of her hand over the fine linen on the table, the ages-old caress that signals the female's propensity for textile plushness. Her large eyes, following the sensuous movements of her fingers, seemed to have an inner light of their own. "In Abendsee, a hamlet in the high country. He had just completed his studies at Heidelberg and was vacationing there."

"And you were also on a vacation?"

Her eyes clouded. "Not really. I was there to take care of my father. He was ill, you see, and he needed a long rest in the mountain air. Abendsee was one of his favorite places."

"How about your mother?"

"My mother left the country when I was a child," she said stiffly. "She went to America in 1934."

I felt suddenly as if I'd strayed into a ladies' lounge. I sought for a way to steer the conversation elsewhere but, as if sensing my discomfort, she waved a hand and displayed a practiced smile that signified a long-made adjustment to a distasteful truth.

"Please, Herr Jaeger," she said, "it's no longer a tender subject. My mother had little choice, really. There had been the slightest injection of non-Aryan blood in her ancestry, and she was lucky to get out, I suppose."

"Why didn't she take you with her?"

"As I say, she had no choice."

"How so?"

"My father wouldn't permit it, among other things."

"I see."

I didn't see, of course. My natural inclination was to blurt that it seemed a hell of a thing for a mother to do, blood lines, politics, or whatever. But I caught myself, realizing that I was supposed to be one of this woman's German contemporaries and therefore expected to be sophisticated in the ways of Nazi sociology. This was something I'd have to concentrate on: I must never forget, even for the slightest moment, that my German heritage could never be strong enough to assure my accurate reaction to German realities. I must never react in a characteristically American way —never apply American ethics—to a uniquely German situation. When in doubt, I must be silent, being careful even then that silence itself wasn't an indiscretion, an inconsistency in a Germanic psyche, so to speak. Again the sense of total inadequacy rushed over me, and to erase a building vision of the infinitude of trifles that could destroy me, I asked another question. "What about your father. Is he still alive?"

The murkiness in her eyes became more pronounced, and I suspected that this was one area in which Frau Werner had not yet made her peace.

"Yes. He's still alive."

"Where is he?"

"In Obermenzing. That's a little place on the west side of the city. He was an officer in the Luftwaffe, but he's on pension now. His health has been failing for some time. . . ."

"How is it he doesn't stay here with you?"

She shrugged. "He insists on keeping his own place."

"It must be a difficult thing for a sick man to do—"

"Oh, he has his ways," she said with a trace of irony. "You see, he once had considerable rank in the military, and even though he's on the retired lists he's not without various compensations. Among them is Leopold, his long-time orderly, who keeps things going and tends to Father's few needs."

"Do you ever see him?"

"Once a month, on the average. He says it's not necessary, but I go anyway. A sense of daughterly duty, I suppose you'd call it. I plan to go there tomorrow, as a matter of fact. I don't look forward to it, either. It takes a whole day, what with transportation the way it is."

"I'll take care of that. I have a car. Remember?"

She shook her head, blushing, and suddenly there was new tension in the room. "I didn't intend to hint such a thing. But I suppose it sounded that way. Forgive me."

"Nonsense. I have the whole day to familiarize myself with the city. What better way than to take you to see your father?"

"I'd rather you wouldn't."

There was something in her voice now that suggested alarm, and I tried to imagine why she would prefer a day-long trip across the snarl of Munich to what at worst could be an hour's drive. Why, I wondered for the thousandth time, did this woman seem so peculiarly diffident when it came to Heinz Jaeger? I decided to press the issue.

"No more argument, Frau Werner," I said as pleasantly as I could. "What time do you want to leave. Early? Noonish?"

She shook her head again, a tightening about her lips. "No. I wouldn't think of it."

"What time?"

"I said no, Herr Jaeger."

"Noon?"

"I said *no!*"

There was immediate regret in her face, and I was startled by the contradiction between the tacit apology and the sharpness of her tone.

"Is there something wrong, Frau Werner?"

"No."

"Something I could help you with?"

"No. Why do you ask?"

She was struggling with something more than embarrassment, I could see that. "Why don't you want me to drive you? Why are you afraid of me? Tell me, won't you?"

"It's simply that Father's not well, and he becomes easily annoyed—even by me. There's no saying what he might do if a complete stranger were to show up. . . ."

"If I were sick and you came to see me, I wouldn't be annoyed."

She raised her eyes, and I felt my face become exasperatingly warm. My voice had betrayed me again. I'd intended no more than a mild crack at her father; instead, because there had been an unexpected tone of indignation, it had come out smacking of tribute to her. I didn't want the woman to get any funny ideas, so I added gruffly, "Anyone would be pleased to have his daughter come to see him when he's sick."

But this only made too much of a bad job, and I felt sort of silly.

Her face softened a bit and she drew a deep breath. "I don't want you to think I'm ungrateful, but Father's somewhat of a trial and I don't want to risk upsetting him more than necessary. But thank you, anyhow. It was a kind offer."

I toyed with my water glass, challenging, recognizing, and passing the curiosity that demanded admittance and action. I formed a conspiratorial expression. "I'll take you to within one block of his place and then lurk in the bushes until you're ready to leave. How's that?"

Her confusion was apparent. "Well—"

"He'll never know I'm anywhere around."

"It's simply that—"

"I'll sit in the shade and read a newspaper."

"I—"

"And write a poem or two."

She laughed, and the transformation was extraordinary. It wasn't just that she looked better when she laughed (and she certainly did that, God knows); she simply became another person.

I closed the agreement. "You be ready at noon. All right?"

She nodded. "All right."

As I helped her from her chair she asked gravely, "You say you're going out again?"

"Yes. A melancholy errand, I'm afraid. I didn't want to mention it earlier because, well, frankly, I didn't want to spoil a pleasant dinner. But I received word where I'll work that Klottner will not be coming back. He was killed in yesterday's raid."

There. That disposes of Klottner as far as Frau Werner's concerned, I sighed silently.

"Oh," she said.

From her expression she was about as moved by Klottner's death as if I'd just told her it would rain tomorrow.

It was more than forty miles one way from Munich-Bogenhausen to Landsberg, but with my new War-Important Work Pass and a streak of good luck I covered the distance before midnight— driving the Opel because I wanted no hard-to-explain mileage building up on Behncke's Mercedes. I parked the car in a thicket about a mile out of Landsberg and walked for about five minutes to reach the crucifix. Message safely stowed, I was back in Munich by dawn.

I slept hard, satisfied that I'd brought Smith along with me this far, at least. If Peter Klaussen—alias Schaue, alias Jaeger— were to die tomorrow, Smith would know where to begin picking up the pieces. . . .

✠ ✠ ✠

Incoming via Zombie   26 March 45

Putzi:

Schaue visited Kaufmann offices for an hour yesterday. Drove away
in Behncke's car, then shuttled it and Klottner's car to Werner residence
Bogenhausen. Later made trip to Landsberg. Lost him near there due
to flat tire on my own vehicle. Have instructed Werner woman to pump
Schaue re these events.

                                                    Peppermint

To Zombie Radio: Please send as follows, Code M
URGENT 26 March 45
    Peppermint:
        I am appalled by Schaue interference. Absolutely cannot under-
        stand how he learned of Kaufmann, let alone how he ingratiated
        himself sufficiently to borrow Behncke's car. Have you told Spike
        about these developments?

                                                    Putzi

Incoming via Zombie   26 March 45

Putzi:
    Spike not yet told. I think he still suspects Schaue to be your double-
check on us. As a matter of fact, so do I, since Schaue seems suspi-
ciously sure of himself for a lost courier.

                                                    Peppermint

To Zombie Radio: Please send as follows, Code M
URGENT 26 March 45

Peppermint:
   Destroy Schaue at once. Repeat: Destroy Schaue at once.

                                             Putzi

By courier, night shuttle plane:
26/III/45

Spike:
   Putzi has ordered destruction of man called Schaue. Do you
   concur?

                              Peppermint

*Soon perhaps. Not quite yet.
Schaue intrigues me.
                    Spike*

EIGHT

The modest Wurm, glassy with sullen eddies, marked the common cause around which the village had rallied centuries before. If it hadn't been for the military signposts and the Flak battery dug in at its rim, Obermenzing, with its onion-steepled church and whitewashed cottages, could have been a tourist poster.

We'd made the trip in comparative silence. I'd been kept pretty busy by the traffic, the roadblocks, and the detours, but whenever I managed a glance her way Frau Werner's face had reflected its own grave preoccupation. Now, as we drubbed over the road paralleling the stream, I sensed her return from deep thought. She stirred, and the paper-wrapped packages on the seat between us crackled under her feminine probing.

"You'll have to direct me from here, Frau Werner."

"Straight ahead to the fork, then the left lane to its end."

"Forget anything?"

"No, it's all here," she said busily. "The little I've been able to pull together, that is. Thank heaven Father's needs are few."

"What does he think about your needs?"

"I have no needs," she said, giving me a quick look.

"Does your father believe that?"

"I don't know what he believes."

"I know what my father believes."

"My father doesn't say much. He never has. . . ."

"A man doesn't have to say much to let his beliefs show through."

"You don't even know my father, Herr Jaeger, and already you judge him."

I regarded her for a moment, then reconsidered the winding lane ahead. "Judge him?"

"Yes. You've never met him, yet you dislike him."

"I didn't say that."

"No. But as you say, a man needn't say anything to let his beliefs show through."

I could find no answer for my own argument, and once more I experienced the peculiar irritation this woman could generate.

The house at the end of the lane was a low-slung cottage with broad sweeps of roof that gave the place a frozen frown. I eased the Mercedes to a halt behind a rambler bush which, piled thickly at a corner of picket fence, formed a screen between house and lane. Turning off the motor, I sank back in the seat, and stretched.

"This is a pretty place," I said, trying to sound agreeable.

"Yes. It makes the war seem very far away."

There was that tenseness again. "You seem nervous, Frau Werner."

"Drives through traffic always upset me."

"Well, you can go in and sit with your daddy now and take some of the wrinkles out of your psyche, eh?"

This time her glance had more expression. "You needn't wait for me, really."

"I will, though."

"I may be quite a while. . . ."

"See if I care," I said.

I sat deep in the car seat, huddled behind the wheel and sucking at one of the cheap cigars I'd found among Klottner's things. The sky had abandoned its earlier efforts to muster good cheer, and now low-scudding clouds, somber as drifting lampblack, threw a nasty spittle against the windshield. Determined to make the wait fruitful, I tried to do some sorting, my mind struggling with the elusive calculus that seemed to go with deceit. But it was like eating soup with a fork, because my thoughts went their own ways, running through the past, erratic and aimless, like the icy rivulets on the glass in front of me. After a while I gave up the job, suspecting vaguely that there was a kind of therapy to be found in the idling of my mental machinery. The past few days had been a weird push and pull of pride, conscience, and duty versus fatigue, fright, and loneliness—and over it all had been the almost psychotic compulsion to win one more fact, to answer one more question. So it was good simply to sit, to watch the grumpy sky, to listen to the squall's liquid pinging on the roof, to think of everything and nothing, to recollect the things I loved and the things I loved not to love.

I had decided to light the cigar and sustain the mood when war reasserted itself. And jerking back to now showed me I'd never been away, since my reaction was immediate—a reflex born of what must have been my subconscious speculation as to what might be going on inside the cottage.

A brace of Mustangs—those long-nosed, square-tailed fighters so dear to the Hotshot Charlie set—dipped soundlessly over the trees ahead, the airscoops on their dirty gray bellies seeming to scrape the street. The car rocked with the shock of their passing, and branches bent and gravel spattered and windows sang and puddles became furious whorls of spray. Then, while the universe filled with their tardy howl, I was out of the car and running, bending against the sleety rain, squinting and grunting as I vaulted the picket fence, panting from exertion when I reached the cottage and pounded on its dark brown door. I was knocking a third time when the door swung open and I bumped against Frau Werner and spattered her with wet and stumbled over a rug and felt suddenly foolish.

"What's wrong?" she demanded, faltering backward, her eyes wide and her hands shaking the water away.

"Strafing run. Didn't you hear the planes, for God's sake?"

As if I'd spoken a cue line, there was the distant crashing of machine guns and the thump of cannon over the meadows and beyond the horizon where the planes teased some luckless caterpillar of traffic to death.

"Why are you so upset?" Her face was pink with anger. "It's a common thing—"

"Common or not, I'm not going to sit in an officer-type car while Ami fighters are prowling."

"Well, you shouldn't have come in. My father is ill—"

I felt my cheeks grow hot. "I don't understand you *or* your father, honest to God, I don't. I'm not bothering anybody—"

She moved to the door and flung it wide, her desperation undisguised. "Get out. Right now."

"Why, damn it?"

"He might hear."

"Well, what if he does? I'm no goddamned tarantula."

"But he's right in the other room and—"

"What in hell is going on here? Who is this man?"

The new voice rapped harsh and indignant. Before I broke off my glare to confront the source, I caught the heat-lightning revival of that thing smacking of terror in Frau Werner's eyes.

"Well, Christl, I said who is it? Is he another of your little playmates?"

"No, Vati. No. He's—"

"I'm only a man who wants some cover from the planes. What's so unreasonable about that?" I gave the other a full-faced stare, making no attempt to control my rage, taking in the worn red ski sweater, the uncreased trousers, the tattered carpet slippers, the whiskered chin, the thin and tousled hair. The eyes, ice-blue and hostile, ignored me.

"I thought I told you, Christl, that I didn't want anyone coming around here."

"I tried to keep him out, Vati, but—"

"Well, get him out now. Right now." The voice was like glass breaking. "And you get out, too. I'm sick and tired of being pestered."

Another man, short and bland and chunky, appeared out of the dusk beyond the inner door. His small, deep-set eyes were bright with interest. "Anything wrong, General?"

"Get these people out of here, Leo. You know how I hate to be pestered. Get them out."

The man called Leo said in an easy voice, "All right, sir. Just take it easy. Your daughter meant no harm, I'm sure."

"Leo! Whose goddamned orderly are you, anyway?"

"Yours, of course, General."

"Well then, get these ninnies out of my house!"

I snapped free of the odd paralysis that had seized me at the moment of recognition. In a voice that was less than cocky now, I said, "Come on, Frau Werner. Let's get out of here, like the man says."

I drove back to Bogenhausen via a modified great-circle route —heading the Mercedes east by northeast along the hem of Nymphenburg to Moosach, then straight east over some secondary roads to the Isar, finally cutting south to Bogenhausen after crossing the river on a dejected pontoon span above Hirschau. I chose this roundabout way for two reasons: I was tired of fighting the jam of Munich proper and I wanted to see what was to be seen on the city's northern perimeter. It had been just more of the same, really, and once I'd regretted my choice of routes when I spotted more low-roving Mustangs and realized the black car stood out like a spider on a napkin on these back roads. I'd pulled into a thicket behind an abandoned gas station, continuing on only after the planes had disappeared, snarling, into the brightening western sky.

Frau Werner had sat silently through it all.

In fact, it wasn't until we had entered the house and hung up our soggy raincoats (she had unearthed one for me in the attic) that she made a sound. Through pale lips she asked, "Would you like some of the Kirsch to take away the chill?"

"Sounds good."

"Go into the library. I'll bring it in there."

I sat in the easy chair and absently studied the garden, which was awash in pallid afternoon light and seemed somehow to have taken on its owner's somber muteness. In the stillness, broken only by the soft sounds she made in the kitchen, I drifted into one more assessment of the lugubrious events in Obermenzing.

The General might indeed have deteriorated in his term of disgrace, but his physical appearance remained basically unchanged, and I chafed over the length of time it had taken me to recognize Joachim Kolb. There was gray in the hair, sure, and there was a discernible shrunken quality in the frame which in all the early photos seemed so square and hard and flat-planed and self-assured. But there was still no accounting for the delay in recognition. There had been one picture in Father's file—that big black box that filled the lower drawer in the upstairs study in Deerhurst —that had shown Joachim Kolb seated in the cockpit of his Fokker D-7. For a 1918 photo the quality had been superb, and Kolb, helmetless and sunlit, had gazed into the camera's lens, eyes level and faintly amused. As a kid I'd often studied it during my airplane-buff phase, since it was really the only one of all those pictures Father had gathered in the old war that showed something of the personality portrayed. Most of the photos were furry with age, poorly lighted, over- or under-exposed, and the men and machines they'd caught were no more than two-dimensional caricatures. But this one had picked up the animal essence of Joachim Kolb, and in later years, when Kolb had outgrown his renown as a World War I ace and become the internationally disreputable playboy and dedicated bootlicker of Hermann Göring, Father had received a considerable sum from *Chronos,* the weekly news magazine (*Chronos* reported it superciliously as "a whopping $1,000"), for the right to use the picture to lead off a sidebar in a cover story on "The Fabulous, Fatuous, Fat Man of Fascism." The main article on Göring had been illuminating and witty, but the sidebar on Kolb had been only depressing. It had been inconceivable to me that Kolb, a brave, colorful, and—from his picture—apparently self-possessed fellow, could degenerate into the role of Nazi court jester and panderer. *Chronos* had spoken darkly of Kolb's wound-induced descent into morphinism and had hinted that some thought him incurably mad. I'd asked Father about this, of course, but he'd shaken his head and muttered something about how "every man has his tragedy" and hadn't said anything after that.

Frau Werner came through the archway, her face averted. She placed the tray on the coffee table, then stood back. She, too, stared fixedly at the garden. "Help yourself, Herr Jaeger," she said tautly.

I took a glass and said, "I'm sorry, Frau Werner. Honestly sorry."

Her gaze remained fast on the garden. "You mean my infamous father?"

"More than that. I'm sorry for butting in."

"There were planes. You had to hide."

"I was being nosy. You knew that, and I knew you knew, and that's why I got so angry, I guess. Not at you. At myself."

She moved a hand listlessly. "Let's forget it, shall we? You know my dark secret now, and I don't particularly care. Really."

"What's such a dark secret? The fact that you happen to have a daddy who was such an irresponsible rakehell even Hitler fired him? I don't see how that's something for you to feel disgraced about. The disgrace is his; it's not communicable like measles or something."

"You're a very fortunate young man, Herr Jaeger."

Struggling to follow the eddy in her thoughts, I asked, "What do you mean by that?"

"You're very fortunate to have lived in Germany for so long without learning that one man's transgressions can be a whole family's crucifixion."

Careful, Klaussen. Don't use American arguments in a German situation. When will you learn?

"I didn't mean it that way," I said cautiously. "I meant that there's no reason for you to go around gloomily *accepting* the cross that belongs to him. It's not yours to lug around—no matter what the current philosophy. And why should you be so rattled about my finding out? What do you think I'm going to do —run out in the street and yell 'Christl Werner's old man is a cashiered Luftwaffe officer? Christl Werner is therefore a cashiered woman'? Not likely. Not at all likely."

"Let's drop the subject, shall we?"

"All right. But don't think for a minute that I, personally, hold you responsible for your nutty daddy. . . ."

✙ ✙ ✙

By courier, night plane
26/III/45

Spike:

The following is a transcript of a recording made today via bug planted several weeks ago by the Werner woman during one of her visits to her father's house. She was driven there by Schaue this p.m., which makes this particular conversation all the more interesting.

Peppermint

TRANSCRIPT:
(Door opening; footsteps; rustling.)
General, are you awake? (Voice identified as that of Artur Leopold, see messages M28 et seq.)
Yes. Thanks for checking, though, Leo. (Voice identified as that of Gen. d. Fl. Joachim Kolb.)
Did you get (word lost here) sleep at all? You need your nap, you know.
I know. But I'm still playing with our puzzle, I'm afraid. (Furniture creakings.) What do you think, Leo?

About the man? Your daughter's doorway sparring partner?
Yes.
Hard to say, General. I just don't know.
He looks German. Talks German.
He does that, all right.
Which could make him a Mueller plant, eh?
To be sure, General, to be sure. (Sigh here.)
However, I don't think he is, Leo. I'm just about convinced that he's our missing American. Who but an American would leave his hat on while arguing with a handsome woman? (Rustling; footsteps; garbled comment, presumably from Leopold; door closing.)

Via return plane
27/III/45

Peppermint: Seems to confirm our suspicions. But what did Kolb mean by our missing American? Determine soonest.
Spike

NINE

The single most dangerous aspect of my situation, I knew, was my isolation from truth. In my moments of self-pity (and these were coming with increasing frequency) I could consider the combat GI, and feel envy. There was probably no one more wretched than the front-line dogface, but the GI had no more to do than to look at the color of his pants for a reminder as to who he was and why he was where he was. And, in case he forgot now and then what his pants signified, the GI could hear a broadcast, maybe, or get briefed or read the *Stars and Stripes* or even listen to the latrine telegraph and regain a generalized notion of belonging to something important enough to justify his misery. But Peter Klaussen? No, sir, I'd moan inwardly, Peter Klaussen's pants aren't even his own. When Peter Klaussen hears a broadcast or reads a paper, the only truth he can be sure of is that there's nary a truth in any of it. And lacking truth, by God, Peter Klaussen can lose his sense of belonging to something and, drifting and waiting, devoid of rationale and theoretically attainable goals, he can screw up good and die, say.

By the end of my first week in the Third Reich I'd established a three-part program by which I hoped to forestall such unpleasantness. First, I'd make little speeches to myself: Who is Peter Klaussen? Well, here are some of the things he is. What's he doing alone in Germany? Here are some of the things he represents. That kind of thing. Second, I made a game of speculating on the truth, using as a base the facts as I'd known them the night I dropped from the plane. I'd known then that three weeks earlier units of the First U.S. Army had crossed the Rhine and established a bridgehead at Remagen; I'd also known that on the night before my jump elements of Patton's Third had crossed the river at Oppenheim and were expected momentarily to be joined on the east bank, north and south of Worms, by the U.S. Seventh. So, with the fact of the Rhine's breachment as my benchmark, I could listen to the German radio and read the ragpaper press sheets and, allowing for Goebbels' windage, make reassuring guesses as to how long it would take the U.S. Army to overrun me—provided I could stay alive in the meantime. If the radio proclaimed the destruction of 400 American tanks southeast of Dortmund, I could suppose that the U.S. First had broken out of Remagen to turn the southern flank of the Ruhr; if the news sheets reported the rout of an American division near Darmstadt, I could presume that the Third was knocking down doors in Frankfurt.

With each bulletin I sought some clue as to how things might be going for that chunk of the U.S. Seventh that had carved a foothold below Worms, for it was this piece of military, I suspected, that held out the greatest promise for one Peter Klaussen. But with god-awful perverseness the communiqués ignored developments along the upper Rhine, a blackout possibly due to the rumored Nazi efforts to set up a redoubt in the Bavarian Alps. And so I would console myself with the obvious: chaotic comings and goings of poorly trained, over-age Volkssturm units; hopeless jams of civilians trying to get out of Munich and hordes of ragtag refugees trying to get in; the increasing number of U.S. fighter planes working over the area like snuffling hound dogs; the decreasing willingness of the radio to say anything at all about anything. The moral: As close as I was to my private panic, the Germans were even closer to their collective one.

And this gave me heart.

The third phase of the program conducted by the Society for the Prevention of Cruelty to Peter Klaussen was my studied effort to avoid inertia. It could be fatally tempting, I knew, to dig in, hoping by my very immobility to remain undiscovered in the rustlers' camp until the sheriff's posse arrived. But I also knew that suspended animation of this sort would be akin to a freezing man's going to sleep, so even when I wasn't physically active I kept my mind occupied with anything and everything that could possibly pertain to the mystery I'd loused myself into. It was all very depressing, though.

Otto Behncke did very little to make it easier.

Behncke was a desk-bound executive of purest grain, rarely leaving his office for anything but the evening return to his place off Consulate Row or a quick run to City Hall on some murky mission. Since my standing instructions were to be available at all times, I began eventually to feel as if I'd been welded to my chair in the bleak garage behind the office. By week's end the call to bring the car around front would send me hopping into the Mercedes like an Elk heading for a convention.

Schultzi had been a godsend. Schultzi was an irrepressible former SS Scharführer who had had his backside stove in when his motor repair platoon had been caught by partisans in the Ukraine. He'd been declared unfit for further active duty—a development he claimed "made me about as put-out as a satyr locked up in a barn full of whores." Mostly to gain Schultzi's confidence, I had let him chatter along, feeding him only enough questions to keep him going, watching for the time when he'd be sufficiently un-guarded to provide some specifics.

It was on Friday night when I felt the time had come. Behncke, as usual, was working late, and Schultzi, as shop foreman of Kaufmann Kompanie, was trying with little success to align the wheels on one of the firm's big wood-burning Imberts. The other help had gone home, but Schultzi had nothing at home and so he'd remained in the garage, which, I suspected, was really his home after all. But Schultzi, being Schultzi, made loudly certain that no one would get the idea he was staying on the job because he liked it. For fully ten minutes he had given an outrageously obscene speech on the insanity of trying to operate a hauling company with vehicles that had log-burning fireplaces in the rear. In a climactic burst of frustration, Schultzi had stood up, face livid, and stepped back from the Imbert, his hands shredding a wiper cloth. Lips trembling, he delivered a heroic kick to the already battered flank of the truck.

I looked at him over my newspaper. "What's the matter, Schultzi?"

In monumental inarticulateness Schultzi sputtered: "The frig-ging frig won't frig, that's what's the frigging matter!"

I laughed, and it surprised me. It had been a long time since I'd laughed. Really, I mean.

"Well," I said, "why don't you knock off for a while? You've been going pretty hard these days. Everybody has to rest now and then."

"Why bother, eh? There's nothing ahead anyhow."

"Oh, I don't know, Schultzi. Things are rough, all right. But where there's life there's hope, they say."

"Horse manure, I say. Germany's finished. And so am I."

"Come on, now. Where's all that fire I saw a minute ago?"

"I mean it. I don't know why we bother. We're finished."

I showed him a smile. "Careful, Schultzi. That's traitor talk. And I'm a Gestapo man, you know."

"Frig the Gestapo. And you too."

"Sit down and have a smoke." I pulled out a box of Zeniths, selected one, and broke it in two, handing the larger half to Schultzi. Sighing elaborately to cover the flicker of honest grati-tude in his eyes, the shop boss pulled up a toolbox and sank onto it. He placed the cigarette stub in a corner of his mouth, screwed up his face and tilted his head to take a light from my outstretched match. He inhaled deeply, then blew a long stream of smoke toward the ceiling.

"How did a nice fellow like you get into the Gestapo?"

The question was unexpected, and I sought a neutral answer. "Just one of those things, I guess. I'd been an apprentice dick on the force in Berlin, assigned to a district out in nowhere. There was a call for volunteers, and I was bored with chasing kids who wrote dirty words on sidewalks and so here I am."

Schultzi nodded philosophically. "Funny how people drift into things. Even funnier in your case, though. Most any Gestapo man I ever saw was a big pain in the ass. You just don't seem the type."

I thought it was time to turn the questions 180 degrees. Lighting my own portion of the cigarette, I asked, "How did you drift into Kaufmann Kompanie, Schultzi?"

"I was wounded. I told you that."

"Yes. But I mean why here? Why did you end up here?"

Schultzi removed a shred of tobacco from his lip with a delicate plucking of his soot-black thumb and forefinger. Studying the fiber, he said: "I've often wondered about that myself. It just sort of happened. I was fresh out of the hospital and had holed up in that craphouse room the Housing Authority had allotted me and was coming off a several-day toot. Well, I woke up one morning and was sitting in that craphouse room and thinking about how in hell I was going to get out of that crappy construction job the Manpower Authority had assigned me when Behncke walked in. Just like that. Do you want a mechanic's job, he asked me, and I said you can bet your ass I want a mechanic's job, how did you know. Behncke gave me that simpy goddamned smirk of his and said, oh, I have my little ways. And that's all there was to it, really. I came over here and have been here since."

"You mean you didn't go looking for Behncke—Behncke came looking for you?"

"Me look for Behncke? Hell, I didn't know Behncke from a maharajah's piles. How could I go looking for him?"

"How about your men? You're the foreman—did you hire your own mechanics?"

Schultzi snorted twin streams of smoke from his nose. "Are

you kidding? Nobody gets hired in Germany these days—they do what they're told to do. That's what's so queer about Behncke. He goes around selecting people he wants and seems to get away with it."

"Regardless of specialty?"

"Well, if you ask me, Behncke's not so much interested in anybody's specialty as he is in their background. Where they've been, what they've done. That sort of stuff."

I tried not to show the true measure of my interest in this. I asked: "Why do you say that?"

"Why, hell," Schultzi grunted around his cigarette, "I wasn't allowed to set foot in this garage until Behncke had finished grilling me in his office on my first day here. Christ, you'd think I'd been pinched the way he went at me." Schultzi seemed irritated at the recollection.

"Questions? What kind of questions?"

"Like if I'd joined the Party, and when; how did I get in the Waffen SS, and when; who was my C.O., and did I like him (he was a bastard, by the way); what did I do in my spare time and did I drink too frigging much; who I was sleeping with these days. A lot of crap like that."

"Sounds sort of personal to me. You answered him, did you?"

"Why not? I don't have any secrets."

"The girl you're sleeping with might," I suggested.

"Her?" Schultzi laughed, and the rumble of it was pleasant. "Why, Gretl's registered. She only gives me free privileges because I'm such an adorable fellow."

I had no choice but to join the laughing because I liked Schultzi and was glad that a registered prostitute liked him too. I remembered the old saying: You want to know about a particular man? Just ask a whore. Nobody can size up a man faster than a whore, and if a whore says a guy's all right, then he's got to be all right.

Schultzi's laughter subsided into a quizzical smirk. "Hey, how about you? Didn't Behncke give you the interrogation routine?"

I went carefully. "Who, me? Why, no. I'm Gestapo, remember? Behncke respects the Gestapo. Which is more than I can say for some shop foremen I know."

Schultzi gave me an amiable wink. "Go to hell."

The intercom buzzed, and Schultzi leaned backward to pick the phone from the wall. "Garage. Schultzi here." He listened for a moment, nodded once, and signed off with, "Yes, sir. Of course."

"He want me?"

"'Please tell Jaeger to bring the car for me,'" Schultzi intoned in a really excellent imitation of Behncke's voice. He added then: "Pompous bastard. Never said a word about my being here so late. Why are people so goddamned inconsiderate of others?"

"It's a cruel world, Schultzi." I sighed, standing up and pulling on my coat.

Easing the Mercedes away from the curb, I asked over a shoulder, "You're going home?"

"Yes. Don't you think it's about time?" Behncke's voice was heavy with self-pity. *God,* I thought, *everybody's a martyr.*

"You're a hard worker, all right," I said.

"Well, somebody's got to do it."

"I suppose so."

"Honestly," Behncke grumped from the back seat, "you'd think I'd have been given more help on this thing. Why are people so inconsiderate of others?"

"It's a cruel world, Herr Behncke."

"Maybe so. But it would be a lot less cruel if I could only get some good vehicles and a full inventory of spare parts. The Food Authority is absolutely insane, I swear it. They have forty tons of potatoes that somehow were mis-shipped to Augsburg and they want me to send enough trucks over there to redeliver them to Regensburg. Fine, I say, but I need seven sets of tires, three crank-shafts, and two universals before I move another inch. Well, do you know what they said? They said: 'Very well, Herr Behncke, after you've made this delivery we'll authorize your spare parts.' Now, tell me, does that make any sense? And then there's that double-damned Labor Distribution Group or whatever they call themselves. I am four drivers short and I line up three very good ones—all fully discharged officers of the Leibstandarte Adolf Hitler—and when I notify the Labor Group they tell me I have my quota for the month and the men are now pushing pencils in the Reichsbahn accounting office. There's not one of them who knows a goddamned thing about accounting, incidentally. So I threaten to appeal the matter to Berlin, and that pompous bastard in charge over there says Go ahead, and if you get any answer out of Berlin I'll come work for you myself because you must be Jesus Himself if you can get any answers out of Berlin these days. I honestly don't know how I'm going to pull off this business if I don't get more help at it."

The whole thing mystified me, of course. Behncke was obviously thoroughly engrossed in his efforts to operate a really rather large trucking concern. How was it, then, that he could find it sufficiently critical to the job to run around Munich hiring mechanics and drivers? Not only that, it was a gross inconsistency to hire former officers of the Leibstandarte Adolf Hitler as truck drivers, that's all there was to it. And why highly personal interrogations such as Schultzi described? Hiring mechanics was one thing; hiring mechanics on the basis of their political histories and bedroom habits was something else again.

Behncke was setting up a cover, by God. But for what? I was thinking about this when I realized Behncke was asking me a question.

"I said how are you making out, Jaeger?"

"Just dandy. I've never had so much restful sleep in my life."

"Well, you're just going to have to content yourself with that for a while."

"Still don't trust me, eh?"

"Time, Jaeger. Things take time."

"I suppose. But time has a way of running out."

"I should know. My day's too short."

"Sounds to me as if you could use an assistant. A real smart assistant. Like me."

"Oh, I could use one, all right," he said noncommittally.

"Why not me?"

Behncke cleared his throat. "Because, Jaeger, I don't have the feel of you yet. You sound all right, you act all right—except for that smart-aleck attitude of yours. But I don't have the feel of you yet."

"Well, it's your loss. I don't mind sleeping."

There was no further comment from the back seat, and so I concentrated on my driving. When we had rounded the monument and rolled to a halt in front of Behncke's large, tree-hidden house, I climbed out and opened the rear car door. "Regular time tomorrow?" I asked, taking the brief case Behncke held out.

"Yes. Now, though, I have one more errand for you tonight." Behncke wheezed as he pulled himself from the car. Once erect, he reclaimed the brief case and pulled an envelope from the inside pocket of his Chesterfield coat. He handed it to me. "I want you to deliver this to Fräulein Meier. You have her address, I believe."

"Well, it's pretty late. She—"

"She'll be expecting you. I told her you'd be by."

"Oh. Well, good night, then."

"Good night, Jaeger. The regular time tomorrow, hear?"

As I drove off I decided the envelope was a test. If Behncke thought Heinz Jaeger was going to fool around with an envelope probably filled with trickily arranged worthless contents he had another think coming. . . .

TEN

Nikki Meier's apartment was like the woman: a glossy island in a sea of decay. Schwabing, as an adjunct to Munich, was the retreat of high-class bohemians—a sort of chromium-plated Teutonic Greenwich Village. The war had smudged the chrome and bemused the Teutons, obviously, but as I topped the stairs and rapped at Number 62 I gathered from the chipped murals in the hall and the piping of a flute nearby that the bohemian cadre had stood fast. And, when the door opened and the inner lamp light revealed the tiger rug and the sunken fireplace with its zebra-striped masonry frame, I perceived Nikki Meier as a dame who would connive a sweet-water bath in mid-Sahara. (*God—a tiger rug, yet.*)

She was dressed in a severe black dress and patent-leather pumps—the symbol of puritanical propriety against a background of the gauche.

"Right on time, Herr Jaeger."

"Like Mussolini's trains, that's me."

She displayed her beautiful teeth in a carefully managed smile that showed she recognized the cliché. "Let me take your hat."

"Thanks. Behncke said to give you this." I handed her the envelope. "Nice place you have here."

"It suffices. I once had a nicer one." She placed the envelope on the coffee table.

"C'est la guerre."

"Sit down, won't you? There—on the sofa. But watch out for the springs. They have a nasty habit of asserting themselves." Her heels clicked busily as she crossed to a closet, and I saw that the black dress fitted in a manner not altogether puritanical. "Would you like a drink? I have some whisky."

"That figures."

"What's that?" she called from behind the door.

"I said not now, thanks."

"Strange man. Any man I know would grab the bottle out of my hand and gulp. Whisky's impossible to get."

"I'm not like any man you know."

She returned across the tiger rug, smoothing her skirt as she came. "What kind of man are you, Herr Jaeger?"

"First of all, I'm a man who prefers to have beautiful blondes call him by his first name."

"Hans, isn't it?"

"Heinz."

"Do you really think I'm beautiful, Heinz?"

"You'll do."

"I think you're beautiful."

"You'd be crazy if you didn't. To see me is to swoon."

"You're amusing, too."

"God, yes."

She sat on the edge of an insect-like chair, her hands clasped primly in her lap, her eyes traveling over me in new appraisal. I tried to think of myself as she saw me, sensing that this could help me to attain and hold a woman-wise façade. I was very ill at ease in roles like this and I suspected the reason was that, having grown to adolescence in an atmosphere virtually devoid of femininity, awe of females had become a thing with me. I was very fond of women, but in their presence I usually felt an inward uncertainty, and I knew better than anybody that frequently, in the effort to compensate, I'd come across not as woman-wise but as a mere wiseguy. Oddly, I found myself wondering now if Frau Werner thought me a wiseguy. And, even more oddly, I found myself hoping she didn't.

"Are you a native Berliner, Heinz?"

"No. I'm a Hessian."

"I'd love to go to Berlin."

"I'm afraid you'd find it a bit noisy these days."

"No more than here, certainly. The raids have been terrible."

"Are you a native of Munich?"

"Oh, no," she said, smiling that fantastic smile and tossing her head. "I'm from Tegernsee—a real hick, I am."

"They make their hicks right beautiful down Tegernsee way. But there I go again. We've already established your good looks."

"You're sweet."

"Mm."

"How did you get along in your first week with Kaufmann Company?"

"So-so. Most of the time I sit around the garage and swap war stories with Schultzi."

She laughed easily. "Schultzi is a hundred-carat buffoon, isn't he?"

We traded smiles that agreed that this was so.

"Tegernsee, eh?" I said, still searching for a solid base from which to launch a more fruitful conversation. "What's it like?"

"Like any other place, I suppose. Only smaller. It's a sort of tourist trap, actually. People come from all over to sop up the scenery and to take fizz baths and drink the cure waters and to lie to each other about how rich and influential they are back home. My parents operate a modest little pension at the edge of

113

town, and I didn't want to spend the rest of my life as a scullery maid daytimes and as a tourist's mattress nights so I took the best offer I could find and came to Munich with Herr Linck."

"Who's he?"

"He's my boy friend. Or was." She threw me a little pout. "He's the owner of a nightclub here and he'd come down to Tegernsee for the baths and he met me at a band concert one evening and he asked me if I wanted a job at his place and I was dying to get out of that little burg so I said Sure, why not? But the war's been hard on nightclubs like his, so when there wasn't enough business to justify my salary I decided to branch out a bit. It wasn't too difficult because I'd had secretarial training of sorts, and help is very hard to come by these days—even for War-Important Work administrators."

"So I hear. Seems odd, too, what with all the females there are sitting around making like housewives in houses that are barely standing up."

"Well, the Führer's against conscription of women, you know."

I nodded toward a gilt-framed photograph on the bookcase beside the overwhelming fireplace. The man was bald, with a heavy square face and eyebrows that met in the middle over his box-like nose. "Is that your former boy friend?"

"Yes. Oswald Linck."

"He doesn't look like a nightclub operator. I always think of nightclub operators as having sleek black hair and jeweled stick-pins in their ties."

"Well, that's what he is." She made another face at me, arose, went to the bookcase, and put the portrait in a drawer. "So much for Oswald Linck, eh?"

"Suits me."

"Are you sure you don't want something? To drink, that is."

"I'm sure. About the drink, that is."

We smiled our little smiles again, and she returned to her chair.

"How long have you been working for Behncke?" I tried to make the question sound casual, but I knew immediately from the slight narrowing of her eyes that I'd tried too hard and had set her defense mechanism to working.

"For about three months," she said, herself somewhat too casual.

"What kind of fellow is he? I mean, to work for."

Nikki Meier gave me a cool blue glance, and there was a discernible tightness about her lips. She said crisply: "You're try-ing to pump me, aren't you? I want you to know right off that I'm no talker. If you have any questions about Herr Behncke, I suggest you ask him. If you can't accept this, then we might as well keep our future relations formal and confine them to the office."

I shrugged. "No offense intended. After a few years in the Gestapo, questions become a way of life."

"Just don't question me. About anybody else, that is."

I leaned forward, arms across my knees, making my face somber and my eyes hard, as I'd seen the movie Gestapo men do. "Don't challenge me, Nikki. That's something else we might as well have understood right off: I ask anybody anything I want to ask at any time."

"Well, ask away," she shot back, her color rising. "Ask me some-thing and see what it gets you."

"All right," I said. "Here's my first question: What's it like to kiss you?"

She shifted slightly, easing the pressure against me, and once again I was conscious of the peculiar duality in which the female could be at once a hardness and a softness, a heat and a coolness, a roundness and a flatness, a dry and a damp. Against the lamp-lit sheets she was a subsiding radiance, and I studied her through half-open eyes, listening to my heart and savoring the scent, and drifting.

Somewhere in the long glowing she whispered: "There. You see what your question got you?"

"I should have asked it sooner."

She laughed and then prepared a new offensive.

"Don't you want me to turn out the lights?"

Her voice was muffled. "You leave those lights alone, beautiful man. I like to see what I'm doing."

I became aware eventually that for all its roaring my mind held a pocket of quiet, and in the pocket, Christl Werner.

Even in the silent cataclysm I could find it possible to wonder why. . . .

I got back to Bogenhausen in that quiet twilight that comes before dawn. The air was fresh, and moisture beaded the trees so that they twinkled against the lavender sky.

The remorse was pretty bad.

I'd had twinges of this kind of thing before, back in the school-days when I'd done some pioneering research into the theories set forth in the locker-room jokes and the Tillie and Mac cartoon books sold under the counter down at Manny's novelty shop. Each time I'd tested the girls (and myself), I had come away feeling a little disgusted, the extraordinary stimulation and gratification having turned at once to—well, remorse is the only word for it, I guess. I'd asked Father about this in one of those weird discussions in which you talk all around, saying everything but what you mean, and about the only thing I got out of it was that most men feel this when the liaison has lacked solid love, or at least unselfish affection.

So it was probably due to this truth that I felt so lousy this morning. Nikki Meier was a pazazz-model sex machine, no two ways about it. But I had about as much affection for her as I'd have for a third nostril, and I felt lousy, lousy, lousy.

As I stopped by the door, fumbling for the key Frau Werner had given me, there was a polite cough in the hedge by the gate behind me.

I turned, saw nobody there, shrugged, yawned, turned to the door again, and found that there'd been alterations in the wood.

Belly-high, at a point just above the key lock, Frau Werner's front door sported a new knothole. I'd guess it was a 32-caliber knothole.

Somebody had shot at me, sure as hell.

I thought about this for a long time, say about two seconds, and didn't even touch the carpet on the way upstairs to my room.

ELEVEN

It took me about a week to get used to looking over my shoulder. Somebody had shot at me, and this made me very nervous. However, after a week or so, the lump of anxiety just north of my navel became a living part of me, and I was no more aware of it than I'd be of a piano in my bed.

But Errol Flynn had never let a few bullets keep him from liberating Norway, so I tried very hard to make like Errol Flynn. Toward this end, I began to analyze various comings and goings.

It soon became apparent that Kaufmann truck drivers would routinely visit Otto Behncke's office at the end of their runs. The company operated out of Munich, housed its vehicles in Schultzi's garage (with the overflowing lining the long alley to the rear), and administered its affairs from the one location. Schultzi had passed along the rumor that Behncke was planning branch offices and subsidiary maintenance shops at Augsburg and Rosenheim, and Schultzi had bellowed a profane prayer that it was more than rumor because only God knew how unworkable it was to try to cover the whole of Bavaria from one crappy hole like this. According to my count, Kaufmann had fourteen trucks of various sizes and capacities, eight trailers, a heavy-duty tow truck, three Volkswagen Type 82's, the Mercedes, and four bicycles. A driver and one assistant were assigned to each transport truck, while Schultzi and a myopic fellow named Groos would handle the auxiliary vehicles when necessary.

Schultzi seemed to double as a sort of superintendent of operations and shop foreman. As super, he was responsible for the technical operation and maintenance of all vehicles and was expected to keep Behncke informed of the exact condition and location of any one of them; he instructed the drivers and assistants, inspected rolling stock before it left the garage and when it returned, procured spare parts, selected routes the drivers were to follow on their trips, supervised the paperwork, and raised general hell. As shop foreman he straw-bossed five mechanics and saw that the drivers were trained in on-the-road repairs and up-keep of lubrication records, trip tickets, and accident reports. He was a thoroughgoing martinet in these roles, but was talented enough to make it stick.

In one corner of the garage, in a little glass-enclosed cubicle, Willi Blatz, a wispy sixty-year-old with a consumptive's cough, spent his lonely days as clerk-dispatcher, and maintained payroll time records, memo receipts, supply records, mileage sheets, and any number of other forms—all complicated and all a delight to the Germanic mind. Schultzi and Blatz pretty well ignored each other. Blatz, I suspected, also viewed me as a good-for-nothing freeloader.

But what interested me most (besides survival, of course) was the ritual followed by the drivers. Most of them seemed well disciplined, observing Schultzi's mandates to the letter and generally keeping out of the way when off duty. Not one of them, though, went off duty without first spending some time behind Otto Behncke's closed door. This was another inconsistency in the maze of inconsistencies that bugged me, but it was, it seemed, one of the more significant ones. Otto Behncke, enchanted with Otto Behncke's image as the big businessman, was not likely to pass the time of day with wage-roll truck jockeys. Unless the truck jockeys were making reports of a special kind.

But what reports?

What in hell was going on here, anyway?

In my efforts to answer these questions, I took two steps. The first was right out of a correspondence course on How To Be a Spy and Find Happiness: I began to visit Willi Blatz's cubicle in the wee hours. Willi kept his office and desk locked, of course, but the real Heinz Jaeger's handy-dandy jimmy set made short shrift of these puny barriers and it wasn't too long before I'd filled a pocket-size notebook with the dates, routes, stops, and cargoes as copied from Willi's meticulous records. This I kept under the bookcase in my room at Frau Werner's, and it was my plan to study the data for a possible pattern. The second step was born of chance, as so many of my steps seemed to be these days. While in the toilet one morning, I'd thought I heard Behncke talking outside in the garage proper. The voice had been muted and garbled but unmistakably Behncke's. After a time I discovered that I'd heard Behncke's voice coming down an airshaft—an opening of which was directly over the seat in the toilet stall. Merely sitting and listening wouldn't do, I found, since the sounds were so indistinct. The air-duct opening was quite wide, however, measuring some three feet square. With a screwdriver and some luck I could climb into the duct—at least a little way—and perhaps things would go better.

I was now attempting to implement this little ploy.

A driver called Pfennig, a lean and silent man, had brought in an Imbert from Landshut, and while he and Schultzi talked with their heads bent over the truck's gasogen compartment, I'd gone into the toilet to remove all but four of the screws from the duct screen. Then, returning to the garage and taking post behind my copy of the *Tageblatt*, I'd waited until Pfennig concluded his report to Schultzi, signed the truck over to maintenance, and headed, hat in hand, into the office. I had had a bad moment when I hurried into the men's room and found the booth occupied, but with the sound of flushing I'd been able to stifle my worry and busy myself at the washbasin until the man had left.

I locked myself in the booth, removed my shoes and trousers, and placed them so that to anyone who might glance under the door they would appear to belong to an occupant. Then I removed the duct screen, hung it on the clothing hook, and hauled myself into the opening.

It wasn't an air duct at all, but a mere corridor-like empty space between the supporting walls of two badly joined buildings. A narrow skylight formed the roof cover, and there was an even narrower door at the far end. It was cold and dim in the space, and in my abbreviated costume I felt the chill all the way through. I located a duct opening that was the twin of the one I'd come through, and, hoisting myself up on a set of water pipes, I could manage a fairly good view of Behncke's office.

Behncke was making notes in a large multiple-ring looseleaf book. The man called Pfennig sat in one of the oak chairs, looking bored.

"How about Keller? Any word of him?" Behncke was asking.

"No," Pfennig said, "Klostermann said he'd checked at the address Zeumer had given him, but the landlady said she'd never heard of him—Keller, that is."

"Think he might have gone to Zell am See? He once had relatives there, I think."

"Your guess is as good as mine, Herr Behncke."

"Well, keep your eyes open. Your next trip's tomorrow, isn't it? To Rosenheim?"

"Mm. A load of coal."

"All right. See if you can sniff out something from that lard-belly Weiss. He's made no decent report since the Year One."

"Very well. Oh, by the way: I'm supposed to attend a wedding party tomorrow night. It'll be late when I get back from Rosenheim, so may I make my report to you the next morning?"

"That'll be all right," Behncke said. "I won't be here tomorrow anyhow. I'm going out of town tonight and won't be back until about noon Thursday. Since you have no runs scheduled for Thursday, you can see me then."

"Thanks. I'll kiss the bride for you."

"I'd rather have you pinch her behind for me."

They both laughed, and Behncke disappeared into the outer office with Pfennig. The looseleaf book was still on Behncke's desk, and I was wondering how I might wangle a look at it when the door opened again and Nikki Meier entered. There was something odd in her manner, and this jazzed my curiosity immediately. Why, in an office in which she had every right to be, would Nikki Meier appear to be furtive? I watched, fascinated, as she hurried to Behncke's desk, flipped open the notebook, took one of those tiny microfilm cameras from the bosom of her dress, and made an exposure. Closing the book then, she returned the camera to its hiding place, peered once around the room, then went through the door, skirt swinging.

Nikki Meier was a most unusual secretary.

Someone was in the washroom when I got back to the duct

opening. Just as I heaved halfway through, the door of the booth rattled and Behncke's voice said irritably: "You in there. Are you going to spend the whole day?"

"Be out in a moment," I called, heart thumping. I wondered how I could pull on trousers and shoes without all the fuss arousing Behncke's suspicions. And there was the duct screen to replace, too. *Jesus.*

"Well, hurry up, will you? If I do nothing else around here, by God, I'm going to build another toilet. This is ridiculous."

"Good idea, Herr Behncke. But in the meantime, be a good fellow and get that newspaper I left out there in the garage on Schultzi's workbench, will you?"

"Just who in hell do you think I am? The upstairs maid?"

"Well, if you want in here you'll have to get me out first. And I can't come out the way I am."

Behncke slammed out the washroom door and, in a frenzy of speed, I had dressed and anchored the duct screen by the time the Big Executive returned, muttering testily.

"Well, damn it, here you are."

"Just pass it under the door, please."

"Oh, for God's sake. Really, now!"

"Please?"

I took the newspaper and, tearing off a piece, rattled it vigorously between my knees. Under cover of the noise I completed the fastening of the duct screen. I flushed the john, gave my clothing a final check, and opened the door.

"Sorry, Herr Behncke."

"Oh, get out of the way, will you? And give me the rest of that paper."

Just before noon the intercom buzzed and, being nearest, I lifted the phone off the hook. "Garage. Jaeger here."

"Oh, Jaeger? Good. Come into the office a minute, will you?"

"Right away, Herr Behncke."

Behncke, no doubt, wanted to tell me we'd be going out of town tonight. It would be a pain, since I was entirely out of fresh underwear and socks, and the socks I was wearing were soggy from my shoeless tour of the inner architecture. As I passed

Nikki's desk I gave her a knowing wink, and she smiled, coloring a little, then blew me a quick kiss. I felt a sudden depression.

"How do you feel, Nikkichen?"

"Sore. All over."

"Atta girl. Exercise is good for you."

"Not when you're not used to it."

"You haven't seen anything yet. Olympics begin soon."

I knocked at Behncke's door and went in. Saluting, I said, "Loafer-in-chief reporting as ordered, Herr Feldmarschall."

Behncke looked up from his work, glasses glinting. "Why must you always be so flip, Jaeger? Can't you just act normally?"

"As the psychiatrists say: What is normal?" I reached for a chair.

"Don't bother to sit down. This won't take long." Behncke cleared his throat and shuffled some papers. Then he said: "It may interest you to know, Jaeger, that I've checked Berlin on you."

An iciness formed, and I thought I heard a roaring. Fighting to demonstrate calmness, I shrugged: "I wondered why it took you so long. So what's the verdict?"

My pistol.

Was it loaded?

"Well," Behncke was saying, "you check out in most respects, I'd say. But I'm still not thoroughly convinced."

"How so?" I forced the words through what seemed to be a wet bath mat. "Berlin's usually pretty good at this kind of thing."

"Berlin is a madhouse, and you know it."

"Well, so what's the complaint?"

"I can't say exactly. They've sent me your picture, and all your vital statistics seem to check out. But I still don't feel right about you somehow."

The roaring had become stupendous.

"Would it help," I managed, "if I sang the 'Horst Wessel Lied' every hour on the hour? Or maybe 'Deutschland über Alles'?"

"Oh, stop it."

"Well, I mean, honestly—What do you want of me, for God's sake?"

"I don't know. There's something about you that's phony, though."

122

"You're no cherry bonbon yourself, Behncke. But I assume you're on the level until you prove otherwise. Why don't you do me the same favor?"

Behncke bounced a pencil on its eraser several times, cleared his throat again, and said, "Impasse again, hm?"

"Not impasse. I have you checkmated."

Behncke sighed and put the pencil in a drawer. "All right," he said in a reasonable tone, "let's calm down, shall we? Let's just let things ride the way they have been."

"No. I want in. I'm sick of playing the sedentary chauffeur."

"Well, I have to go out of town tonight. I'll be gone all day tomorrow. We'll talk about it more when I get back Thursday."

"Why can't we talk about it while I drive?"

"Because you're not going, Jaeger. I'm driving myself. Give me the keys to the Mercedes."

"I'm your chauffeur, remember? What's this about your driving all of a sudden?"

Behncke made a pouting smile. "This is personal, Jaeger. I don't want you hanging around when I'm romancing the lady."

I thought about that for a moment, then decided I didn't believe it. Romance? Behncke? However, I could see no way around this one. "As you wish. What about me? Do I sit around the garage all day anyhow? Like always?"

"Why not? You're being paid, aren't you?"

"When are you leaving?"

"Three o'clock. I have to go home and pack first."

"Don't you want me to drive you to your place?"

"No need. Keys, please?" Behncke held out a pudgy hand.

"Well, how will I get home myself tonight?"

"I dare say you'll work out something. You're one of those clever Gestapo fellows."

Something was in the wind, no doubt about it, and I knew that my only chance to discover what was to post a continuous watch on Behncke. I had talked Schultzi out of one of the four bicycles and had nearly broken my neck getting to Bogenhausen and the Opel, which I now steered around the Maximilians Anlage at a speed that made the tires howl. Behncke had left his office at exactly three o'clock, and I prayed half aloud that the fat man had really gone home to pack a bag, as he'd said.

Clearing the monument, I headed the Opel south on Maria Theresa Strasse, and when I neared Behncke's big place I maintained speed and tilted my hat more so as to cover most of the left side of my face. I went past the house at what must have been fifty miles an hour, but not without catching a glimpse of the Mercedes under the porte-cochère and, just ahead of it in a hedge-bordered parking area, a military Volkswagen. Breathing a bit easier, I made a U-turn at the next intersection and drove back to park about thirty yards from where Behncke's driveway entered the street.

I turned off the motor, pushed back my hat, and said, "Jesus."

I was cold and hungry, my feet were still wet, and I had to go to the toilet. The waiting was very hard on me, and it was made more so by the maddening questions.

Who in Berlin Gestapo headquarters had vouched for me? Why? Who had furnished that headquarters with a photo of me? How? When? Why? Nikki was a camera bug—had it been Nikki? But when? Why? How? Hadn't I had my eyes on her at all times whenever we'd been together? But cameras can operate remotely and automatically, so what difference would that make? Nikki had taken a passport-type picture of me for my cover passes, but Behncke wasn't so stupid as to miss the precise likeness of that photo to the one sent down from Berlin. No. It would have to be another picture. But if it was Nikki, who was she working for, anyway? But why Nikki, anyway? Anybody could have taken my picture at any time; granting this, who and why? Heinz Jaeger had been a bona fide Gestapo agent; who in Berlin now said I was Jaeger? And why?

I felt a chilling renewal of that old sense of vulnerability. I had a friend in the Gestapo's front office. And this frightened me. Very much. Like the knowledge that somebody had shot at me and probably would do so again. . . .

I was wondering if there would be any therapeutic value in screaming and kicking my feet when I saw the Mercedes coming down the driveway, its black flanks flickering among the tree trunks and shrubs. Sitting up, I started the Opel and released the brake.

The Mercedes paused at the driveway's end, then turned smoothly to the north, heading away from me, its exhaust making discreet little swirls in the cold.

This was becoming an extraordinary day indeed.

The big sedan was being driven by the man called Leo.

Behncke was in the rear seat.

And beside him was—of all people—Joachim Kolb, disgraced General der Flieger.

TWELVE

I finally found a place to stay in Tegernsee, the so-called Sunny Child of the Bavarian Alps. I'd waited in the street outside the hotel that had engulfed Behncke, Kolb, and Leo until well after midnight, watching uncertainly for additional arrivals or further clues as to just what had brought everybody down to this godforsaken hole. I would have passed the night in the car except for three things: first, a black Opel could not be parked overnight at any point commanding a good view of the hotel without being as obvious as a wart on a baby's bottom; second, I would most certainly have fallen asleep; and, third, I would most certainly have frozen to death if I had. Since it would have been insane to attempt quarters in the hotel here in Südberg, I'd driven to the roadblock outside town to ask the fat little Hipo man in charge for some suggestions. For two cigarettes I had been directed to a place just off Hochfeldstrasse near the railroad station in Tegernsee, more than ten miles away. It had been a clammy place that once catered to minimum-budget tourists, and when I'd left before dawn for the return to Südberg I was as cold and bone-sore as if I'd spent the night in a slit trench.

Day had helped me find my observation post. At the edge of Südberg's Kurpark, across the square from the hotel, was a tiny restaurant that featured a reading room to one side. Even at this ungodly hour the place was jammed with transient soldiers whose sullen sloughing of the watery mock coffee, served by a hunch-back behind the counter, was observed in silent disdain by a knot of meerschaum-sucking Bürgers. I'd been able to scrounge a seat in the corner window of the reading room and, dug in behind a three-day-old copy of the *Völkischer Beobachter,* had established my watch—half afraid that Behncke and his friends might have left during the night. But when my anxiety had reached unman-ageable proportions and I was about to make a move—any move—Leo had come out of the hotel, squinted at the sky, spoken briefly to the doddering doorman, and then disappeared into the lobby.

By eight o'clock I was numb from sitting, and the hunchback was beginning to send lowered-brow looks my way. Someone had turned on a radio, and the news was horrible or exhilarating, depending on whose side you were on. I pondered this, remind-ing myself that as an American it was stimulating indeed to hear that two American divisions had been wiped out in the heavy fighting near Heilbronn. That must mean, I deduced by the Klaussen Method for Judging Windage in Newscasts, that the Seventh U.S. Army was well on its way to Stuttgart and the Danube. It couldn't be long now, and I was half excited over this prospect and half depressed with the realization that many a man was known to have died on the last day of a war. . . .

A gray Horch drove up to the hotel.

I lowered my newspaper, leaning toward the window.

Three men and a woman climbed from the car and, after much slamming of doors, went inside. The hotel door closed, the creaky doorman resumed his slouch-shouldered vigil, and all was serene again.

For a few moments only. Then two more cars squeaked to a

halt in tandem to disgorge eight passengers, two of them women. The women were dumpy and thick-legged and wore mannish clothing.

Twelve arrivals, all told. With three already in the hotel, that made a minimum of fifteen.

Behncke was holding a meeting, obviously. Or was he attending a meeting?

A meeting of whom? For what?

"Can I get you something, buddy?"

The voice, close and wine-tainted, was unfriendly. I glanced over my shoulder at the hunchback. "No, thanks, just waiting for a friend," I said cheerily.

"You've been sitting here a long time, buddy."

"Is there a law against it?"

"Maybe."

"Well, you run along to the law library and research the point. You come up with something against it, I'll leave."

"See that fellow at the end of the counter, buddy? The one with the thick neck and the mustache? He's a cop. We're real good pals."

"He's adorable. You're lucky to have made such a catch."

"Beat it, buddy. I've been watching you, and I know a bum when I see one. So beat it."

"Oh. You mean I haven't bought anything. Well," I said, slapping some bills on the table, "how about breakfast?"

"Out. I just don't like your looks. Out."

I went out, partly furious over the humiliation, partly relieved that the cop had been kept out of the act. How many times had Smith warned me against the little things? It's not so much the big things that go wrong for agents, Smith had said, but watch out for those unexpected little things. Objectively it cost nothing to defer to a hard-nosed Bavarian hunchback. But the incident was irritating as hell: it had disrupted my surveillance and put me out in the weather again.

I crossed the cobbled street and went into the park, an expanse of soggy lawns studded with dripping, rumpled-looking trees and crisscrossed by a network of cracked concrete walks. I followed one of these, keeping a line of ragged shrubs between me and the

127

hotel. At the end of the walk was a summerhouse standing aloof and bleak in an arc of enormous, winter-blackened azaleas. Leaning against one of the flaking white columns, I resumed my watch.

I remained on this Calvary for more than three hours. Somewhere in the interval I became aware that I was not the only one who watched the Brannenberger Hotel.

It was the odd regularity of a salt-and-pepper topcoat that eventually caught my attention. The man was so inconspicuous in his little patrol he became conspicuous. Since nine, when the sun had begun to show through the dregs of last night's storm, there had been a swelling stream of pedestrians in front of the hotel—soldiers looking lost, women haranguing chalk-faced children, peasants in town to confirm that there was nothing in town —and the topcoat kept reappearing in their ranks.

At eleven-thirty there was renewed activity at the hotel entrance. The old doorman pulled himself together and began opening car doors, and the three squat women emerged, pulling on gloves and gabbling amiably. They were followed by the men, who bowed stiffly and shook hands all around before helping the women into the cars. After a final curbside bobbing of heads, the group of men split up and the cars moved off in a concert of protracted burps. At eleven-thirty-five, a Daimler sedan, faultlessly waxed, pulled up near the hotel and the salt-and-pepper topcoat sidled up to it. The man in it leaned through a window of the car to talk with somebody in the back seat. At eleven-thirty-six, Behncke's Mercedes swished around a corner and braked to a halt, and a leather-jacketed adolescent clambered out to hand the keys to the doorman.

The salt-and-pepper climbed in beside the driver of the Daimler.

I trotted across the park, my legs boardlike from the cold, to the tiny parking lot where I'd left the Opel.

Everybody was going someplace, and I was in no mood to be left behind.

The Opel was cold, too, and started only after filing vigorous complaints with the management; but I finally kicked it into life and headed clockwise around the park so that I could pass the Daimler and see who occupied its rear seat.

I saw quite clearly who it was.

Oswald Linck. Nikki Meier's ex-boy friend.

It was eleven-forty-five when Behncke, Leo, and the General appeared at the doorway, and their appearance was the signal for Linck's driver and the salt-and-pepper fellow to leave the Daimler and close in. It happened very quickly. The driver strode up to Behncke, pushed him against the Mercedes and frisked him, while the topcoat led Leo and the General to the hotel wall, which he made them face, hands outstretched. Then all five men bundled into Linck's car and drove off.

Behncke and company had been pinched.

I eased the Opel into cruising speed at a discreet distance behind the Daimler, which cleared town in moments and began the descent down the winding macadam ribbon toward the flatlands to the north. As I drove, I hated Oswald Linck. Oswald Linck was complicating things beyond all manageable limits. Oswald Linck had to be stopped.

But must he be?

Whose side was he on, anyway?

Maybe he was one of the good guys. One of those who had vouched for me in Berlin. Or maybe—

I caught myself up short. Common sense said that my overriding mission was to penetrate Behncke's secret, to sort out and label all the true colors in the yarn box of hints and clues and scents and hunches and guesses and intimations and implications that comprised the Behncke portrait. I could not do this if Behncke were to vanish.

So good guy, bad guy, or just plain schnook, Oswald Linck had to be stopped.

The U.S. Army Air Corps was the first to stop him.

As I cleared a curve on a flank of hill, I could see into the broad valley below, where a pair of Thunderbolt fighters was working over a string of freight cars on a siding at the outskirts of a village. The big potbellied planes sent up a distant bass rumble as they circled and dived, and I could see the smoke trailing from their wing guns long before the sound of their firing reached me. There was a bubble of flame at the railhead, with four of the freight cars spinning toy-like in the air. Then the planes were arcing up and around for another pass.

Oswald Linck's driver was no fool.

An official-looking car on a mountain road would be an intriguing target for a pair of flyboys already tiring of the easy shots in the valley. The Daimler slowed, its taillights winking under their blackout hoods. I applied my own brakes. I was not that kind of fool, either, and the planes had given me my cue.

The car ahead stopped, ground into reverse, and backed into a niche in the woods where a roadside crucifix presided over a cluster of benches installed in a more gentle day for use by those who would ponder the eternals. As I wheeled the decelerating Opel onto the gravel and yanked it to a halt behind the Daimler, my eye caught the carved figure suspended on the cross and I felt a sick something very much like guilt.

I was out of the car then, running, my hand clawing in my coat.

Pounding on the window beside the Daimler's driver, I shouted, pointing skyward and muffling the words: "Hey—your wheels are going around! Didn't you know that?"

I could see Behncke sitting white-faced and handcuffed to the General in the back seat, next to Linck. Leo was in the front seat, jammed between the driver and the salt-and-pepper topcoat.

"I said your wheels are going around! Didn't you hear me?"

The driver rolled down his window. His voice was mean. "What in Christ's name is the matter? Who are you, and what do you want?"

My hand came out of my pocket below the windowsill. "I said your wheels are going around and there are planes all around," I choked.

"What did you say? Who are you? A nut?"

"I want to help you, that's all."

"Get the hell away from this car—"

The three shots came so fast they seemed to make a single sound, like the stuttering snap of dry wood. The driver grinned foolishly and sat back, his eyes wide open and bemused. The man in the topcoat bounced high in the seat and slammed against the far door, which banged open and tumbled him half to the ground. Linck's head jerked sideways, and his hat spun into the front seat. He turned as if to say something to the General, then rolled to the floor, his bald head making a dull sound against the carpet.

For long moments there was nothing but the faraway moan of the planes.

Eventually Leo stirred and said thoughtfully, "Holy loving Jesu von Jesu."

"You shot them," Behncke whispered.

"Of course he did, you idiot," the General sighed.

I was shaking.

"Well, my hero," I heard General Kolb say from a long way away, "do you have any other brilliant plans? Or are you simply going to stand there and shake?"

"I shot them."

"So you did. What do you want—the Iron Cross?"

"He goddamned near shot me, too," Leo said through pale lips. "I could feel the slug brush my coat. Jesu von Jesu."

Behncke cleared his throat. "You were taking a hell of a chance, Jaeger. You could have killed us all."

"For God's sake," the General said, "are we going to sit here all day, gossiping like a bunch of women? You, Jaeger, or whatever your name is, get these cuffs off of us."

"I shot them."

"It was a hell of a chance, that's all I can say."

"Jesu von Jesu."

"Will *somebody* get these goddamned cuffs *off?*"

"What are we going to do now, Jaeger?" Behncke croaked. "What are we going to do, now that we're up to our asses in dead Mueller men? You just tell me that, Jaeger."

Leo whined, "Yes—what? Christ, if we had gone with them we'd have had a chance to talk our way out. But now—Jesu von Jesu . . ."

"Will you please stop saying Jesu von Jesu, Leo?" the General grated. "This young man has just saved our skins, and you know it. We're in a jam, I think, so let's get out of here to where we'll have a little time for the shock to ease up and we can talk more sensibly."

"No—wait," I managed finally. "I have a plan."

"Ah," the General said, "our hero is regaining his wits. What's your plan, my boy? Eh?"

I stared at him, blinking. "You're not retired in disgrace, are you, General?"

"Disgrace is a relative thing, young man."

"But you're not what they say you are. Not really."

"Let's hear your plan, shall we? There's not much time."

I realized the pistol was still in my hand. I stuffed it in my coat pocket. The skin on my face felt tight and hard, and I wondered if I had a fever.

"Your plan?" Kolb repeated.

"Put that man's body back in the car," I told Leo, pointing to the topcoat spilling on the ground. "And bring me the keys to the handcuffs."

"What are you going to do, Jaeger?" Behncke hissed, watching Leo wrestle the thing into the front seat. I ignored him.

"All right, Leo," I said when Kolb's and Behncke's wrists were free. "Now drive the car to the edge of the road. Out there on the curve. Park it facing up the hill, as if it's on its way to Südberg, sort of. Make sure it's out in the open. No trees hiding it. Behncke, you and the General help me gather some leaves and twigs."

The Daimler's wheels spun on the gravel as Leo pulled out of the parking area and onto the road. Its tires squealed as he made the sharp turn uphill. Somewhere in the valley the Thunderbolts hummed.

I piled the branches and damp leaves under some trees across the road from where the Daimler now sat shining in the pale sunlight. The others dumped their armloads on the pile, then stepped back, looking at me.

"Now we hide, eh, young man? While the smoke attracts the planes?"

"That's right, General. All of you take cover. Quick."

I touched my lighter to the driest leaves on four sides of the pile. I did not run until the flames snapped brittlely and the white clouds gushed.

132

Within four minutes the planes had come and gone and the Daimler, its now rust-colored flanks gashed and torn and holed, had been reduced to an incandescent hulk.

"What I don't understand," Behncke was saying, "is how Linck got onto us. I didn't even know the man."

"That's quite a secretary you've got," I said, watching the smoothness with which Leo eased the Opel into the Munich-bound lane.

"Nikki?" Behncke thought for a long time. He said finally, "Why, the little bitch. I'll take care of her."

"Oh, no you won't," I said. "You'll not say a word to her. We want her right where she is."

"Who do you think you're talking to, Jaeger?"

"Shut up, Behncke," the General said mildly. "Let's hear what Herr Jaeger has in mind."

I said: "We've got to assume that Linck was not the only Mueller man interested in Kaufmann Kompanie. By making it look as if Linck and his men were strafed en route *to* the hotel we've settled nothing as far as Mueller's Gestapo is concerned. We've only bought a little time. Nikki will continue to feed the Gestapo information on Behncke's operation. But with one difference: it will be information we decide she should pass along."

"We? What do you mean by that?" Behncke huffed.

"I mean we. You, Leo, the General. Me."

"Oh, no. Not you, Jaeger. You're not in yet. Not until I decide to let you in."

The General stirred, and when he spoke his tone was flat and angry. "How long will it take you to understand, Behncke, that this young man has saved your miserable life? Moreover, he's shown audacity, presence of mind, imagination, and ruthlessness. He's shown his loyalty to you and to Leo and to me and to all those we represent. If you can't see that, then I'll simply have to assume that you're unsuited to your present job. And if that's the case, we'll have to eliminate you. Now, do you accept Jaeger as one of us or do I take steps to remove you as a member of my command?"

133

Behncke's face was cherry red, and he fought to control his furious embarrassment by stroking his mustache with quick, nervous little motions. Seeming to take Behncke's silence as an answer, General Kolb patted me on the shoulder.

"All right, Herr Jaeger. Let's go to my house and talk it all out. I'll wager you could use a cup of coffee, too, eh?"

"As a matter of fact, General, I'll settle for a pair of fresh socks."

PART 2 *DEVELOPMENT*

THIRTEEN

On April 29, 1945, soldiers of the Seventh United States Army took Munich.

I had known they were coming, as had everyone in the city. It had been my plan to be standing at some meaningful location when the event took place, such as the Odeonsplatz, where I could see the Rezidentstrasse and the spot where Adolf Hitler had chickened out in the first true test of his leadership, or, perhaps, the Burgerbräukeller, the Haidhausen beer joint from which der Führer had launched his campaign to make the world cry. But partly by ironical coincidence, partly due to the astonishing speed with which the Seventh had swept in from the west, I'd been caught in probably the most ignominious location of all: the men's room off the garage of Kaufmann Kompanie, produce and fuel haulers.

I'd been drying my hands on a piece of cast-off coveralls, and then Schultzi was opening the washroom door and saying, his eyes misted and his voice thickened with awe, "They're here."

"Who's here?"

"The Amis."

"You're joking."

"No. They're here."

"American *soldiers?*"

"Jillions of them. All dressed alike."

I went across the garage and stood at the personnel entrance for a long time.

There weren't jillions of them, really. First there was a recon jeep bouncing by, radio aerial whipping, its whine diminishing to become a part of the city's waiting silence; then came the slow, almost thoughtful stride of the olive-colored wraiths representing the point of an advance party of an enormous main body still trailing miles to the west. I found somewhere in the passing interval that who these men were, where they had been, or where they would go was a matter of peculiar indifference to me, possibly because the tremendous ram they spearheaded was so vast, so abstract, so impersonal itself. What eventually did get to me was the sound. I decided that the sound—an odd blending of rhythm and irregularity—was more indicative of my country's grandeur than all the bands, all the flags, all the pomp and glisten of all the parades in history.

The soft slap of GI combat boots, it was. A kind of whispering shuffle punctuated by the muted clank of metal.

Nothing more.

Just: slap-slap-slap, clank; slap-slap-slap, clank.

The United States of America, imposing its will.

I waited until nightfall to make my move. Civilian traffic was at a standstill because of the fluid military situation, and so nothing had entered or left Schultzi's garage. And, since Behncke had gone to Kempten for the weekend after picking up his abandoned Mercedes in Südberg, the office, too, had been dark and empty. So Schultzi and I had merely sat around, playing double solitaire and speculating on what Germany would be like under the Eisenhower fist. But after a small supper of beans and potatoes boiled in a can on Schultzi's alcohol burner, I stretched, yawned, and announced that I'd make a stab at getting back to Bogenhausen and a real bed, American army or no.

I had no more than started the Opel and swung down the Briennerstrasse when a jeep squealed out of an alley and jerked to a halt across my path. In the twilight, two men—huge and malevolent, they were—dismounted and stalked toward me, Tommy guns and helmets beaded with moisture.

I wanted to hug them. Honest.

"Wo in das hell thinken Sie du are gehen, Kraut? Getten Sie aus von das friggin' car," the bigger one said in a South Carolina baritone.

"Yeah—and make it schnell, too," the other one put in.

138

I laughed, unable to control the relief and jubilation and solemnity and all the mixed things you feel when you find something precious you thought you'd lost.

"What's so friggin' funny, Kraut? I said get your ass out of the car."

I climbed out, and through the gauze in my throat I said, "I'm an American."

The GI's glanced at each other, then back at me. The Southerner broke the silence finally. "Heh-heh. Well, I declare. You're an American, eh?"

"That's right."

"Well then," said the baritone, "that must make me John Philip Sousa, hm?"

"I'm not kidding, soldier. I'm an American officer. And I'm very glad to see you."

"Well, people always did sort of warm up to me quick."

"He's clean," the one called Lou grunted after a thorough patting of my clothes. "I got his papers."

"O.K. We'll take him to the lieutenant. Come on you, get in the jeep."

"What about my car here?"

"You won't be needin' it for a while."

"Well, let me take the distributor cap, at least. That car's an old pal of mine."

"Go ahead. I don't give a damn. Do you give a damn, Lou?"

"I don't give a damn. But he might have a gun or suthin under the hood, like."

"Look, goddamn it," I broke in, "do you guys think for a crummy minute I'd pull a silly frigging stunt like that?"

The South Carolinian looked at Lou. "Sure talks American, don't he?"

Lieutenant Haley was a Princeton man who looked as if he smelled something bad. He had given me a haughty appraisal, listening with no apparent interest as the baritone described the capture of this here friggin' Kraut spy that sure talked American and said he was and can we go to chow now, sir.

"Get Lieutenant Champion for me first," Haley said in his

Basil Rathbone way. "I want him to sit in on this, since he's the S-2." Obviously Lieutenant Haley did not at all approve of Lieutenant Champion's being the unit's intelligence officer.

When they had gone, Haley, who was seated behind a desk built of two crates and a door that still had its knobs, traded silent, unfriendly inspections with me. After a time the door banged open, filling the little confectioner's shop with a chill wind and a really enormous fellow in a balloon-like field jacket who boomed, "Well, Your Royal Scrotum, I hear you've captured Eric von Stroheim."

Haley said archly, "Close the door. It's cold in here."

"Of course, Your Arrogance." The big lieutenant (he was another second John) made the door fast with thumb, forefinger, and extended pinky. He turned, faced Haley, and made a sweeping bow.

"Oh, cut it out, Champion," Haley chafed. "Don't be a boor all your life. This man claims he's a first lieutenant in the U.S. Army. This may be of academic interest to you inasmuch as you're the S-2 and he's wearing civilian clothing and was driving a German car."

"To be sure, to be sure." Champion looked me up and down, his ample mouth turned up quizzically at the corners. He motioned to an ammunition box. "Sit down, won't you? You look a little tired around the poopdeck."

"Thanks," I sighed, sinking to the box.

"Now, what's the story, my friend? Who are you and what's up?"

"I'm Peter Klaussen, First Lieutenant, Officers Reserve Corps, Serial number 0-545169. That's all I can tell you at this stage."

The big fellow pulled some Luckies from the pocket of his stained jacket, selected one, then held out the pack. "Smoke?"

I nodded my thanks and took the light from Champion's Zippo. The tobacco tasted so good I nearly fainted from holding it in my lungs so long. "It's been quite a spell since I've had a real smoke."

"How come?"

I waggled a sly finger. "You're a sneaky one, all right."

"Well," Champion said, pulling up an ammo box of his own, "what happens now? Do we send you off to a detention Lager for trial as an impersonator of a U.S. officer? Do we get out the rubber

140

hose and sweat you? Does John really love Sally? Will Marcia give up her baby?"

"For heaven's sake, Champion," Haley grumped.

I studied the end of my cigarette. "As S-2 of this unit, Lieutenant Champion, you can assist me in the completion of my mission."

"Now, how could that be, Marcia?"

"You can relay a message to G-2 at SHAEF."

Champion chuckled, and the room echoed the rumble. "Oh, come on, now, pal. Ever since Marseilles I've had characters asking me to do the same. Every damned town, every crummy crossroads has produced some kind of boob who tells me all wide-eyed and breathless that he's really an American agent who has a message for Ike which he'll gladly deliver after he's had a bath, a beefsteak dinner, a cigar, and a good lay."

"I don't want any pay-off to deliver. I'll give you the message right now. Free."

There was a flicker of interest in Champion's eyes. Haley looked up from the study of his nails.

"Ah-so," Champion said with a Japanese inflection. "Honoraber spy leady to terr arr he know without blibe? Velley intellesting."

"Not all I know. Just a message."

"And what is the message, pray?"

" 'Mairzy Doats.' "

" 'Mairzy Doats'?"

"That's right."

"That's the message? All of it?"

"Yes."

"Seems so aloof and distant, somehow. It lacks warmth and understanding and all those crazy, wonderful things I've found to be so meaningful and endearing in our life together. Oh, Peter, why can't we *communicate* any more?"

"Sorry, Sally. Why don't you run over and watch Marcia have her baby?"

✠ ✠ ✠

TWX: TO AC OF S, G-2, SHAEF, 30 APRIL 45 (THRU: ALPHA CHANNEL)
FROM G-2 7TH ARMY: S-2 OF MUNICH-BASED RECON COMPANY
IS HOLDING CIVILIAN CLAIMING TO BE PETER KLAUSSEN, 1ST
LT, ORC, ASN 0-545169, ON ASSGMT UR HQS. CIVILIAN MES-
SAGES YOU AS FOLLOWS: MAIRZY DOATS. PLS ADVISE.

L. T. COONEY, MAJ INF

TOP SECRET

Memo to Smith, OSS Liaison   1 May 45
  1. Please note attached TWX.
  2. Query: Does this revive *Scab* affair? Advise soonest.

For AC of S, G-2, SHAEF
M. S. Manning, Lt Col Arty

By Courier—Most Urgent   1 May 45

Peppermint:
  Have info that reports survival of Ludwig Schaue. If true, advise
soonest (1) why he survives and (2) why I was not so notified.

Putzi

2/V/45   Via Courier

Putzi:
  Report true. Schaue has become friendly with Kolb and is obviously infatuated with Kolb's daughter. Moreover, Schaue seems
to be a remarkably resourceful chap. Thus Spike feels Schaue

offers one more potential lead to Bormann's cache. We need all the leads we can get, remember.

Peppermint

By Courier—Most Urgent   3 May 45

Peppermint:

Schaue survival immaterial to me for the moment. But I am incensed over your failure to report this development. Such a lapse could cause me extreme embarrassment at this headquarters. More important, it is arrogant disregard of my control position. You and Spike must not let this happen again.

Putzi

TOP SECRET

Memo to AC of S, G-2, SHAEF   3 May 45

Attn: Col Manning; Ref: Ur ltr 1 May 45

1. Klaussen survival does not yet revive *Scab* affair. However, I have elected to keep him on assignment this office to pursue investigation related to Operation *Appleseed*.
2. I will proceed Munich TDY 7 May 45 to debrief Klaussen.

Smith

TOP SECRET

TWX: TO G-2, 7TH ARMY, 4 MAY 45 (THRU: ALPHA CHANNEL) ATTN: MAJ COONEY

FROM AC OF S, G-2, SHAEF: REUR TWX 30 APRIL 45. CONFIRM IDENTITY CIVILIAN CLAIMING TO BE PETER KLAUSSEN, 1ST LT,

ORC, INF, ASN 0-545169. PLS HOLD KLAUSSEN CURRENT LOCA-
TION FOR DEBRIEFING BY MANLEY SMITH, MAJ, INF, REPRESENTA-
TIVE THIS HQS, ARRIVING UR HQS 7 MAY 45.

MANNING, LT COL ARTY

FOURTEEN

Smith had elected to hold the debriefing in one of the offices
Military Government had commandeered at the rear of the
Rathaus on the Marienplatz. He was in Class A's, and with all
the service ribbons and the spade-shaped SHAEF shoulder patch
with its brilliant sword, he looked quite elegant and soldierly. I
still couldn't warm up to him, though, and I wondered how much
this showed. Not that I cared, really.

Smith was studying some notes and, without looking up, said
unenthusiastically, "Glad you made it, Klaussen."

"Thanks. Glad to be back."

"I've talked to Lieutenant Champion and he's given me the
details of your arrival."

"Good man, Champion."

"All right," Smith said blandly, "we might as well get our little
post mortem under way. What went wrong, and where did you
hole up? Step by step, please, since even little shreds of information can be useful in my business."

"Hole *up*? You're kidding, of course."

Smith looked at me directly for the first time. "You mean you
didn't hole up?"

"Why, heck no. I've been a very busy little katzenjammer.
Didn't you recover my message by the crucifix?"

"Not yet. I've asked Seventh Army CIC to look for it."

144

"Well then. Just don't go assuming things until you know the whole story," I huffed. "I went to a lot of trouble to get that message to you, as skimpy as it is."

Smith, a tinge of color in his carefully shaved cheeks, said, "So you didn't hole up, eh?"

"No. I pursued the mission."

"Well, this brightens my day," he said opaquely. "What's the story?"

"I've managed to penetrate the Werewolf high command."

"*Werewolf?* That's ridiculous. The Werewolf organization was a figment of Goebbels' sick imagination, nothing more. Interrogation of some very high-horsepower Nazi prisoners has already confirmed that. I'll admit SHAEF strategy has been badly warped due to the propaganda about Werewolves, the Last Redoubt, and all that, but propaganda it was."

"Do you want to hear this, Smith, or don't you? I don't give a good damn one way or the other."

"Don't get snotty, Klaussen."

"Don't rub me, then. I've completed my obligation to you. Treat me nice."

"Very well," Smith murmured, evading the challenge. "Take it from the top."

I lit a cigarette and stared out the small window at the spring-washed Munich skyline. Somewhere a GI radio crackled something about Doenitz and the imminent unconditional surrender, and outside, above the traffic noises, I could hear summer birds arguing in the eaves. I worked very hard to be calm and cool, but it wasn't easy.

"Last autumn," I said, "Martin Bormann called General Joachim Kolb into his Berlin office and—"

"Good God," Smith broke in, "you *do* take things from the top, don't you?"

There was a flip of malicious pleasure under my ribs. For once I'd scored on Smith, and it was a happy event. "You ain't heard nothin' yet, Sam," I said.

"Why would the deputy Führer call in Kolb? Last we heard of Kolb was that Hitler fired him last year, certified as mentally incompetent."

"I'll get to that."

"Please do." Smith wrote something in his little notebook and scrawled a big question mark after it.

"Bormann told Kolb," I went on, "that Germany's military efforts seemed doomed and that Hitler's plan to fight to the last German was asinine, that whatever happened to Hitler something had to be done to assure the Nazi Party's survival."

Smith coughed dryly and said, "I find this hard to believe already. Bormann has been notoriously loyal to Hitler, and even to entertain such a thought was pluperfect treason. It simply doesn't fit, my boy."

"Are you going to hold on to conventional opinion or are you going to hear me out for some possible new ideas?"

"You're very irritating, Klaussen. You know that, don't you?"

"I'm very irritated."

I could see Smith was honestly struggling to control himself, and it occurred to me that I was rapidly becoming the very kind of person I disliked the most. And so, half depressed, half contrite, I tried to stop talking between my teeth.

"Bormann said that although everybody was talking about the Werewolf idea he was preparing to do something about it. Down in Munich, he said, there was a hauling firm called Kaufmann Kompanie which had barely survived the Nazi corporate dissolution laws of October, 1937, by qualifying with capital of some 200,000 Marks. Kaufmann, hamstrung by all the small business controls, had never been able to climb away from the raw edge of insolvency and now was about to fold. Bormann said that about five million Marks had been quietly removed from the Hitler Youth national treasury and placed in the Munich bank account of Otto Behncke, ostensibly a simon-pure, nonpolitical businessman but actually the former comptroller of the National Youth Education Bureau and an SS Hauptbannführer. Behncke, posing as a well-heeled manipulator on the make, was to buy in as owner-manager of Kaufmann. His mission: to get Kaufmann on its feet; then, in the event of a complete collapse of the German armies, to ingratiate himself with the incoming Allied troops so that when the occupying forces moved in he'd be able to present himself and his firm as being approved by Military Government officials. With this cover, he could carry out the real plot."

Smith stirred. "Which is?"

"Which is as follows. Bormann has ordered certain key personnel of the SS, SA, Reichsjugendführung, Hitler Jugend, and Bund Deutscher Mädel to take up residence in Bavaria, where they're to organize systematic operations designed to support long-range Werewolf resistance to the occupation. Behncke's trucks, hauling loads of coal and food blessed by the Allies, are to be driven by SS, SA, SD, and HJ characters with carefully prepared cover identities who keep Behncke informed of progress in the provinces and carry Behncke's orders to those working in the provinces. Meanwhile, Behncke's company is supposed to become self-supporting, so that the remaining portion of the HJ five million can be used to buy arms, equipment, and food needed by the Werewolf workers."

"Wait a minute," Smith said, holding up his pencil and shaking his head. "You mean Bormann expects a third-rate clerk like Behncke to be father and mastermind of the new Nazi Party? God in heaven."

I shook my own head. "Easy does it, Major. I'm still taking it from the top. Behncke's no more than an errand boy who's supposed to have things set up and clicking by the time Bormann himself can risk crawling out from under his rock to take charge."

Smith blinked slowly at his notebook, three times. "I see. But why Kolb? Why did Bormann ring in Kolb?"

"As you say, Behncke's a third-rater. But he has one great attribute: he is unknown, unobtrusive, so lacking in notoriety as a Nazi he has the best possible chance of hiding his true past from the Allies. Therefore he makes a very good front man."

"But Bormann feels Behncke needs a chaperon and Kolb is it, hm?"

"Yes. As you know, Kolb's been famous for years as a World War I ace turned playboy, dope addict, lush, and thoroughgoing bastard who climbed to a cushy job in the Luftwaffe by riding Göring's shirttails. But the record shows that from about 1940 on there are no reports of Kolb's cutting up like there were in the twenties and thirties. From what I gather, Kolb kicked his habits and settled down to become a first-rate administrator in Luftwaffe GHQ. However, Hitler never liked Kolb, and indulged him in the same watchful way he had the fairies who permeated the

147

early SA. If it hadn't been for Göring's sponsorship of Kolb, Hitler probably would have purged the General long before the war—"

Smith coughed again and said testily, "The point, the point."

"Bormann, like Göring, saw a lot of talent in Kolb, apparently. After sending Behncke off to Munich, Bormann called in Kolb, described the plot, and informed Kolb that he, Kolb, was to be the secret leader for the Werewolf project—providing Behncke with over-all policy guidance—until Bormann himself could work his way south from Berlin and assume command. Bormann told Kolb to feign a huge drinking bout, to raise hell, insult some important people, blow his stack, so that Hitler would be sure to fire him. Object: to build a cast-iron cover for Kolb as the leader of a lot of hanky-panky under, first, Hitler's nose, and, second, under Eisenhower's nose. In other words, when the Werewolves begin to prowl who's going to think their leader is an irresponsible drunken nut who even Hitler couldn't put up with?"

Smith sneered faintly and said, "Awfully melodramatic, isn't it?"

I sneered faintly and said, "Major Smith, you just show me one damned thing about Germany's past twelve years that isn't melodramatic."

"So all this is what's going on then, hm?"

"All this is what Behncke—and Bormann, wherever he may be hiding—think is going on. General Kolb has had other ideas. Namely, collaboration with us good guys."

"Oh? So then Kolb is our man, Scab, eh?"

I stubbed out my cigarette. "Yes. Even when Bormann was giving him his orders, Kolb says, he could see that the plan was unworkable, stupid, and not in the German national interest. Primarily a military man and only a nominal Nazi, Kolb thinks the Nazis are political onanists, and he believes the best thing that could happen to Germany is their complete eradication. But more than that, he saw the Bormann plan as the means by which to escape his own prosecution by the Allies as a Nazi of general officer rank."

"How so?" Smith put in.

"Kolb saw it this way: If he were to collaborate with the

Americans in smashing the plot, the Americans would let him free to take care of a very personal matter."

"Which is?"

"Amends to his daughter. He says he's given her a bad time for years, and the only thing that counts with him now is a chance to repair their relationship."

Smith made a cynical sound in his chest. Then he said, "Soft violin music is heard here, hm?"

I shrugged. "You asked why. I told you."

"All right, so what did Kolb do to implement his little counter-plot?"

"Kolb asked Bormann to assign Eugen Klottner to him as an aide. Klottner, a Gestapo man and Kolb's best friend, had long been disillusioned with the Nazi crap, and Kolb knew he'd be amenable to his plan to screw Bormann and Behncke. And, as Kolb found, Klottner was not only amenable—he was delighted to find a route he could use to earn some goodwill from the Americans for himself. To ring in the Americans, Klottner suggested that he pinch a U.S. agent he knew to be operating a radio near Wiesbaden. Kolb agreed, and they both convinced the agent that big things were afoot and that a U.S. officer should be dropped into Bavaria on March 24—the date Kolb, accompanied by Artur Leopold, his orderly, was to move into a little place in Obermenzing and assume his secret command. The American agent radioed SHAEF, and I, dear Peter Klaussen, got pushed out of a Liberator one misty night. The only fault with this latter, incidentally, was that you thought I was to be a courier, while Kolb and Klottner awaited me as a kind of resident U.S. of A. partner. I can't tell you how embarrassed *I* was over this little misunderstanding."

Smith made no acknowledgment of this sarcasm. Instead he said: "Which brings me to the very obvious question. How did you end up knowing so much of the melodrama unfolding?"

"Partly by plain brass, partly by good luck, partly by logical circumstance."

"Explain, please."

I groped for another cigarette and discovered I was out. Smith did not offer me one of his. Pretending I didn't care, I said:

"Behncke, in one of his earliest conferences with Kolb, pointed out that if he were to keep Kaufmann Kompanie running he'd need a first-rate black-market specialist who speaks English. He anticipates trouble operating under American occupation—trouble getting tires, spare parts, that sort of thing—and he wanted a man skilled in black-market operations to head up that activity for him. Kolb didn't know such a man, so he asked Klottner. Klottner suggested that Bormann be asked to transfer Heinz Jaeger to Munich. Jaeger, an old pal of Klottner's, would be just what Dr. Behncke ordered. But Behncke didn't like the idea of another Gestapo man being cut in on the plot. He argued that Gestapo Chief Heinrich Mueller was very loyal to Hitler and the special transfer of Jaeger might tip Mueller to the Bormann plan. Besides, Jaeger might be very loyal to Mueller, and if so, they'd be dead. Klottner said Jaeger was quite safe, since Jaeger hated Mueller and had often said privately that he'd like nothing better than to fix Mueller's wagon. So Kolb decided in favor of Jaeger and arranged his transfer to Munich on March 23—the day before the U.S. officer would arrive. Klottner was to meet Jaeger at the airport; then both of them would rendezvous with the Ami parachutist early the following morning. All three would then go to Obermenzing for a thorough briefing by Kolb. The idea was to have Jaeger report to Behncke as the black-market specialist and the Ami—me—to stay on with Kolb as U.S. counselor, sort of, pretending to be an old pal of Kolb's who had no place else to go. My true role, of course, was to be a secret shared only by Kolb, Leopold, Klottner, and Jaeger—the ringleaders of the counterplot against Bormann and Behncke and Company."

Smith turned in his swivel chair to gaze out the window, his eyes distant and cool in the reflected sunlight. "So what happened?"

"After a bad landing I finally made contact with Klottner and Jaeger. I told them I was a courier, no more, and that I had to get back with their proposal. They said no, that I'd have to talk thing over with a third man. As they drove me toward Munich there was an air raid and Klottner and Jaeger were killed. My cover had been broken, so I had no choice but to assume the identity of Jaeger—his clothes fit me—and go to Klottner's home address.

"Which was what?" Smith asked, pencil poised to make the note.

"Freudestrasse 449, Munich-Bogenhausen. It's owned and occupied by Christl Werner, widow of a Wehrmacht physician killed in Russia and daughter of none other than General Kolb."

Smith looked up from his notebook. "Now isn't that cozy."

"Luckily, Frau Werner had never heard of Jaeger, so I was able to con a room by telling her I was Jaeger, an old friend of Klottner's. In Klottner's room I found this business card." I passed Smith the card, face down, so he could read the notation on the back. "I assumed 'Despair' meant me, so I went to Kaufmann to ask for a job, still posing as Jaeger. I was interviewed by Behncke, and after some horsing around, Behncke gave me a probational job as his chauffeur and—"

"Probational? You mean he didn't buy your story all the way?"

"No, he didn't. He took Klottner's death very hard, because without Klottner's voucher nobody—least of all Behncke—could be sure I was really Jaeger. In Behncke's suspicious little mind I could be one of Heinrich Mueller's loyal Gestapo men who'd somehow learned of the Werewolf plot and had knocked off Klottner and Jaeger and taken Jaeger's place. He accepted me conditionally until I could demonstrate where my true loyalties lay."

Smith nodded. "And why didn't he check Bormann to see if you were really Jaeger? Hm?"

"For security's sake, Bormann had ordered a halt to communications between the Munich group and himself. So with this impasse we went to work. I subsequently learned by snooping around most of what I've told you here. Plus a couple of other things I haven't covered."

"Like what?"

"Like the fact that Behncke's secretary, Nikki Meier, was an informer for Oswald Linck, a Mueller Gestapo man. Like the fact that Christl Werner, Kolb's daughter, is scared silly of something I can't pin down. Like the fact that somebody's been shooting at me. Like the fact that Behncke *did* check Berlin to see if I was really Jaeger, and somebody in Berlin said I was—even provided pictures of me, yet."

Smith looked at me sharply, and I could see something very much like worry flicker through his eyes. This impressed me, because I didn't think Smith could worry about anything.

"Ouch," he said. "Who do you think vouched for you?"

"I haven't the slightest."

"Kolb?"

"The idea of somebody in Berlin vouching for a Yankee spook seemed to frighten the hell out of Kolb."

"It frightens me, too," Smith said tartly.

"You should see it from here," I said tartly.

There was a pause, and Smith bounced his pencil on its eraser several times. Eventually he said, "How did you get so friendly with Kolb?"

"One day Behncke and Kolb held a meeting of their field commanders at a hotel in Südberg, a run-down spa not far from Tegernsee. When they started back for Munich, Oswald Linck, apparently tipped by Nikki Meier, pinched Behncke, Kolb, and Leopold on charges of treason to Hitler. I managed to rescue them by doing in Linck and his hoods"—despite myself I stumbled over the words—"and, convinced that I was really the American he'd suspected I was all along, Kolb took me to his place in Obermenzing and told me the whole story as I've told it to you. Behncke, of course, assumed that Kolb had accepted me simply on the basis of my, ah, dispatching some Mueller Gestapo men. In other words, Behncke still does not suspect I'm an American. On the contrary: reassured by Kolb's acceptance of me, Behncke now tolerates me as the real Jaeger."

Smith hid a yawn behind his wrist, then glanced at his watch. "Well, Klaussen," he said, "what are your next steps?"

I felt a peculiar sinking feeling. "You want me to continue, then? That's official?"

"Certainly. Why not?"

I went slowly. "Well, I don't know how you professional spy people work, but as for me, I don't particularly like this kind of thing. I keep stumbling over my scruples."

"You'll get over that. We all do."

"I'm not sure I want to."

"You haven't any choice, actually."

152

"The old 'your country needs you' routine, eh?"

"Something like that. Now: What are your plans?"

"Well," I said, trying to shake off the fast-building depression by making words, "I guess I'll try first to get a look at those pictures of me sent down by my unknown benefactor in Berlin. If I could see them, I think I could figure out who took them, and when. And in the process, I think I'll rent a tank. To be shot at makes me very unhappy." I hesitated, then added, "I also want to find out what's bugging Christl Werner."

Smith snorted. "Details, Klaussen, details. More important, I want you to keep an eye out for Bormann; to try to determine whether Behncke's bank account is the only source of Nazi funds; to look for evidence as to whether Mueller, the Gestapo chief, is still alive; to find out what Kolb's *real* motives are. Those kinds of things are what I want to know."

Because I didn't know what else to say I said, "All right."

Smith closed his notebook, placed it in his jacket pocket, screwed the lead into his pencil, and stood up.

"And now," he said, "you'd better get going. There's a peace on, they say."

FIFTEEN

The Abendsee filled a chink in the Alps, its placid, deep-green waters forming a moodily shifting mirror for the colossal peaks above. The mountains, deployed in a jagged semicircle, were faced on the lake's northern rim by a fan-shaped sweep of valley land that snoozed in the sun and exuded the mixed scent of wildflowers, pines, and rich black earth tilled for centuries by occupants of the Disney-cute cottages dotted around. The road cleared a highland rise, then went out across the valley like a lazily tossed rope, and giving the Opel its rein, I relaxed and tried to absorb the majesty of it all.

I decided to make some conversation. "Abendsee. The Evening Lake. That's a pretty name, isn't it?"

"Yes. I once loved this place," Christl Werner said beside me.

"Once? Why once?"

"You forget, Herr Jaeger. It's where I met my husband."

I felt a flash of annoyance with myself. "Of course. I'm sorry. I should have remembered."

"No reason why you should have."

"Your father also came here for his illness, didn't he? Is that why he decided to come back again now?"

"No. His house in Obermenzing has been taken over by the Amis as an officers' quarters and, since he's had a place here for years, it was the logical move to bring him here."

"I'm surprised he didn't come here in the first place. Who'd want to live in Obermenzing when he has a house by the Abendsee?"

She shrugged a shoulder. "I don't even try to fathom my father any more, what with his condition and all."

"How did he get down here?"

"It was while you were being held by the Ami troops. The second morning after your—disappearance—an Ami officer drove up to my father's house and told Leo that the two of them would have to get out—the house was needed as a barracks for the officers of a military police unit, or something. Anyway, Leo bundled Father into the VW and down they came."

"Oh."

"I was worried about you, you know."

I gave her another glance, but she kept her eyes on the road.

"Worried about me? What do you mean?"

"When you didn't come back for such a long time, I worried about you. I remembered how Herr Klottner went out one morning and never came back."

"Well," I said, strangely pleased, "that's nice. It's nice to be missed."

"It's rather nice to have you around the house."

"You really don't know very much about me, Frau Werner," I said, the warmth in me fading.

There was a period of silence, and I could sense that she, too, was having trouble finding a conversational base. "You've often mentioned your father," she said. "You like him very much, don't you?"

"Very much."

"What kind of man is he?"

"Oh, he's many things. A flier in the First War—he was in the Richthofen squadron, and very proud of it. Then a writer. And after my mother died when I was born, he traveled a lot. Physically, he's not very big, but he gives you the impression he is. And when he says something you listen, because even if he's joking there's something about what he says and the way he says it that's sort of special. It's hard to explain."

"It must be wonderful to have a father who jokes."

I gave her a sidelong look. Her hair shone deep red in the sun, and her eyes, half closed against the glare, were iridescent. With her blouse and black vest-like jacket, she was very young and small, and I felt a rush of—of something.

"I wish you'd had one," I said.

She did not answer.

Teufelsschwert—the Devil's Sword—was the name of the incredible minaret of granite that rose from the lake's southern arc to hold a giant finger of warning over the valley. Even on this spring afternoon the peak was blackish and malevolent, and the snow on its summit was more blue than white, except for the sparkling cascades caught up and sent sifting into nowhere by the hellish winds roaming aloft. In its shadow I felt the chilling presence of a hundred million years all congealed.

We had turned right at the village square on the lake's northern shore and followed a gravel road, which climbed up and around to the west and south to carve a tortured S up the north-facing skirt of Teufelsschwert. High above the Abendsee, the road had leveled off to cross a grassy plateau and end at crag's rim. There an impossible house clung to an impossible lip on the impossible precipice the Teufelsschwert presented to the lake and valley beyond. The place was an inverted L-shape, with the main house forming the crosspiece along the cliff's edge and the right-angled wing—presumably a garage and utility area—cutting into an ankle of the mountain proper. The road had broadened to become a combination driveway for the garage wing and a parking apron filling the hollow of the **L**. A hedge separated the parking area from a massive sundeck that jutted into space over the glassy water some two hundred feet below.

I stood at the railing of the deck, smoking a cigarette and wondering if my slight giddiness was due to the thin mountain air or to a real case of vertigo. I had just turned to enter the house when General Kolb came out through the expanse of sliding glass that fronted the living room inside.

"Welcome to Fliegerfreude, Herr Jaeger. Quite a view, eh?"

"Hello, General. Is that what you call this place—'Flier's Joy'?"

Kolb nodded, a smile ghosting his face. "Yes. When you sit in a chair by the railing and half close your eyes and listen to the wind you get the impression you're flying. I did it once, shortly after the house had been built, and being in a soddenly romantic mood, I suppose, I gave the place its name. It's trite, to be sure, but the name has stuck."

"It's one hell of a place. How come you bothered with Obermenzing when you could have come here all along?"

"Convenience, mainly. I had to be certain that Behncke was set up and going, and I couldn't do that in this godforsaken birdhouse. I would have stayed there, too, if your little friends from across the sea hadn't changed my mind."

I humphed. "They might change your mind again if they see this. Just think how fast you'll be out of here if some general from Wilkes-Barre spots this elegant joint."

Kolb shook his head. "I don't think so. I dare say you, with your connections, can keep generals from Wilkes-Barre from cluttering up my mountain home."

I couldn't help smiling. "I suppose so. In any event, it's quite a place. It has everything you could need."

"Not everything. There's no piano."

"Piano?"

"Yes. I once played. Quite well, they tell me. I miss it now. Behncke says he'll try to get Ami permission to locate one and haul it up here. Maybe you could help."

"Maybe. You're full of little surprises, aren't you, General?"

"Oh, it's not much, really. My mother once had fond notions of

ιy becoming a concert pianist. I might have, too, if the First War
ιnd dope and drink and politics hadn't eventually intervened.
Ϳut that's life, as they say."

"I guess so."

"I'd like to play again, though. It's not only a pleasure in itself
—it also helps me think. Do you play an instrument, Jaeger?"

"I'm afraid not. It must be fun, though." I paused, then asked,
How long have you had Fliegerfreude?"

"Oh, since '37 or '38. I'd have to look it up. Those years are
ιomewhat fuzzy."

"Fuzzy or not, you must have been in the chips. You don't build
. place like this with trolley tokens."

"True. But the land was granted to me by a grateful Führer,
he house was built by a grateful Göring, and I was built by grate-
ul distilleries. I can't imagine how it was I never happened to
ιll over that railing. They tell me that once, during a sleet storm,
climbed over it and chinned myself twenty times."

"You must have been a hell-raiser, all right."

"Yes. They don't make men like that any more. I hope."

Remembering, I asked: "Where's your daughter? It wouldn't
ιo for her to see us chatting away like old war buddies, would it?
ϳhe made me promise to keep out of your sight."

"She helped Leo with the supplies you brought, then decided to
ιake a nap. I checked, and she's really sawing it off."

"Well, it's only security we're fooling with."

"Speaking of security, you had me worried, disappearing among
he Amis for a whole week. Everything all right?"

"Yes. I merely got snarled in red tape. But it's all set now. All
ιve have to do is sit back and watch Behncke operate, take down
he list of recruits he compiles, then, when Headquarters decides
ι's time, round up the whole bunch."

The General humphed. "You make it sound easy. He may look
ι, but Behncke's no fool."

"Neither are you and I, General. We can take Behncke."

"I like to think so. But there are some things still bothering me."

"Such as?"

"For one thing, your unknown angel in Berlin—who was he,
ιnd why did he cover for you?"

Studying the valley, I murmured, "That's what I'd like to

know." After a pause, I asked mildly: "Tell me, General, why d Oswald Linck and his men choose to arrest you in Südberg? Yo were right under their noses in Munich all the time. Why wa until you had gone to a motheaten hotel in the hills?"

Kolb clamped his Tyrolean hat lower on his head, placed h elbows on the railing, and stared off at the northern sky. "It's n guess that they wanted to catch us in a seditious act. Under Hi ler, my boy, such a meeting as we held in my father's hotel wa precisely that—sedition, treason. Also, I suppose they wanted watch the faces that gathered. After all, they were in your kir of business, and you're not rushing in to pinch Behncke, are you'

"Your father? You say your father runs the hotel in Südberg'

"Mm. He and I get along like cats and dogs. He remembe only my bad days, and he won't let me forget them either, ur fortunately."

"Why did you meet there, then?"

"It was centrally located for those who attended, and relative remote from Ami action. Also, it gave me a cover. What's mor natural than to go visiting your own father and having in a fe old friends in the process?"

"I see. Tell me something else," I put in carefully. "Just wl was it you agreed so readily to demolish your manfully built ne image when Bormann asked you to?"

Kolb looked at me. "I didn't agree so readily, young man."

"But you did agree. If you despised the Nazis so much and r garded your hard-won personal reconstruction so highly, wl didn't you tell Bormann to find another boy?"

"To refuse was to die. Alive and thinking, I could fix the wagons."

I nodded. "Still—"

The General interrupted, and there was an edge to his voic "This means, I suppose, that you still don't trust my motives, eh.

"Perhaps."

"This is the last time I'm going to tell you: I have only or reason for helping you Americans to squash Behncke. I'm tryin —in the classic stool-pigeon manner—to trade Behncke's defe for my personal amnesty. Yours is a nation of emotional nincom poops who categorize everything in absolutes of good or ba

158

You recognize no shades between; if it isn't good by your definition, it's entirely bad. Is a man a German? Then he must be a Nazi. Is a man a Nazi? Then he must be Satan incarnate, and off to jail with him. There's no pause for consideration as to who and why the German is, how and when he might have become a Nazi, or if, as a Nazi, he was a hero or a heel. There's—"

I broke in testily, "You Nazis will get your hearings—"

"Oh, certainly," he scoffed. "We'll get our hearings. Before judges who predicate their judgments on your Casablanca philosophy, in which a man like Schultzi, say, or a woman like Christl, say, are of the same stamp as those monsters who ran the ovens at Buchenwald. Schultzi: an enlistee in the Waffen SS. Why? The little man's hunger for status. Christl: a Party member and a worker in the Bund Deutscher Mädel. Why? Because her drunken old man demanded it. Joachim Kolb: a Nazi general. Why? A sick career officer's opportunism. But your precious hearings will see only the fact of participation, never the mitigation. Well, Jaeger, I want none of that. I want to be left free to make amends, deeply personal amends, to some people I've hurt—Christl first and above all. Understand: I'm not afraid of your squalid little hearings—I'm afraid that if I become ensnarled in them I won't have the time to make my daughter laugh again. By helping you I hope to buy the time. If this sounds like sentimental hogwash to you and your suspicious superiors, then you all can go to hell."

"All right," I grumped. "But tell me something else, General?"

"Well?"

"What happened to the American agent you and Klottner used as a go-between with our intelligence people in the beginning of all this? The agent in Wiesbaden."

"We had him hanged to a telephone pole, of course. Maximum security was involved. Why?"

"Just wondered," I said. "As an emotional nincompoop, I try to keep my emotions oriented."

✠ ✠ ✠

Dear Herr Hartmann:

Here is the recording of a conversation between my father and the man called Jaeger, made with the distance microphone as they stood on the sundeck at Fliegerfreude. I could not hear what they said, nor have I played the recording, naturally. I hope all their remarks were picked up by the machine, but I can't say for sure. Mechanical things have always confused me.

Any further word from my husband? Please let me know if there is.

Christl Werner

Via Courier:

Spike:

Here's the recording the Werner woman made at Fliegerfreude. As you'll note, it's quite good and reveals some interesting things.

Peppermint

To → What have you done to keep the woman under our control?
S.

Via Courier:

Spike:

I've used the usual procedures with Frau Werner—letters from the prison camp, a picture of her husband in PW togs, etc. She's very pliable.

Peppermint

160

SIXTEEN

Nikki was not at her desk, so I rapped twice on Behncke's door and swung in without ceremony. He was standing in a corner, blowing his nose delicately into a dazzling handkerchief. Nikki was there, too, her face quite flushed. She spun about and busied herself at a file cabinet.

"Hello," I said. "Anyone for World War Three?"

Behncke placed the hanky in his breast pocket, fussing at it until it was precisely casual. But not precisely casual enough to hide the lipstick on it. "Don't you knock at people's doors, Jaeger?" he asked irritably.

"I knocked."

"Well, I didn't tell you to come in."

"I thought you'd be deliriously happy to see me after my long absence and I got carried away, I guess."

Behncke glanced at Nikki, gave her the raised eyebrow, and watched her start for the door. She nodded coolly in my direction, then disappeared into the outer office, leaving a wake of scented soap. I had a fleeting sense of all this having happened in exactly the same way at some other time.

"Where in Christ's name have you been?" Behncke asked in his jolly way.

I did not wait for him to offer a chair. I lifted one away from the wall and sat on it backward, saying, "I've been lolling about assorted Ami prison camps, smoking Ami cigarettes, and lying like hell on an Ami Fragebogen. They let me go Friday, and I spent the weekend helping Christl Werner take supplies to the General at Fliegerfreude. I missed you terribly every minute, naturally."

161

Behncke straightened his glasses, pulled a little note pad from a desk drawer, and, lips pursed, delicately adjusted the lead in his mechanical pencil. I wondered why it was this man galled me so. I had only to glimpse Behncke's face, and the adrenalin would begin to flow in rivers.

"Well, it's good that you're back, actually," Behncke was saying, "because there are a few rather important things you can take care of. And considerable time has been lost already, I'm afraid, what with Germany under total occupation and all."

"What would these things be?"

Behncke cleared his throat and jotted a few words in his pad. Without looking up he said: "It's time we have our little black-market contacts established and working. Before the Americans came, I handled all our supply problems, but now it's your turn as our black-market specialist from the late lamented Gestapo. I've already had exploratory talks with a Major Sneed—Silly name. The Americans have the silliest names, I think—and he seems to be the big cheese in charge of keeping people in Bavaria from freezing and starving next winter, and this Major Sneed was happy, very happy indeed, to discover that Kaufmann Kompanie is ready, willing, and able to cooperate in the considerable logistics problems he faces. But there are two snags, from what I was able to gather from his bureaucratic gibberish, only one of which really concerns you."

I interrupted mildly, "Everything concerns me now. I'm a full partner, remember?"

The plums behind his glasses regarded me indifferently. "Well for one thing, Major Sneed says he can't throw us into the breach as he puts it, until Military Government checks all our personnel and commercial background through something called CIC which is the American Gestapo, I believe. That's one of my headaches, making all the cover data sufficiently tight and all that. But what you can do is to handle the second one. Major Sneed gave me a general rundown on how much we can expect by way of operating supplies—if we're cleared by CIC, that is—and even with the rosiest estimates they'll be horribly inadequate, horribly. We foresaw this, of course, and that's why Klottner arranged your transfer from Berlin in the first place."

I nodded. "What do you need the most? Right away, I mean."

"Tires. Tires. As many as we can get. Schultzi says each truck is on its last rubber right now. There isn't a spare in the place. If we don't have tires we don't run at all, Jaeger. I mean it. The situation is desperate. There are many people to contact. We haven't even scratched the surface yet. If our trucks don't move we can't contact another soul. Desperate."

"Schultzi can give me the sizes he needs, I suppose?"

"He has a list all prepared for you."

"All right," I sighed, "I'll see what I can do. It will cost you, you know. Black markets aren't cheap."

"Pay what you must," he said darkly.

"How are we coming with our contacts these days?" I asked, deciding that the money question made Behncke uncomfortable. I knew that I had my own little problem of ingratiation: somehow I had to establish a solid working relationship with Behncke. I could not do this by constantly baiting the man. But it wouldn't be easy, that was for sure, because baiting a pompous fop like Behncke was a reflex kind of thing for Peter Klaussen.

"As I say," Behncke answered, "we've only just begun to hit a significant lode of friends. Bavaria and the Tyrol are rapidly filling with people, especially since our meeting at Südberg."

"There were three women and nine men at that session. Who were they?"

"Don't interrupt me, Jaeger. It's one of my few idiosyncrasies. I despise being interrupted," Behncke said sourly.

"Sorry." I drew a memo pad from my inside coat pocket. "Mind if I make a few notes?"

Behncke ignored the question, and went on: "At present we're restricting our operations to the Ober- and Nieder-bayern areas, with Munich as our base, naturally. The object of the Südberg meeting was to delineate the geographical zones in which future operations will be conducted and to name the individuals who'll be responsible in each. Oberbayern and the Alps proper will be under the direction of Kurt Bednar, SS Brigadeführer and a delightful chap, incidentally, who is working as an orchestra leader in a winter sports hotel near Mittenwald; Niederbayern is the job of Alex Heide, now a dairyman but formerly a Gebietsführer in the Reichsjugendführung; the Allgäu is under Robert Kohl, who was, I believe, an Oberbannführer in the HJ and an old pal of Klottner's; Schwaben and Oberschwaben are the responsibility of Gustav Singer, Wehrmacht colonel and SS Sturmbannführer; the Schwäbische Alb is Klaus Bergmann's—he was an Amtchef in the RJF; and the Schwarzwald will be under Karl-Heinz Enzminger, a former bureau chief in the Sicherheitsdienst who came very highly recommended by Klottner." Behncke referred to his notebook again, cameo finger worrying his mustache. "Let's see. The other six men—Fritz Schaefer, Dieter Kugel, Max Schilling, Heinrich Weigand, Wolfram Gutermann, and Horst Matzdorf—are understudying the district leaders and are all SS or HJ personalities who, I hope, will get their own districts when we expand into places like the Odenwald, the Pfalz, Hesse, and on to the north."

Behncke paused, so I put in another question: "How about addresses for all of these people? I'll need to know where I can get in touch with them as time goes by."

"I've asked Nikki to type them up for you and the General."

"Good. Quite a crowd you're gathering. How about the women?"

"Hilda Zimmer, Anna-Marie Schwarz, and Gretl Kranz. All former Bund Deutscher Mädel executives. I've asked them to consider the hospital, canteen, and other auxiliary functions."

"I see." I stared at my notes for a time, then muttered, "Still brass-heavy, hm?"

"What do you mean?"

"These sound like good types. But they're all pretty old. When do we start rounding up the fighters? If we're going to set up a crack Werewolf operation we'd better get humping. All the money and supplies in the world won't be worth a peach pit if we haven't got plenty of hard-bellied, iron-chewing people who like to scrap."

Behncke's face clouded and he gave a little snort of impatience.

"Well, don't you agree, Behncke? It's basic, I'd say. We need combat types if we're to fight the Yankee occupiers."

Closing his pad and placing the pencil in his pocket, Behncke seemed to struggle to keep his composure. But, failing, he blurted:

"Oh, come off it, Jaeger. You know our chances of setting up armed resistance to the Occupation are absolutely non-existent. The whole idea's hogwash."

I studied Behncke very closely. "Oh?"

"Hogwash, that's what it is. Hogwash."

"Interesting," I said reasonably. "But what in hell are we supposed to be doing here, then? If not Werewolves, armed resistance, what's all the shouting about?"

Behncke appeared to make a decision. When he spoke there was an odd new air about him, and I took a long moment to recognize it for what it was: candor.

"The way I see it," he said, leaning forward on the desk, "our single greatest value to Germany at this or any stage is our political-economic potential."

"What's that supposed to mean?"

"I'm going to lay out my thinking for you, Jaeger. I'll need your help if my plan is to work, and despite your frequently irritating manner I sense that you are astute, knowledgeable, and courageous. You demonstrated this last quality quite clearly that day you freed us from Oswald Linck. I've never really thanked you properly for what you did that day, but I am very grateful. Very grateful indeed. Thank you."

"Don't mention it."

Behncke was obviously out of his depth in this role, and I was glad when the good old truculence reappeared.

"I believe, Jaeger, I honestly believe that any active attempt on our part to sabotage the Occupation would be foolhardy and doomed to failure. I think our most constructive program lies in a more subtle direction."

"Go on."

"As I see it, our effort should be a long-range one. We should bend all our efforts toward making Kaufmann so financially healthy that we, as a sort of nucleus surrounded by a galaxy of like-minded people in Bavaria—even beyond—will be able to influence the future politics of Germany along National Socialist lines. With the company as a nation-wide complex, for instance, with a treasury loaded with the liquid assets derived from our legitimate business operations, with our employee roster of well-covered Nazi faithfuls, with the blessing of occupying powers anxious to be free of the trouble and expense of distributing goods to a destitute population—with such strengths as these we could make Nazism once again the dominant factor in German politics."

I held up a hand. "Wait. You mean you'd like to abandon the active-resistance idea altogether? There'd be none at all?"

"Precisely," Behncke said, his magnified eyes brittle. "No shoot-'em-up at all, but a long-term, twofold program: first, the formation of a strong economic structure which would afford cover and financial backing for the second phase—the protracted, sly, covert influencing of any eventual German government toward the Führer principle."

"An attempt to revive the Party some day?"

Behncke shook his head. "Of course not. That would be silly. The Party's dead. It holds no enchantment for anybody without Hitler. And to re-establish the Party would only invite a lot of distracting acrimony and hullabaloo. I simply propose to employ the Nazi ideologies in whatever national government may evolve in the years ahead, that's all. Think of it. We'd all become stinking rich and we'd have a nice, vigorous government ready to genuflect every time we sneezed."

We sat silently for a time, considering each other. I said finally, "What do you propose to do?"

That guarded look crept in behind Behncke's spectacles again. Toying with his mustache, he murmured, "Nothing. Yet."

"Nothing? I thought you were all heated up with this idea."

"I am, Jaeger. I am."

"Well then—"

"It's just," Behncke said, "that the General's frequent comment might be right. Maybe we haven't given Bormann enough time. And if he does show up and I haven't followed orders—" He paused.

"Then that," I smiled, "would be the soccer game for good old Otto Behncke."

After a long soak in the tub, I dried myself on one of the fat red towels Frau Werner had set aside for my use, threw the towel around me, and went down the hall to my room. Lighting a cigarette, I sank onto the desk chair, lifted the phone, and dialed O. There was a buzz, a click, another buzz, and then the Munich operator's haughty voice came on: "Zentrum."

"Would you connect me with Central in Frankfurt-Main, please?"

Click, buzz, click, buzz. Buzz. "Your number, please?"

I gave it.

Another voice, this one a man's, and sounding very far away: "Zentrum."

"Sugar-Daddy, please."

Buzz, click. Buzz. Then: "Number?"

I blew a stream of smoke and said carefully, "23778."

Buzz, click.

"Schmidt here."

"Jaeger."

"Oh, hullo. This is a surprise." Smith's voice was supercilious even in German.

"Are you going to be home tomorrow?"

"Let's see. Sunday? Yes, I guess so. Why?"

"I'd like to drop in for a spell. Just to say hello to the family and so on."

"Sounds like fun."

"Any special time?"

"Well, there's church, and—Wait: how about meeting us at the Hauptbahnhof at noon? We can go to the house from there."

"Sounds fine. Noon at the main railroad station. Right?"

"Right."

"See you."

"Delighted. 'Bye."

Pale night came through the open casement, and a summer breeze, fresh with the recent rain, stirred the curtains.

"Nikki?"

"Mm?"

"Tell me something, will you?"

She shifted, taking her face from the hollow of my throat. "What would you like to know, beautiful man?"

"How much is Behncke paying you?"

She chuckled and rubbed her nose against mine. "Now what kind of a question is that? Here you are, lying on the couch of love and thinking of salaries and Behncke and heaven knows what other dismal things. I've lost my hold on you, I'm afraid. . . ."

"No. I'm serious. How much?"

"Not enough, that's certain," she chortled. "There's never enough. Not for Nikki."

"Five hundred a month?"

"Me? Behncke pay *me* five hundred a month? You've had too much wine. He pays me three. As salary, that is. He also picks up the tab for this apartment."

"Would you like more?"

There was a tentative silence. When she spoke again, the amusement had left her voice. "More? What do you mean?"

"Just that."

"Doing what?"

"Just what you are doing."

"I don't understand."

"How would you like say, an extra 800 Deutschemark, every week."

She raised up quickly, pressing her hands against my chest for support. I could see her eyes in the dimness, wide and puzzled. "Eight hundred? Each and every *week?*"

"Yes."

"What would I have to do? Assassinate Eisenhower?"

"Would you?"

She snickered. "No. I wouldn't do that. Ike's adorable."

"Would you kill Ike for a thousand a week?"

"Of course. He's not that adorable. Why? Is that what you want me to do?"

"No. But would you gossip about Behncke?"

She thought about that for a time, then shook her head dubiously. "Oh. My. I don't know. That could be dangerous. . . ."

"Nothing worth anything comes easily."

"Well. My goodness. This is something sort of against my principles. You know that. I've told you that."

"I know. But you love money. That's one of your principles, too, isn't it?"

She giggled and pinched me. "All right, beautiful man, what would you like to know about Behncke?"

"I want a photograph from his secret file. That's your first job. Get me a photograph he's hiding." I paused. "It's a picture of me. Sent to him from Berlin. I want that picture."

"It won't be easy. Behncke watches his strongbox like a hawk."

I sighed. "Your uncanny ability to open strongboxes is your most endearing quality, Nikki."

SEVENTEEN

The charcoal-hued Mercedes followed me all the way. It had picked me up on the Nymphenburgerlandstrasse, and never left its station some several hundred yards to the rear, even during the tortuous detours outside Augsburg, Ulm, Stuttgart, and Karlsruhe. I had watched it in the mirror, of course, but my mind, independent, interfered and demanded an explanation of the extraordinary remorse I felt.

I had left Nikki Meier in the deceptive innocence of slumber—face composed, legs spread, arms outflung—and throughout the 230-mile drive I pondered, in a sort of sullen anguish, the grossly immoral person I was becoming. I had never been a prude, nor was I a victim of the puritanical sex tyranny that seemed to oppress so many Americans. But I simply knew with some unforgiving instinct that I had left an important part of myself tangled forever in Nikki Meier's scented sheets. I had sold myself. And I hated it.

To break away from the depression I had tried to break away from the Mercedes. But, like my conscience, the gray-black car was omnipresent. There was one time—on the stretch of Autobahn that swung west below the Neckar and crossed the great plain to Mannheim—when an enormous convoy of Seventh Army six-by-sixes, standing radiator to tailgate amid a buzzing swarm of jeeps, had cut me off from my shadow. But after I'd cleared Darmstadt and was on the final leg to Frankfurt, the other car resumed patrol, taking its post with maddening precision.

As I swung into the teeming Bahnhofsplatz, I saw a huge, white-gloved traffic MP presiding at the base of the triangle made by the old trolley tracks in front of the railroad station. Leaving the Opel in high gear, I took my foot from the accelerator and let the car come to a jerking stall in the triangle's center.

"O.K., buddy," the MP said, leaning into the window, "you'll have to get this heap out of here. You're friggin' up the traffic."

"I'm an American intelligence agent," I said quickly in English, "and I need your help."

"How do I know that, buddy? That you're an American, I mean."

"I'll prove it later. Meanwhile, please make as if you're bawling me out, will you? I'm being followed."

The MP, one of those smooth-skinned, crew-cut Coca-Cola ads, was (thank God) sharp. He pointed a finger threateningly at my chest and said, jaw outthrust, "What do you want me to do?"

"Three things, please. First, order some of these pedestrians to push my car to the curb. Second, order me out of the car, make a fuss over my papers, and run me in. Third, send one of your pals to get me a good cop's description of the guy in that blackish Mercedes parked second in line over there at the corner of Kaiserstrasse. O.K.?"

The MP stole a glance at the Mercedes. "How about its license number?"

"Get it if you want, but it's probably a phony."

The big corporal smiled and showed why the world esteemed American dentistry. "Cloak and dagger, eh? Heh-heh. You've brightened my day, buddy. I was bored."

I winked and smiled back. "You take care of those things, Corporal, and a letter of commendation goes to your C.O."

"You're on, buddy."

It had taken Smith no time at all to find me in the MP shack at the corner of the great barnlike railroad station and even less time for the corporal to return with an A. Conan Doyle word picture of the man in the Mercedes. The description, duly noted in my little pad, had proved to be meaningless. Just another man, except for a large mane of wavy gray hair and a kind of gentle look about him. After getting the name and APO of the noncom's commanding officer (I'd meant every word about the commendation), Smith and I had driven in Smith's car to the big brownstone on Myliusstrasse which, Smith told me, was headquarters for CIC's Frankfurt city team. Over coffee, sipped in a bay-window alcove on the second floor, I ticked off the last note in my little book. "There. That covers it: Behncke's political strategies, Kolb's motivations."

"Interesting," Smith conceded in his dry way. "So Behncke yearns to run somebody for president, hm? No more shoot-'em-up. Well, that something, I guess. Anything else?"

"Couple of things," I said, placing my cup on the table and taking a sheaf of papers from my cardboard brief case. "First, here's a list of all the personalities Behncke's contacted to date. Almost all of them are Nazis in MG's automatic-arrest categories. Several of them, I think, are wanted for war crimes." I placed the papers beside the cup. "I'll give you supplementary lists as they're forthcoming."

"No problems there?"

"No. Behncke gives me a carbon of all list additions. As his black-market specialist, I'll have to know where everybody is. For instance, if there's a tank of red gasoline to be hidden in Rosenheim I might have to know who's there to help me hide it. And so on."

"Handy for us good guys, hm?"

"Peachy-keen."

Smith nodded. "All right. I'll keep a master list in my office, keep G-2 informed as the list grows." He paused. "You said there are a couple of things. What's the other?"

"I'm setting up Nikki Meier as an informant. She wants eight hundred DM's a week to snitch on Behncke."

Smith gave me a cool glance. "Pretty expensive snitching."

"She's an expensive dame. But I think it's worth it. She can give us more perspective on what Behncke's doing. I can see and hear only so much, you know." I waited, expecting an argument.

"Very well," Smith said indifferently. "Confidential Funds will take care of it. I'll ask them to set it up so the money is couriered to you through CIC in Munich."

Leaning over to pour another cup of coffee, I asked: "Do I notice a creeping emphasis on CIC lately? Or am I just imagining things?"

Smith brushed a piece of lint from his carefully pressed pinks. "Perhaps. That's something I wanted to brief you on, as a matter of fact." He paused for a gentlemanly yawn, then explained: "Now that the war's over, there's considerable shuffling around of functions and responsibilities. SHAEF is no longer SHAEF—it's USFET, or U.S. Forces, European Theater. OSS will gradually disband and reorganize into a sort of Central Intelligence Agency under the State Department, I think. This agency will be responsible for all of OSS's current jobs—with one major exception. Here in Occupied Germany the counterintelligence function will break down by geography: anything of CI nature outside the U.S. Zone will be OSS or CIA handled; anything of CI nature inside the Zone will become the province of the Army Counter Intelligence Corps under USFET. CIA outside, CIC inside."

I said, "So where does all this leave me?"

"Since the Behncke thing is an internal matter, confined so far to the U.S. Zone of Occupation, it now falls into CIC business. Therefore, I'm having you transferred back to CIC."

I worked to conceal the smile that wanted to form. "How about you?"

"That's unimportant right now. I'll still be on the job and, for the foreseeable future, will continue to be your case officer."

I no longer felt the urge to smile. "I see. Well, where am I assigned for administration and all that?"

Smith lit a cigarette and blew a stream of smoke at an ash that had settled on his row of chest ribbons. "CIC's undergoing a change, too. As of July 17, all the CIC army slash teams will be absorbed into geographical regions under the Chief of CIC here in Frankfurt's Farben Building. Under what's to be known as the 970th CIC Detachment, there will be eight regions: Number

One in Stuttgart, Number Two in Frankfurt, Three in Bad Nauheim, Four in Munich, Five in Regensburg, Six in Bamberg, Seven in the Bremen Enclave, and Eight in Berlin."

"So I'm to be assigned to CIC Region Four, Munich?"

"Only for communications. Operationally you'll be a special agent on detached duty, reporting directly to me. Actually, the only man in Region Four who'll know you at all will be the Ops Chief, and even he will know you only by code name."

"And what will that be?"

Smith smiled his wan smile. "What's wrong with 'Despair'? The name's still uncompromised."

"I don't like that name," I said, not knowing why.

Smith looked at me again, and there was a silence. Then: "Is it getting to you, Herr Jaeger? Hm?"

"What do you mean?"

"I suspect you might be having a case of the Spook's Spooks."

"If it isn't too much to ask, what in hell are you talking about?"

The corners of Smith's mouth turned upward sufficiently to hint at a secret joke. "The Spook's Spooks—the peculiar melancholy the secret agent can fall victim to now and then. Especially the U.S. of A. Presbyterian type who loves to feel unclean and contemptible for sneaking around back alleys and spying on people."

"Oh, come off it, Smith. I'm no Boy Scout," I lied.

Smith gave me a long, thoughtful appraisal. "Actually," he said finally, "you're showing gratifying promise. Back at Home Plate you were a bright-eyed, pink-faced character all aglow with that disgusting air of right-will-prevail-so-long-as-we-keep-God-and-the-good-on-our-side. Well, you're no longer quite the same fellow. I perceive a distinct air of surly meanness showing through, and I'm glad."

"Thanks a heap, Coach."

On the return to the railroad station, Smith was in a reflective mood. Eyes straight ahead, lips compressed, he let the little Renault take us through the mountainous ruins to Bockenheimer Landstrasse, then left along the trolley line to the disheveled Opera House, right into Taunus Anlage and the Mainzer Landstrasse, and finally to Karl Strasse and the Bahnhofsplatz. I was not disposed to break the silence, so I simply sat and watched the last fingers of sun gild the endless moonscape of rubble.

When the car halted in a cul across from the big old post office, Smith switched off the motor and lit another Chesterfield. "Well, here we are," he said, watching a rust-colored locomotive chuff off toward the sunset. "You should be back in Munich by midnight, with luck."

"Yes."

"How's Frau Werner making out?"

"All right, I guess. Seems still to be mourning her husband."

"Killed in Russia, wasn't he?"

"Yes. There was a lot of dying in Russia, and he was part of it."

"What do you think of the Russians, Klaussen?"

It was a peculiar question, asked in a peculiar tone and in a peculiar context. I hesitated, thinking about what I thought of the Russians. Keeping neutral, I said, "They're our allies. That's about all I need to know, I guess. Why?"

"Just wondered. I've been delving into the Rote Kapelle recently, and the Russians are on my mind, I suppose."

"Rote Kapelle? The Soviet spy ring the Nazis smashed back in '42? That's sort of ancient history, isn't it?"

Smith shrugged and glanced at his watch. "Yes. But there are dibs and dabs still dangling. They've got to be cleaned up before we have the full picture. And one of my additional duties around headquarters, I regret to say, makes me a historian. G-2 is compiling a history of intelligence ops in Europe during the war years, and everybody who has a desk here—even the mail girl, I think—has been assigned a piece or two to write. The Rote Kapelle is one of mine."

I nodded, squinting at the dying sun. "As I recall, the Rote Kapelle was a bunch of German society snobs who turncoated on the Nazis and ran a wireless network for the Soviets. The Abwehr pinched them all, and they were executed after a big propaganda trial in Berlin. Isn't that it?"

"Mm. Messy affair. But this reminds me: keep your eyes open for any trace of Mueller, the Gestapo chief, will you? His part in breaking up the Rote Kapelle is still fuzzy."

"The way I get it, Mueller was killed in the defense of Berlin. Behncke danced a little jig when he got the news."

Smith smiled faintly. "I know. But there's no proof yet. And if he's alive I'd sure like to talk to him. He's one of the best the Nazis had. . . ."

"O.K., I'll watch."

Smith arced an arm and consulted his watch again, signaling dismissal of the subject. "I'll set up the Nikki Meier fund, and I'll message the Ops Chief in Munich to expect word from you. As for the black-market tires and things, you'll need some help on that, I'm afraid. Somebody who can front as an American officer who's making black-market deals. Somebody safe and smart and not too nosy. I'll have to think about that. . . ."

"No you won't," I said. "I have the man I want."

"Who's that?"

I took out my notebook, found a page, and tore it out. "Here's the unit address and this is the man: Second Lieutenant Robert Champion."

As I drove the long black road south, two things kept bugging me. One was Smith's bizarre interest in Peter Klaussen's opinions on the Soviets—and here I had the distinct impression that I'd been given a test and had flunked. The other was Smith's bizarre lack of interest in the matter of the charcoal-colored Mercedes.

Smith had not asked a single question, had not offered one speculation of his own, as to who might be tailing me.

It was almost as if Smith didn't care.

Smith was a creep, all right.

✠ ✠ ✠

To: Central Registry, G-2, USFET, for Appleseed File 4/6/45

From: Ira B. Tolley, Clerk, German Desk

Please file this transcript of a one-end German-language conversation via telephone. Speaker: Putzi.

Peppermint? Putzi here. You want to see me? (Pause) What do you mean, how did I know you were in town? Christ, you might as well have taken an ad in the newspaper. Despair tells me you followed him all the way from Munich. (Pause) Well, you've simply got to be more careful. Despair is a very inexperienced, moral young man addicted to stubborn patriotism and to taking hellish chances on sheer luck. He's the unpredictable type who might just do something foolish about you, and you know how that could foul me up. After all, you're my only route of contact with Spike, and if I lose you I lose Spike. I cannot under any circumstances lose contact with Spike. (Pause) You let me worry about the gold. You hear? (Pause) Don't worry. (Pause) Will you stop worrying about that? You and the gold and Spike are the only things I give a damn about. If Despair gets in your way, you know what to do. (Pause) All right. All right, I said. (Pause) Very well. But be careful.

EIGHTEEN

The Kleinhesselohe was a restaurant on the lagoon in Munich's Englischer Garten. It was now a sort of halfway house, where Americans and Germans could square off in a tentative public exploration of the repeal of the ill-advised no-fraternization rule

SHAEF had issued at Occupation's outset. Many raunchy stories had sifted through the population, each of which mirrored the idiocy of a rule prohibiting conversation between soldiers and civilians compelled to share the same real estate. One of these, passed along by a cackling, thigh-slapping Schultzi, had to do with a GI whose commanding officer had caught him in bed with a plump Fräulein. The GI, shivering at attention in the nude, admitted to his irate lieutenant that, sure, he had been in sexual congress, but, "Honest, sir, I never said a word to her."

The rule had finally deferred to logic, though, and now good old enemies met under the influence of music and wine to peer eye-to-eye for clues as to what all the shooting had been about.

I could see all this from the lagoon-side bench where we had settled during our walk through the park. We sat, not saying anything, watching the restaurant's Japanese lanterns make bobbing diamonds in the water and listening to the sounds made by people who have discovered how sweet it is to have survived.

I'd been very restless since my trip to Frankfurt, and it was worse than ever this evening. On my way home from work (God, I sounded like a Westport commuter . . .) I had seen two GI's walking down the street with a pair of Fräuleins, and something about their arm-in-arm familiarity had made me very homesick. After supper I'd asked her to take a ride.

Turning off her radio, her solemn eyes showing a flicker of something, she'd said yes, it's a fine idea for a fine evening. And so now we sat, and I wondered why I had bothered.

Stirring, she asked (without looking at me, naturally), "What happened to that nice smile you once had, Herr Jaeger?"

"Smile? What do you mean?"

"When you first came here to Munich, you were different somehow. You seemed very tired and worried, that's so. But you also managed to smile a lot. These days you're simply worried, sort of. And you don't smile so much, and that's too bad, because it was a nice thing to see. . . ."

"Life's getting tougher all the time," I said. For once she returned my inspection. Her eyes caught a last shred of sun, and there was something strangely moving about the greenish luminescence in them; I had a sense of looking into small, glowing crystals and seeing all the longing and hope and hurt and nobility and loneliness that made man God's most unhappy creature.

"You haven't changed at all, Frau Werner. You're exactly the same as always: unwilling to be yourself."

The eyes didn't waver this time. "What is that, Herr Jaeger? What is myself? If you know, will you please tell me? All my life I've wanted to know what I am."

I felt myself shrugging. "I don't know who you are. But I do think you'd do yourself a distinct favor if you'd take off the ashes and sackcloth and get on with being Christl Werner and to hell with the past. I don't know anything about your husband, but if he was a good type, as you say he was, I think he'd be the first to agree. You're young and alive, and he's dead, and you can't change that. It's no dishonor to a dead man to do a little living on your own."

She looked away, her lips compressed. "You are being presumptuous, Herr Jaeger."

"Not really. I simply regret your wasting all the woman I suspect to be hiding behind those eyes of yours."

She hugged herself against the night's coming chill. "There's nothing behind my eyes. Not a real woman, anyway."

"Oh, come on now. That's just plain maudlin nonsense. If you're trying to play the languishing tragedienne, I suggest you don't. You're too pink and sexy for the part."

She remained motionless for a long time, arms folded about her, mouth set, eyes thoughtful. Somewhere in the silence she seemed to make a decision, and I sensed that whatever it was it had cost her plenty.

"Herr Jaeger," she said, "I'm going to tell you something. About me. I'm going to tell you because I think you're beginning to like me, and this is something you can't afford. You're the first person to treat me with consideration and respect for more than four years, and I like you for that. I like you so much I'm going to make you not like me."

She cut off my attempt to interrupt with a wave of her hand. "No. Wait. I know my father, and it won't be long before he manages to tell you about me. I'd simply rather tell you myself, that's all."

I sat back, watching her search for language.

"I am a person," she said, "who cannot be trusted. I am, for reasons I can't understand, full of treachery. When I married Franz Werner, I vowed I'd be everything a man could want in a wife. He was very much in love with me, I think, but as much as I wanted to, I couldn't be much more than deeply grateful to him for giving me a chance to break away from the memories of my mother and the cruelties of my father. But he was a physician on the rise, and I saw very little of him, and there were times when I wondered if I'd really escaped, what with the sitting alone, thinking and remembering and resenting and fearing and daring not to hope. One afternoon something happened to me. I'd been thinking of my father and hating him, and the hate grew and grew until I could hardly stand it. And then the gardener, a thick young man standing at the laundry sink, washing up and looking at me in that leering, arrogant way my father always did, and suddenly I wanted to debase and degrade and lower and triumph over my father, and I degraded him in the only way I knew and he became a gardener and a whining animal, and when it was over I laughed and spat in his face, and that's when I realized that my father was really standing in the doorway from the garage, and the gardener ran and I don't remember much except my father shouting how I was no better than he was and I was hitting him and screaming. My father called Franz home and made me tell him what I'd done, and all Franz could say was why, why, why, and my father asked him what he was going to do about it and Franz kept asking why, why. Well, Franz refused to do anything about it—why he hadn't killed me on the spot I'll never know—but he did nothing, and to show his contempt for him my father had Franz posted to the Russian front as a veterinary where instead of a fine career in medicine he earned a Russian bullet while tending ailing pack animals. . . ."

Her voice fell off, and in the dusk her face was a ghost's face. I drew a deep breath, then said, "So?"

"So you see the true extent of my capacity for treachery."

"Is it really treachery when a treacherous act takes place in an emotional collapse?"

"Treachery is treachery."

179

"I'm not convinced of that. Not in this case. And I have a hunch your husband was unconvinced, too. He must have been quite a fellow."

"I'll spend the rest of my life wishing I could make it up to him."

I shook my head. "I think that's a mistake. If he refused to condemn you, why should you condemn yourself?"

"I hurt him. I'll never forget it. I'd do anything—anything—to make it up to him."

I put my hand on her shoulder. "Well, call it treachery if you want. I call it a nervous breakdown. Come on, I'll take you home and make you a cup of hot coffee. I'm a very good coffee maker."

I stood up and took her hand. In the dimness I could see her downcast eyes, and I couldn't help laughing. "So that's what that was all about, eh?"

"What do you mean?"

"All this is why you haven't wanted your father to see you with me, isn't it? You don't want your father to think I'm another gardener, do you?"

"I'm all burned out where my father is concerned, Herr Jaeger. It's you I don't want to hurt."

"How could you do that?"

"If you don't see that by now, I could never tell you."

"All right. Say your moment of—weakness—actually was treachery. Does one act of treachery make you unreliable and unworthy forever and ever, amen?"

"You don't understand," she said stiffly. "You don't know what self-loathing can be."

"Don't be too sure about that."

"Well, it's as simple as this, Herr Jaeger: you are my friend, and I'd rather dismiss you than lose you. Now take me home, will you, please?"

I did. But throughout the drive I kept wondering.

Christl Werner had made a confession of a kind which, for a woman, was the ultimate in self-vilification.

But I kept wondering: What was the confession she had *really* wanted to make?

She had dismissed me, sure enough.

But not for the reason she'd given. . . .

The phone at the other end lifted with a faraway click. "Schmidt."

"Jaeger here."

"Pretty late for calling, isn't it?"

"I wanted to be sure you'd be in."

"What's on your mind?"

"Did you have any luck with the champion?"

"He reports Friday. He'll call you at your house Friday night."

"Good. I'll need him very soon now. . . ." I paused. I heard it again. An odd clicking.

"Everything all right? Hm?"

"Yes."

"You sound blue. Same old malady? Spooks?"

"No. Just a bit lonely."

"Mm. Well. That all?"

"Yes."

"Good night."

The moon had risen, and from my position in the darkened upper hallway I could see the rectangular patterns made by the faint light on the floor of the foyer below. Remembering the lecture on night vision, the one given by the fat major in the Harmony Church classroom at Benning, I did not look directly at the lower hall but set my eyes on one of its walls. If you see motion in the dark, the major had droned, don't look directly at the object but to one side of it—you'll be surprised at the detail you can pick up out of the corner of your eye in the dark.

The major had been right (they were always right at Benning), because now I could make out Christl Werner. She was stooped beside the telephone table near the front door and, as I watched, she withdrew something from the umbrella urn. It clinked softly and caught a piece of moonlight and sent out a soft gleam.

I waited, motionless in the upstairs dark, while she padded softly down the hall toward the rear of the house, holding her nightrobe close. When I thought I heard the back door open and shut, I sneaked down the stairs and hurried to the library. The drapes were drawn wide, and the garden, framed in the grid of the casement, was awash in moonglow. Standing by the window, I watched her cross the lawn to the shrub-lined picket fence and the gate to the alley. She waited for a full minute before a man stepped out of the shadows. She took something from her robe and gave it to the man, who, after tipping his hat, turned and melted into the alley's murk.

I ran to the foyer and, flicking on my flash for a spasm of time, threw its light into the umbrella urn.

There, packed neatly in its green carrier, spool spindles still uncovered, was a tiny recorder. The urn's false bottom rested against the wall, only inches from where the recorder's lead line joined the telephone junction box. It was amateurish. But adequate.

She arrived at the house sooner than I'd expected. When I heard the back door squeak, I pressed into the shadow of the foyer wardrobe, holding my breath while she passed close by to stoop and replace spool and urn bottom.

When she arose and went to her room, I could hear her crying softly.

And I knew then what she'd really tried to say in the park.

NINETEEN

The headquarters of CIC Region Four, Munich, had been established, of all places, on Maria Theresa Strasse in the former consulate of a banana country a few hundred yards north of Otto Behncke's house. It was a big white place, all ells and gables and balconies and forbidding shrubs. The ground floor was almost cellar-like in arrangement, with heavily plastered walls and alcoves and small doors, closed and inscrutable. The first floor was more open and airy, and high-ceilinged rooms had been converted into offices in which phones rang and typewriters chattered and men in olive drab devoid of insignia hurried about through coffee and tobacco smells.

The Ops Chief had met me at the door and, after a deadpan scrutiny of my Personal Ausweis and MG-authorized driver's license, led me via a winding stairway to the first floor and into an office, whose door he closed and locked. If those in the building had seen me pass through, I decided, they'd gone to elaborate lengths to pretend they had not.

"You're Despair then?" the man asked briskly, holding a chair for me.

"Yes."

"I have some confidential funds for you."

"Good. How about Champion? Is he here yet?"

"Mm. He's upstairs, getting his quarters and rations squared away. We're assigning him temporarily as assistant motor officer. You want to see him?"

"When we're finished here."

"Very well. You can use this office. When you're ready to go, push this button under the lip of the desk and I'll have someone lead you out." He paused, then added: "Anything we can do for you right now?"

"Yes, there is, as a matter of fact. I need some mechanical aids."

"Such as?"

"First, some new clothes. A couple of suits—the works. I've worn these out. And second, I'd like to have a complete bugging job on the house at Freudestrasse 449, Bogenhausen. From cellar to attic and back again."

"Hm. I'll have to check. But I think I can fix you up." He scribbled the address on a pad. "How soon?"

"I'll have to get the landlady out for a day. How about Saturday? I'm driving her down to the Abendsee and shouldn't get back before midnight, at least."

The carefully barbered man stared out the window, his gray eyes pondering Saturday. "All right," he said finally. "Can you have her out of there by nine?"

"Sure. But remember, I need a microphone in every room and recordings from each. Unfriendlies have already tapped the phone and may have planted mikes elsewhere. If your technicians run into these, I'd like to leave them undisturbed. I don't want the unfriendlies to know we're on to them."

"Which unfriendlies?"

"I don't know yet. That's what I want to find out."

"That all?"

I flicked some ashes into a tray made of a sawed-off 88 casing. "One more thing. I'd like a twenty-four-hour stakeout on the place —for a week, at least. And one of the men should have a telephoto camera. I'd like a picture of every soul that goes in or out —including me—and the same for any vehicle that pulls up there, whether at the front or in the alley to the rear, including mine."

The man sat back in his swivel chair, his eyes narrowed dubiously and his lips pressed against the end of the pencil he held. "Ouch. You don't want much, do you?"

"This is top-priority stuff, you know."

"My friend, everything is top-priority stuff these days. G-2 screams top priority, MG screams top priority, Washington screams top priority. Everybody and his uncle has some kind of security ax to grind and everybody expects CIC to do the work. I'm afraid you'll have to wait in line."

"Three days?"

"You can have them for two."

"All right. Start them off the day after the place has been bugged. O.K.?"

"O.K. Now, here's your informant's money." The man pulled open a drawer, removed a brown package, and handed it across the desk. "Four thousand Deutschemark. Smith has signed for them. If you need more, that's tough tit."

"What do you mean?"

"Money. There's never enough. The United States, my dear Despair, provides ice-cream parlors and giant supermarket PX's for its troops, subsidizes nightclubs and golf courses for its officers, provides steamer cruises down the Rhine, ski lodges in Garmisch, trips to Paris and Cannes, tons of motion pictures and paperbacks, shiploads of whisky and condoms, and spends jillions on clearing the Theater of good men and loading it up with fuzz-faced schnooks. But it refuses—absolutely refuses—to spend more than a senator's lunch money on the intelligence it needs to keep everybody safe while they're guzzling and ogling and snoozing and whoring. That four thousand you have there is more than I get to run four chains of informants for a week. And I have to fill out eight thousands' worth of papers a week to explain where it goes."

I nodded sympathetically. "Maybe we'll learn some day."

"Don't hold your breath until then."

"May I see Champion now?"

"Sure. Buzz me when you're ready to go. And good luck on whatever the hell you're doing—hear?"

Champion was even larger than I remembered. He came through the door like an olive-drab mountain, a puzzled frown pulling his brows together above his Roman nose. His eyes registered recognition then, and the frown melded into an easy grin.

"Well, if it isn't Penn State's answer to Fu Manchu."

"Hullo, Champion," I said, working hard to return the smile. "Lock the door, will you?"

"Do I have you to thank for hauling me off that boat to the Pacific?"

"I guess so."

Champion winked theatrically. "May all your days be blessed with riches and honor, your nights with total capability."

"Sit down. I have some things I want to fill you in on. It'll probably take a while."

"Pity. And I did *so* want to get my hair done. . . ."

I slid the cigarette pack toward him and sank into the Ops Chief's swivel chair. "You're looking fit."

"Feel good."

"Feel good enough to become a dirty bastard?"

"I feel good because I *am* a dirty bastard. Next question?"

"No question. A statement: you are now a dirty bastard who sells U.S. Government property on the black market."

"Who snitched? I'll kill the son of a bitch. It was only a carton of Luckies . . ."

Ignoring the broadly feigned indignation, I said: "A group of high-ranking Nazis is hiding here in Bavaria with view toward subversion of the Occupation aims. Their cover is a trucking con-

185

cern called Kaufmann, headquarters in Munich. I've managed to penetrate them by landing a job with Kaufmann. The Nazi front office thinks I'm a black-market operator who can deliver fuel, tires, and spare parts above and beyond those MG authorizes. I need somebody to pose as a crooked U.S. officer who sells these things to me. You're that officer."

Champion crossed his legs and hugged a knee. "Simple enough. Where do I get the goods? From CIC here?"

"I wish it were that simple. You'll have to find yourself a real crook. We've got to make you look legit all the way, since we don't know how deeply the opposition will check on you. You've got to be a real crook and you have to enlist another one. Someone, perhaps, who works at a motor pool somewhere."

"Oo. What am I to do for working capital? Sell my adorable pink body?"

"You get the stuff, you get paid handsomely. Kaufmann's first need is for twenty sets of truck tires. I'll give you the equivalent of thirty-two thousand Deutschemark for them—half as binder, half on delivery."

"What if I get caught by the MP's while posing as a dirty bastard?"

"The Ops Chief here has a phrase: tough tit."

"Oo."

"You want to back out?"

Champion patted a yawn. "No. I was just saying oo. I always say oo when I become a rich crook."

"All right, then, here's a pad and pencil. We've got a lot of work to nail down."

Champion stood up and pulled off his Ike jacket. "Guess who else is here in Munich now."

"Who?"

"Lieutenant John Haley. Now known as *First* Lieutenant John Haley."

"The Princeton man who looks like he smells Limburger?"

"None other than. Front-runner in that great classic *Le Grand Pricks.*"

"What's he doing?"

"He's an MP officer assigned to the City Hall Detachment.

That's what scares me the most about this job I've just hired up on."

"Why?"

"Can you imagine," Champion grinned, "what it would be like to be arrested by that bastard?"

"That's the least of your worries."

"How so?"

"You're going to be too smart to get arrested."

I punched the elevator button out of reflex, but of course it wasn't working, so I took the main stairway, stopping halfway up at the landing with the huge window that overlooked the street below and the city beyond. It offered quite a view now that the lights were on again, and I stood for a time, contemplating it all and trying to will away the depression that was now my constant companion. It was clammy in the cavernous stairwell, so I pulled my coat closer and finished the climb.

I was tired and very lonely.

I had reached the top of the stairs and was making the turn toward Nikki's apartment when I heard the latch on her door click and the faint sound of chuckling good-byes inside. Dancing to one side, I slid into the murk of an alcove a second before the door opened and a man emerged, hat in hand.

It was Otto Behncke.

"Good night, dumpling," Nikki was saying. She gave him a lingering kiss, pinched one of his jowls, then closed the door. Behncke giggled, then passed within three feet of me to disappear down the stairs. I waited, listening to the diminishing sounds, until the place was still again. I watched four minutes march across my watch before moving to the door and tapping softly.

She was in a negligee and looked somewhat rumpled. But she showed her beautiful teeth in a smile that seemed sincere. "Darling. How nice. I didn't think I'd see you tonight."

I threw my hat and coat on the foyer chair and crossed to the bar. Lifting a bottle of Hennessey, I turned it in the light. "I've brought your first payment."

"That's nice," she said from the divan. "Come see me. This very minute."

"I want a drink first." I poured a heavy dose into a tall glass.

"I've missed you. It's difficult in the office, knowing you're around somewhere and not being able to do anything about it."

I drained the glass without pausing for breath.

"My," she said, "you *were* thirsty, weren't you? Or do you have to steel yourself for the coming combat?" Her tone was bantering.

"No combat tonight, Nikki." I did not look at her.

"No? Why not? Tired?"

"Our deal's a money deal now. My money for your information."

"That isn't the way I understood it. There was no mention of my losing a lover. . . ."

"Well, that's the way it is."

I heard the rustling as she arose and crossed behind me. Her arms stole around my waist, and the scent was there.

"Cut it out, Nikki. I mean it."

Her arms fell away, and she moved around to look me full in the face. There was mild disbelief in her expression. "You aren't joking, are you?"

"I'm not joking," I said, studying the empty glass.

"Why? Because I'm an employee now?" Her voice was taking on a flinty sound.

"Because," I said acidly, "you're an employee who has a dumpling."

She laughed, a short sound with real amusement in it. "Oh. Oh, my. You saw Otto leave just now?" She laughed again and took my chin in her hand. "Well, now, don't you pout. Otto is nothing but a fat old man. And I have to do something to earn my eight hundred a week. Now, don't I, beautiful young man?"

I felt my annoyance rising. "Well, all the same, it's just a money deal between us now."

She turned and picked up a glass of her own, her face pensive. "What if I say otherwise, beautiful young man?"

"Otherwise? You pass up eight hundred a week? Fat chance."

"I don't want to give up the money, of course. But you forget one thing. I'm a healthy, lusty young woman, and you're a healthy, lusty young man, and—*pow*."

I shook my head. "I'm not that lusty. I get lusty only when I'm interested, not when I'm compelled."

"I never saw a young man who knew the difference between interest and compulsion once the wrestling's begun."

"You're a real tramp, aren't you?" The question was more a statement of fact.

"Mm."

I placed the bills on the bar. "There's your money, honey. Now, where's that picture?"

She picked up the money and rolled it fondly between a thumb and forefinger. With an air of decision she said, "I can't accept this. Not if it costs me my beautiful young man."

"You mean I'm worth more than eight hundred a week to you?"

"Much more, come to think of it."

"What's so special about me?"

"You're kind. You say nice things. You treat a tramp as if she isn't a tramp. I've never known anyone like you."

I shook my head slowly. "You must be joking."

"No." She smiled gently and placed the rolled bills in my shirt pocket, then sank to the divan like a silent screen siren.

"You mean you're in love with me?"

"Of course not, silly. But you're wonderful for my morale."

"What if I were to beat hell out of you?"

"You won't. I know my men. You're simply not a woman-beater."

"I need information, Nikki. And the main item required right now is that photo. You hear?"

"You'll get it. But there's only one way you can get it."

"No deal. I have a girl now," I lied. "A good girl."

She smiled slyly. "That makes the challenge all the greater."

"You're a bitch, Nikki. A bullying bitch."

"Aren't I, though? But I'm a bitch with a very choice piece of news for you. What'll it be? The news? Or fidelity to your girl? Hm?"

TWENTY

Behncke busied himself with nervous little fussings, and even in my black mood I was able to wonder why. Was he trying to find the offensive, so as to punish Heinz Jaeger for being late? Or was he defending—trying to cover up a case of anxiety, as he appeared to be? Either way, Behncke was not himself today.

But who was?

I had listened to Nikki's lethargic little speech in the small of the night—receiving, weighing, and filing each word as if it had been a tiny, separate reimbursement for the confidence and self-respect my oversight had cost me. Her voice muffled by approaching sleep, she'd told of the secret visit Behncke had received from former SS Brigadeführer Eric Hammer, leader of a faction in Lübeck on the North Sea; of Hammer's insistence that Behncke include the northern group among those being supported by Behncke's company; of Hammer's angry departure, threatening violence, after Behncke's refusal. I'd listened closely, because in the effort I found a minute measure of escape from the self-disgust, disappointment, alarm, and outright anger I'd felt when, in the sordid afterglow, a whisper of intellect had told me that I would not have had to play her game at all.

Even now the question gave me fits: Why hadn't I merely threatened Nikki with her Oswald Linck caper?

Why hadn't I said: Nikki, play the game my way or I'll tell Behncke how I peeked through the air duct in his office and saw you microfilming his records for Oswald Linck.

Nikki was terrified of Behncke, and I was pretty sure she'd do anything to keep him from learning of her former tie with Linck.

Why hadn't I thought of something that significant and useful?

Now, slumped in Behncke's office, I could not decide which was worse: my blind, weirdly willing descent into outright whoredom or the inexplicable void in my thinking that permitted me to miss seeing the trump card I'd held against Nikki all along. In any event, I knew beyond any further doubt that Peter Klaussen was constitutionally unsuited to this kind of work. On the one hand, there was the moral block. Some men would need no justification whatsoever for carnal involvement with a beautiful woman; for others, carnal involvement sanctified by duty would be a rare delight. But for some reason beyond my understanding, the man who was Peter Klaussen seemed to have a limit, and this limit had been exceeded. Period. Moreover, if I could overlook Nikki's single greatest weakness I could overlook anything, and in this game, oversights were as healthy as gangrene.

My lousy curiosity had got me into all this. That was the lousy truth.

So sick was I of my curiosity I would have ignored Behncke's early-morning phone call if I hadn't been so taken with the peculiar sound in his voice. . . .

Behncke was looking up now, giving me a curt nod of greeting. "I realize," he said, "that I called you quite early. But this is important. For one thing, that silly Major Sneed has some papers I need, and since he's leaving for Bad Tölz this morning I want you to hop in VW Number Three—the Mercedes is due for a grease job—and pick them up first off."

"It's only eight-thirty."

"You're late, though."

"As the Amis say, tough tit."

"You've held me up terribly," Behncke grumbled. I gave him a closer look. There was a trace of very real anxiety there. Intuition told me that Behncke was prattling, trying desperately to find a further rationale for this meeting.

"You said for one thing, Behncke. What's another thing?"

The fat man's hands made his favorite steeple. I noted that they trembled ever so slightly. "I'll have to make it short," he said. "We've had bad news."

"What kind of bad news?" I asked with a horrid sinking.

"Some people in Lübeck. They've got wind of what we're trying to do and they want in."

"Are you all right, Jaeger?"

"What?"

"Are you all right? You're not listening to me."

"I'm listening."

"Well, as I say, there's this bunch up in Lübeck, and they are a thoroughly disreputable group and I don't know what we're going to do about them. They have heard of our little operation, and they claim Bormann's intention was that it support all subversives, not only in Bavaria but wherever in Germany they might be. Eric Hammer—he's an SS Brigadeführer, by the way, and I met him several times during the war at cocktail parties in Wannsee, and he's a fat, vacuous, greedy, reprehensible fellow— Hammer says we should merge the forces up north and down here so that his crowd can share in the cover and financial advantages offered by Kaufmann Kompanie. He even proposes to open a Kaufmann branch in Lübeck, with him as the manager. Can you imagine? He—Jaeger . . . Are you listening to me?"

"I'm listening, goddamn it. So what did you tell Hammer?"

Behncke sat back in his chair, trying to look grim and militant. "I told him, naturally, that a merger is out of the question."

"Why?"

"Well, it would seem to me that's quite obvious. First, I don't have enough operating income to support two operations, and, second, Hammer is an activist. He wants to derail trains and shoot Amis and raise hell in general. This, as you know, is entirely inconsistent with my plans."

There was a silence.

"What in the world is the matter with you, anyhow, Jaeger? You're acting very strangely."

"Nothing. What did Hammer say when you turned him down?"

"He was dreadful. Really dreadful. He said either we cut him in or we have a fight on our hands."

Shifting in my chair, I asked, "So what do you want me to do about all this?"

Behncke leaned across the desk confidentially. "You're an old Gestapo hand, thoroughly trained and experienced in counterpressures. I want you to think about ways we can head off this interference from Hammer and his toads."

192

"All right. I'll let you know."

Behncke consulted his watch. "Time for you to run. Think about it, will you, Jaeger?"

"Sure. I'm a real deep thinker, I am."

The garage was cold and smelly, and the urge to gag returned with new emphasis. I glanced around for Behncke's Mercedes and spotted it on the grease rack. A pair of mechanics struggled in a far corner to lift the motor from an Imbert, and the block and tackle made a nasty rattling sound. I called to them. "Where's Schultzi?"

"Who wants to know?" Schultzi boomed as he came from the washroom.

"I've got a run to City Hall, and the car's on the rack. Can I have one of the VW's? Number Three, I think Behncke said."

"Nice to see you again, Herr Chauffeur." Schultzi sighed, parrying my question until his mind could sort his vehicles. "I might say that for a chauffeur you sure don't spend much time chauffeuring these days. Do you realize that along with the seven hundred million duties I have around here I've had to drive Behncke on his little errands for four days this week alone? Where've you been, for God's sake?"

"Sorry, Schultzi," I said. "Behncke has me on a special assignment. Didn't he tell you?"

The garage super spread his black-caked hands. "Nobody ever tells me anything around here, except 'Schultzi do this; Schultzi do that.' Jesus, you'd think I had seventy arms and legs."

"Things are rough all over."

"Maybe. But it all starts here."

"Trucks running?"

"Oh, sure. Every one of them purring along on tissue-paper tires. When they blow it'll sound like Stalingrad all over again."

"I'm trying to fix that for you. That's my special assignment."

"Well, I hope you don't take too long at it. Do you know what 've been doing on those little tours with Behncke, by the way? Trying to find a ten-ton diesel-driven truck. And do you know vhy? So that we can move a frigging grand piano from Munich o the Abendsee so some screwy friend of Behncke's can while away the hours. Can you imagine? A ten-ton truck, just to move a piano?"

I tried to consider that, but it was no good.

"You all right?" Schultzi was asking.

"Great. Why?"

"You look like cold pork gravy."

"Little out of sorts, I guess."

Schultzi humphed in that way of his. "It seems to me, Herr Jaeger, that you've been a little out of sorts for some time."

"What do you mean?"

"You used to be a good sort. But you've changed. Nowadays you act as if you could bite everybody's ass off."

"You, too, Schultzi?" My mind went back to that evening with Chris in the park, and the remorse gave me another bad time.

"Eh?"

"Never mind."

"Well, if there's anything I can do—"

"You can lend me a VW."

"Let's see. Pfennig has taken Number One to Harlaching to pick up a manifold. . . . The keys to Number Three are on the board. Help yourself."

I turned, then hesitated. "Why don't you knock off and come along, Schultzi? It'll be only a half hour or so. Do you good to get some air in your soul."

Schultzi's partial pout lit up in a grin, and I could see that he was genuinely pleased. "Well now, that's better," he said. "That's the fellow I used to know."

It was one of those days when Bavaria seems to glow under a neon sky and the air feels like wine. Schultzi, folded up on himself in the front passenger seat, beamed like a kid at a fair, and I congratulated myself for having asked him to come along because I sensed that his guileless good cheer could do a lot to snap me out of my melancholy. He seemed somehow to recognize this, too, and he was even more ebullient than usual.

The VW was one of the better ones, and although it rattled and snorted a good bit, it was eager and responsive, and with Schultz already launched on what he called the latest joke, I settled to my

194

riving and the reconstruction of my spirit. We pulled out of the
lley onto the main drag and turned south toward the circle,
where I planned to cut east on the Briennerstrasse.

"So this fellow is packing his bag," Schultzi chortled, "and his
wife says where are you going? To America, the fellow says, and
he says, well, why? He says because I hear that over there all the
dames are gorgeous and they have so few men the dames are will-
ng to pay a man up to ten Marks every time he can lay them.
Why should I stay here and work for a living when there's
a deal like that going? Right off, the wife starts packing her own
bag. Where are you going? the husband asks. To America, the
wife says. Well, why? he says. And then, heh-heh-ha-ha, the wife
says, I want to see how you manage to live on ten Marks a year.
Ha-ha-ha—"

I grimaced at Schultzi and wondered what he would say if I
old him I'd heard the first version of that story in Kenmore Junior
High School.

I was thinking how boyish Schultzi's face looked when he
laughed when his teeth exploded and spattered all over me.

The rest was quite clear to me—as clear as anything can be
when you're squinting your eyes and ducking and trying to steer
a car that's already out of control and tipping over.

Schultzi's shattered head, snapping backward and throwing off
its peaked, blue-dyed Wehrmacht cap; his shoulders flexing and
his chest expanding as his body leaped and hurtled against me;
the air singing with glass dust and paint chips; the squeal of tires
and scraping of metal.

Even when the car was on its side and careening into a bomb
crater I could be detached enough to identify the most meaningful sound of them all. I'd fired it frequently in the Weapons Famil-
iarization Course, and I knew the sound of a Schmeisser machine
pistol when I heard it, all right. Like a piece of cardboard stuck
into a fast-turning bicycle wheel, it was. . . .

Somebody came out of the crowd. I could hear boots on the
pavement and, after a time, I saw a man's face against the koda-
chrome sky, peering over the right doorsill and looking down
at me.

195

"They're both dead," he said out of the corner of his mouth t those muttering in hushed tones beyond.

"I'm not dead," I said.

His eyes narrowed. "All that blood on you—"

"It's his, not mine. Get me out of here, will you? I can't mov He's pinning me down."

"Sure," the man said. "Hold on a minute . . ."

I was standing at the curb, trembling and studying the wrec when someone touched my elbow. It was Behncke, and he sai his voice like chalk on a blackboard, "Are you all right? I hear the shooting and the crash and ran out here—"

"I'm fine."

"Who did it, Jaeger?"

"I don't know. If I had a guess I'd say your pal Hammer ha made an early start in his little campaign to muscle in."

"But Schultzi. Why Schultzi?"

"Schultzi just lucked out. I was the target, I think."

"You? What makes you think that?"

"Because I'm the hero in this story."

✠ ✠ ✠

TOP SECRET

To: Central Registry, USFET   2 Aug 45

From: AC of S, G-2, per Abner B. Crowell, M/Sgt, clerk.
    Herewith a transcript of shorthand notes taken at the request o G-2 during a discussion this date in his office. Please file wit Appleseed Case.

G-2:   I've just read the file of Agent's Continuation Reports from Klaussen, Major. The Behncke thing is getting pretty involved isn't it?

Smith: Yes, sir.

G-2:   What do you recommend, Smith? Foreclosure?

Smith: I think it's too early, General. As you know, we have much to do yet in the Appleseed matter, and a large part of the problem is to line up an organization for Spike to take over. I concede that the Behncke group is growing large and unwieldy, as you say, but I think it ought to be permitted to solidify and move into high gear before we weed it out. I—

G-2: Are you convinced that the Behncke group can be handled by Spike?

Smith: Spike can handle any group.

G-2: How about this boy Klaussen? What are your plans for him?

Smith: Klaussen is a freak, of course. I plan to remove him from the case and transfer him to the MIS replacement pool at Oberursel.

G-2: You don't like him much, do you?

Smith: It's not a question of whether I like him or not, General. He's a good sort, I suppose, but that's not the point. He's a rank amateur bashing about in an area of great delicacy. I would not have kept him where he is so long if he hadn't offered a way to keep Spike and Peppermint honest. But—

G-2: But now you see him as a liability rather than an asset.

Smith: Klaussen seems to have a talent for being erratic. I simply have a creepy feeling with him around—as if he might get a burst of zeal at the wrong time, in the wrong place, for the wrong reasons. He—

G-2: It seems to me he's shown considerable get-up-and-go. I rather admire him.

Smith: I do, too. Very much, As a matter of fact, I plan to talk to the Chief, CIC, and Ronny Blackwell over in G-1 to see what can be done to get Klaussen a medal. A Bronze Star, say.

G-2: Bronze Star?

Smith: Yes, sir. I think he's earned it, even with all his bumbling. Unless you disagree, of course, General.

G-2: I disagree.

Smith: Well, then—

G-2: I say he should get the Distinguished Service Cross.

Smith: Well—

G-2: You don't approve, Smith?

Smith: Well, General, there are many top-notch spooks who have done outstanding things and who have gone without so much as a commendation, and after all, I—

G-2: This man is not a top-notch spook.

Smith: That's just it, sir. Klaussen—

G-2: Klaussen is an American officer who has demonstrated exceptional courage and devotion to duty under extraordinary circumstances. He is indeed not a spook, Major Smith. Not in my book. Spooks serve for many reasons—the least of them duty, honor, country. Spooks mainly are malcontents, money-lovers, thrill-seekers—people grinding their own axes. Lieutenant Klaussen has risked his life beyond all reasonable expectations over a protracted period for no reason but the fact that he's an American officer. I'm looking forward to the day I can shake his hand.

Smith: Well, of course, sir, I didn't mean—

G-2: The trouble with you and so many other men in this work, Major, is that you deal for so long with so many spooks that you tend to act like them, think like them, be like them. Well, Smith, now that your transfer will drop you into a more abjectly military environment, it will do you well to reread your Officers' Guide a few times. Those leaves on your collar do have a meaning, and I suggest you search it out. As for—

Smith: Sir, I—

G-2: Don't interrupt me, Major. I despise being interrupted. As for plans, you will remove Klaussen from the Behncke investigation as you propose. It's a reasonable move, I believe. But your intention to assign him to Oberursel requires further study. I will advise you of my decision on this when I complete the schedule for phasing the Behncke foreclosure into G-3 capabilities.

Smith: Very well, sir. But I must go on record as advising against the Behncke foreclosure at this time.

G-2: Sergeant Crowell here is making that note for the record. And, although it's against my natural inclination, I'll explain something to you. If we foreclose Behncke, Kolb, et al., it will be on a highly selective basis. We will arrest only Behncke and Kolb and a few lesser characters and leave their organization essentially intact. The reason for any arrests at all is a political one. Washington is most anxious to have the US taxpayer understand that while Nazism has been licked in the field considerable armed force will be needed in Germany to keep it licked at the source. Therefore, we would arrest Behncke and a reasonable number of his cohorts, giving maximum publicity to the arrests and the basic points of Bormann's original plot. We'd leave out any reference to the real situation, of course. Once the hoopla's died down we'd put Peppermint in Behncke's place and go on as intended. In other words, we'd simply accelerate our true plans and turn things over to Spike that much sooner—providing, of course, we find the gold. If the Appleseed thing is to succeed, we need that gold. We need it very much.

Smith: I'm fully aware of that, sir—

G-2:   And one other personal thing, Smith: you'd better tone down that air of superiority of yours. It doesn't sit well with superior officers.

Smith: I don't understand, General. I was not aware—

G-2:   As much as it may pain you to learn this, Smith, there are a number of things you're not aware of. And one of them is that I do not appreciate your condescending manner in my presence.

Smith: I have nothing but the utmost respect for you, sir. I think—

G-2:   You think I'm a moon-faced schoolteacher.

Smith: Oh, no, sir, I—

G-2:   And another thing you are unaware of, Smith, is that I do not care a whit what you think of me. You may go now.

Smith: Sir—

G-2:   You may go now, Major Smith.

TWENTY-ONE

I'd made a date to meet Champion at Region Four at 3:00 P.M. This was the only business of the day (Behncke believed me to be working on the tire thing—which I was, in a way), so I kept to my room and forced myself to use the early morning hours for sorting things out. Schultzi's death by ambush had had a heavy effect on me, part of it due to exaggerated sentimentality, part of it due to the incredibility of my own escape. In the first instance, I no longer saw Schultzi as a former SS trooper abetting a crooked cause but as an old classmate, sort of, whose major sins had been born of ignorance and circumstance. In the other, I simply could not comprehend a law of chance that could work so minutely as to direct every bullet in a long Schmeisser burst into everything but me. As a result of this two-way stretch, I'd fallen into a kind of prolonged, brooding inertia which, finally, I now struggled to throw off by taking inventory.

Item: Behncke was planning an eventual return of the Nazi system to German national politics, financing the movement from the assets and operating income of Kaufmann Kompanie. *Check.*

Item: My job was to keep U.S. Intelligence (i.e., Major Manley Wisenheimer Smith) apprised of Behncke's maneuvers without Behncke finding me out. *Check.*

Item: My secret ally in this job was General Kolb, who, to Behncke, was caretaker boss until Martin Bormann's resurrection. *Check.*

Item: Behncke's plans and my job were now jeopardized by Eric Hammer and a group in the Lübeck area who had underscored their determination to horn in by killing Schultzi and damned near killing me—at least once if not twice. *Check. No. Double-check.*

Item: I had sent Smith a query via Region Four TWX asking that he contact British MI-5 at Bad Oyenhausen to see what they knew of Hammer and his whereabouts and activities and all that crap. *Check.*

Item: The whole schmeer was now complicated by the fact that my landlady was spying on me for someone unknown to me. *Check.*

And so it went for an hour or so.

I was sitting there, like a guy holding a return-trip ticket on the *Titanic,* when something went through my mind and out.

It had to do with Schultzi. Or was it money? Or both?

What was it?

I began to worry the money thing like a terrier, as they say, trying to recognize holes in the financial statements which Behncke had filed with Military Government and which I'd reviewed the day before with an MG economist named Frisbee. It had all checked out precisely, and Frisbee had assured me that although Kaufmann was no world-beater it should, with care, remain solvent. But if—

Should remain solvent?

Why would Hammer be anxious to get a cut of a company with an acre of problems and an inch of solvency?

It would be understandable if Hammer were to get the hots over a strong working organization with lots of boodle. This would be something to stir the gonads of any political activist— Hammer included. But a loose-knit chain of grumpy, thoroughly beaten outs supported solely by a poor-mouth trucking firm?

It didn't equate. A cut of nothing is nothing.

Unless there *was* something somewhere.

But what? Where?

Was Behncke hiding something?

Like money? Big money, maybe?

With the Opel cruising at medium altitude, I checked my watch and saw that I'd have plenty of time for the round trip to Ober-menzing. Ever since my discovery of Christl Werner's nocturnal recording sessions, our relationship had been delicately altered. Everything continued to be correct and polite and friendly, all right, but I sensed her subtle withdrawal, and every so often I'd catch her looking at me in a tentative way, as if I were a neighbor whose name escaped her. Possibly in her own attempt to search for our former rapport, she'd asked me to drop by the General's old place. She had left behind a sewing bag during one of her visits and she suggested that perhaps the Ami MP's now quartered there would permit me to pick it up. It was on the shelf in the foyer closet, and as tattered as it was no Ami would be likely to covet it as war booty. I'd responded enthusiastically to the mock levity in this little gesture, but it was a bad job, because I only overdid it, and she had returned to her sober self, showing without saying it that she knew something was wrong.

I knew that ultimately I'd have to do something about Christl Werner, but what, when, or how was beyond me. She was playing me for a patsy, and all I could do about it was to run her errands. (Man of decision. That's me, boy.)

My plan, if that's what you'd call it, had been to be direct—to drive right up to the place, flash my new CIC credentials, and ask the MP's if I could have the damned sewing bag they had in their closet. Rehearsing a few gutsy American comebacks I could serve up to the wisecracks I knew they'd make, I jounced down the lane toward the cottage.

But instead of driving up to the gate I turned off the motor and made a coasting turn into the cover of the rambler bush. I needed cover right away.

There wasn't a GI vehicle in sight.

Instead there were a beat-up old pickup truck and three civilian cars—one of them a charcoal-colored Mercedes. And digging in the yard was a party of men.

I watched them for a long time, but didn't learn a thing.

In Südberg, as at Obermenzing, I tried the direct approach. I arrived about noon, propelled by an amorphous but compelling hunch. I walked in the front door of the decaying hotel and asked the old man at the desk if I could see Herr Kolb.

"I am Herr Kolb," he said, his faded blue eyes growing cautious, his faded blue lips growing tight.

"Is there somewhere we can talk privately?"

He studied me for a time as if I were a slide specimen, then swept a translucent hand in a small arc that took in the lobby's creaky iron posts, dusty potted plants, lifeless glass, and time-stained plaster. "In a place like this," he said, "who's to overhear? We are already talking privately, Herr—"

"Jaeger."

"What do you wish to discuss?" His voice was very brittle.

"Well," I said, going slowly, "my request might seem a bit un-usual, and I'd like you to understand that my intentions—"

"I see," he croaked, his eyes suddenly like popsicles, "then I suppose you want to look at my cellar. Is that it?"

I felt myself swallowing. Loudly. "Why—yes. Ah—how did you know?"

The old man sniffed. "I know a gangster when I see one."

"Gangster?"

"You're all gangsters. All of you. Dirty blood-sucking murdering gangsters. Nazi filth. Why don't you just die?" He had switched to the contemptuous "du," I noted.

"You don't understand—"

"You're right," he hissed. "I'll never understand. Not in a million years will I ever understand how vermin like you could do what you did. God will never forgive you for what you did to our coun-try. I will never forgive you for what you did to me."

Despite my astonishment, I had enough sense to try drawing him out. "What did I do to you, Herr Kolb? We've just met."

The parchment hands balled into fragile little fists. Shaking one, he grated: "I once had a fine son, and you and your filthy little Führer turned him into a horror just like yourselves. What have you done to me, you ask. Loving God in heaven!"

"I'd still like to look at your cellar."

The old man sneered, and when he spoke his voice was an inch above a whisper. "Of course you would, you dirty scum. But I can save you the time. Your friends were here two days ago, and they looked, and they dug, and they pounded, and they found nothing. Nothing. So go on down to the cellar and add to the rubble if you want. But you won't find anything, either."

He was right. I didn't.

But my hunch had been right, too. Someone was scouting the General's periphery, looking very hard for something.

Champion came in. He was in CIC uniform—officer's Class A's

devoid of insignia except for the brass US on each lapel. "Guten Abend," he said without enthusiasm. He paused, then said: "God. You look like the Sphinx's sphincter. Sore at something?"

"You'll never believe it, but I've been sitting here wishing I was in uniform."

"Homesick, eh?"

"Everybody's homesick, Champion. Even the Germans, and they're home."

Champion sat down across the Ops Chief's desk from me, and sighed. "Heard about your narrow one last week. Close but no tamale, eh?"

"How did you hear?"

"One of the Ops boys got a carbon of the Landespolizei report on the incident. I recognized the Schultzi name, and Kaufmann, and read the rest. Who tried to knock you off—do you know?"

"No."

"Creepy."

"So how are you making out, Champion?" I asked, in no mood for the amenities.

"Depends on how you look at it. I'm doing lousy as an instinctively moral young man; I'm doing great as a dirty bastard."

A flash of anger swept over me, a surprising prominence of irrational outrage that shot out from the sun in my belly. "Isn't that too goddamned bad, now?" I heard myself barking. "Poor old Champion has the blues because he has to be a bad boy."

Champion, his face immediately and vividly red, said: "I didn't mean anything. What the hell are you so sore about?"

"Just don't moan and groan around me, that's all. I've got troubles that haven't even been invented yet."

"I'm not moaning and groaning, goddamn it. What's the matter with you, anyway?"

"Shut up and give me your report."

"Well. All right. All right, buddy-boy. Pardon me for having hair."

"Come on, come on. The report."

"I have," Champion said tautly, "established myself as a latter-day Al Capone. I have your eighty truck tires. I am ready to deliver them at any time you say. The sooner, the better, because

204

I've found it's as hard to hide hot stuff here as it's reputed to be in State College, P-A."

"All right. I'll check and let you know in the morning."

"Don't you want to hear how I pulled this off?"

"You got the tires. That's all that counts."

"I see. I thought you'd be curious. . . ."

"I'm as curious as hell, Champion. But my curiosity has got me into a lot of trouble lately, and I've got all I can handle without taking on the trials and tribulations of Robert Champion, latter-day Al Capone."

"Paldon me, Honolaber Spy."

"Now beat it, will you? I'm expecting some recordings."

Champion stood up, pulled the wrinkles from his jacket, and ran a hand through his hair. He paused for a moment, then turned and went to the door. From the hallway, before closing the door, he said, "Klaussen?"

"Well?"

"You'll never make it."

"What are you talking about?"

"You can't be a good guy and an intelligence spook at the same time. You've got to be either or. You want to be a good guy? Then resign. You want to be a good agent? Then forget your ethics. But don't try to be both. You'll never make it."

"Get out."

The technician played them all—even those that had recorded nothing but the rattling of dishes, the faint mutter of the radio, the opening and closing of doors, and embarrassing bathroom sounds. There was some footage that included Christl Werner's idle chitchat with the postman, a phone conversation involving the problems of shopping, and the taciturn tabletalk picked up on the evening she and I had shared a modest supper. It was the second to the last set of spools that did it.

"Good afternoon, Frau Werner," a man's voice said in Saxon overtones, "are you alone?"

"I'm alone."

"May I come in?"

"Do I have a choice?"

"Ha-ha. I'm afraid not."

(Another spool, this one from the library.)

"Sit down, Herr Hartmann," Christl Werner's voice said.

"Thank you. I shan't take long. I don't want to risk Jaeger's unexpected arrival. He's a very erratic young fellow. Ha-ha."

"What is it you want now?"

"We've listened to Jaeger's phone conversations with Frankfurt and we'd like you to cover us on a new name that's come up. Please listen for the name Champion in your chats with Jaeger, if you will. We doubt he'll mention it, but if he does, please let us know everything that's said."

"Very well." Her voice was small and tight. "Anything else?"

"Not at this point. Incidentally, we've picked up some really good stuff between your father and Jaeger from that spool you got at Fliegerfreude that day. Excellent stuff. You'll be a real expert soon, Frau Werner. Ha-ha."

There was a lull. Then: "Is anything wrong, my dear? You seem preoccupied today. More so than usual. Preoccupation in our little profession can be a danger flag."

Another pause.

"Are you," the man's voice chuckled, "in love with our Herr Jaeger? Is that your problem, Frau Werner?"

"That's none of your business, Herr Hartmann."

"Oh, but it is. Love is what makes the world go around—in circles. That's what an American humorist claims, I recall."

"It's still none of your business."

"It is very much so, since love for Jaeger could complicate your motivations all out of reason and we'd end up with split loyalties and all sorts of other unhappy breakdowns in our currently excellent relationship."

"Don't worry about me. My sense of obligation overrides any other emotions left to me."

"Tell me outright: Are you in love with Heinz Jaeger?"

Pause.

"No."

"I don't think I believe you, Frau Werner."

"Then why did you ask?"

"I was interested in the tone of your answer, actually. I find that your negative answer is really more affirmative than an affirmative answer would have been."

"I don't understand all that nonsense. Now will you please leave? I'm busy."

"You've got to decide, Frau Werner."

"Decide?"

"Once and for all. Is it us or is it Jaeger?"

"Good day, Herr Hartmann."

"Remember, my dear: you really have no choice. You love Jaeger, I can see that. But what good is love when there's no life to enjoy it, eh? Ha-ha."

"Good day, Herr Hartmann."

The recording ended with a long run of silence broken only by the sound of a single sob.

They were excellent photographs. I could see that as soon as I spread them on the blotter. One showed the man at Frau Werner's door, another showed him striding down the walk toward the gate, a third caught him beside the ivied wall, and the last froze him in the act of entering a Mercedes.

"What color was this car?" I asked the photographer, a bald fellow with bad breath and thick glasses.

"I'm not much on color, but it was the same kind of black you see in a fireplace. Blackish gray, sort of."

"Anybody else in the car?"

"No. I could see that when it went past the house. I tried to get a shot then, but nothing was right. So I settled for the pix you have there."

"All right." I glanced at the stakeout chief. "How about other visitors? Were there any?"

"None to speak of. The mailman. The creep there in the pictures. You. That's all."

"You're absolutely sure," I asked the recorder technician, "that the spool I have here is of this man's voice? The guy in the pictures?"

"Scout's honor."

"O.K." I drew a deep breath and sat back in my chair. "You guys did a good job. I appreciate it."

The stakeout chief shrugged. "Grade-school stuff. There were no bugs in the house but ours, incidentally. The unfriendlies have only tapped the phone."

"That helps."

"Reet. That all?"

"Yes. That's all. Good night."

Curiously, I reached across the desk for the Webster's. I leafed through the pages until I came to it: "Memory—the power, function, or act of reproducing and identifying what has been learned or experienced; the faculty of remembering."

I closed the book and sat quietly, watching the cigarette smoke make ectoplasmic whorls beneath the desk lamp. Somewhere in all the crap I'd gone through in these past months a mote of information had been acquired by my conscious and stored by my unconscious. It hung now in some dark corner, just beyond recollection. But with every thrust of my memory's fingers it swayed further from reach, and I writhed with the special agony that comes with a face remembered but unremembered, a face familiar yet beyond identification.

I had seen Hartmann somewhere.

But where?

When?

The phone at my elbow buzzed politely and I picked it up. "Yes?"

"Sir, this is Ambrose in Ops," the youngish Missouri voice said. "I've checked on that MP billet in Obermenzing like you requested and there isn't much to report—"

"Give me what you have."

"Well, sir, it was a motorized patrol unit that was supposed to police the Autobahn between Munich and Augsburg, according to the poop at MG. But the MP's were moved out of the place a week ago and put in a farmhouse ten miles west."

"Who ordered the change of location?"

"That's what's so fuzzy about all this, sir; nobody can say for sure. The MP commander at City Hall says the order originated from MG Housing Control. MG says it couldn't originate such an order because it involves troop deployment."

"Well, hell, *somebody* must have something definite on it—"

"Sorry, sir. The only other line I could get on it was that the latest Billeting Directory has a notation that the Obermenzing house was to be vacated for the convenience of the Theater Commander."

"*McNarney?* What in hell would McNarney want with a crummy cottage in Obermenzing?"

"Well, that's a catch-all phrase, sir. It means that somebody has something going they don't want to document."

"Can *anybody* use that gimmick?"

"Oh, no, sir. Only somebody at USFET command level."

✠ ✠ ✠

By Courier: MOST URGENT   10/8/45

Peppermint:

Tell Spike that US plans partial foreclosure on Behncke for purely US domestic political considerations. The framework will not be weakened; only the fat is to be pared. You and Spike are to stand fast and, upon word from me, to proceed Munich and assume direct management of Kaufmann under agreed-upon cover. Details follow.

Putzi

12/8/45

Putzi:

Spike agrees tentatively. However, he cautions that if the slightest thing goes wrong he will break off all contact with you and abandon the plan completely. Repeat: the slightest hitch loses Spike to you for good.

Peppermint

TWENTY-TWO

I arrived at the office at five-twenty.

Behncke was so delighted with my report on Champion's progress with the tires he nearly danced, crowing that they would help to keep Kaufmann operating indefinitely. So for the moment, at least, the black-market angle seemed to be established. Whether it was the tires or the prompt delivery or the impressive efficiency I couldn't say, but whatever it was, Behncke had warmed to me dramatically. Some of this was showing through now.

"I tell you, Jaeger," Behncke burbled, "Kaufmann is destined for great things. Great things. And you will grow with it, take my word. It was incredible the way you simply went out and got the tires and came back and that was that. I simply set my price and you delivered. No dickering. Just results. Incredible, these days."

"Money will do anything."

"Ah, yes. But it takes handling. And you've shown you can handle it."

I was puzzled. (Not that this was anything new.) Behncke was entirely out of character, and the inconsistencies were so apparent they were impossible to read—like a line of printed text held close to the eye. As Behncke chattered on, I considered these inconsistencies, trying to back off so that the images could be focused. For one thing, Behncke had been frightened white only a week ago, with Schultzi's murder seeming to reduce him to a state of near collapse. This evening there wasn't a shred of that anxiety in evidence. Moreover, following the Landespolizei's perfunctory investigation of the killing, Eric Hammer and the northern group had become an almost total preoccupation with

Behncke. Today there had not been even a mention of the subject. For a third item, I'd never once seen Behncke anything but grumpy when he talked about money. But today—for all the money talk going on—he was positively radiant.

Behncke was up to something new.

What?

"And so," Behncke was saying, "we've got the truck and the piano and all we have to do is load her up and toddle on off to Fliegerfreude ..."

"Piano?"

"Yes. Damn it, Jaeger, you have the most aggravating habit of woolgathering sometimes. I've been prattling along, thinking you're listening, and you haven't even been in the room."

"Sorry. Piano, eh? General Kolb's?"

"Yes. He'll be delighted."

"When are you taking it down?"

"Tomorrow afternoon. Since it's Saturday we can take our time about getting back. I have the truck en route to Haidhausen, where it will pick up a set of tires." He winked slyly. "Pfennig has six laborers lined up. They'll load the piano in Harlaching and do the unloading at Fliegerfreude, and Nikki and you and I will ride down in the Mercedes."

I lit a cigarette, considering all this. I said then: "Sounds like quite a party. Why Nikki?"

Behncke's cupid's mouth puckered conspiratorially. "We're going to have a council of war. We're going over everything, from top to bottom and back again. And I want Nikki to take it all down. We've got Hammer and his bunch to decide about; we've got a going organization established in Bavaria and the Oden- wald; I have district offices ready to open in Nürnberg, Stuttgart, and Heilbronn; Major Sneed and his fellow idiots in the Military Government are about to authorize our trucks' crossing over into the Austrian Zone; and"—Behncke paused for a theatrical intake of breath and another precious wink—"you, Herr Jaeger, are about to become assistant general director of Kaufmann Kompanie."

It occurred to me that this was pretty good penetration. How many undercover agents work up from probational chauffeur to become second in command of the enemy operation? I thought of Smith, and felt a strange sensation. After a moment I recognized it: I wanted to smile.

"Well," I said, "this is certainly a surprise. Assistant general director, eh?"

"Right. And well earned, too. You've been very good to have around, Jaeger. Your fast thinking that day on the mountain road, the fine impression you've made on the General, your extraordinary adroitness on the black market—all these things make it quite clear that you should be in the firm's active leadership. And all the men like and respect you."

"I don't know if that's a compliment or not."

"It is. I assure you. It is."

"Well, Behncke, I can't deny I'm pleased. I suppose a salary increase goes with the job?"

"Indeed it does. A fat one. Very fat."

"How much?"

Behncke waggled a finger. "Not yet. I want to save *some* surprises for tomorrow."

"I hope you surprise the hell out of me."

"Oh, I will—I will."

I arose and stubbed out my cigarette in the big crystal ashtray on Behncke's desk. "Well, it sounds as if you've been a busy one these past couple of weeks."

Behncke nodded smug agreement. "Indeed I have. You may have been up to your ears in the tire negotiations, Jaeger, but I haven't been asleep the while."

"I can see that, all right. You're a real operator."

"We both are. We'll make a good team."

"It should be fun. Well, I'm off. I've got to see a man about some spare parts."

I went out, pausing to watch Nikki pound out a sentence on the new typewriter Behncke had bought her. She halted in mid-burst, then looked up over her black-rimmed glasses and winked a blue eye.

"Hullo," she said. "Like your new suit."

"Thanks. Schultzi convinced me I should have some new duds all around."

A shadow flicked over her face. But then she showed her gorgeous teeth and brightened her eyes. "Well, it's certainly an improvement."

"Tonight. About ten?"

"Oh, dear. Otto mentioned that he might drop by."

"Tell him you've had a change in plans."

"He won't like that. He'll think something's strange. . . ."

"Tell him you have cramps."

"Well—"

"And have the you-know-what there."

"I haven't been able to get it yet."

"That's all right. You have until ten." I permitted my annoyance to show.

"But—"

"Ten o'clock. With picture."

As I went through the front entrance, I wrestled with still another inconsistency. I couldn't name it yet, but I knew it had something to do with Schultzi. I'd reached the Opel when it hit me. I went back in and asked Blatz, the prune-faced clerk, for all trip tickets dated the day of Schultzi's death. We took all of five minutes to go through the file three times. But there was no doubt about it: the one I was looking for wasn't there.

And now came the action I'd dreaded all along: doing something about Christl Werner.

I threw the towel around me, rinsed away a trace of shaving soap clinging to the bowl, then took a last look at myself in the mirror. Leaning over the tub and raising the window shade, I studied the evening-mellowed garden and ran through a tiny rehearsal. Still unsatisfied, I went to my room and dressed.

My senses were acutely alive but my lips were stiff, my cheeks tight and hot, my legs sluggish, my fingers awkward—much as if a thin coating of paraffin had melted and hardened over me. Bongo Lohmeier, the retired spy who'd taught Order of Battle at Ritchie, had told me about this kind of thing in a rum-soggy monologue one night in the big old hotel on the square in Hagerstown: "The realization that you're about to do things that are altogether alien to your character, codes, and emotions sort of

213

lacquers you over with a dead feeling. Like you've had an enormous shot of novocain, kind of . . ."

I went to the top of the stairs, paused for a moment in the soft inner twilight, then leaned against the banister and called, "Frau Werner?"

I heard her steps in the lower hall.

"Yes? Did you call?"

"Could I trouble you for a moment? A window is stuck in my room here, and I think if you give me a hand I can force it open."

I was fussing with the casement catch when she came in my room.

"What is it, Herr Jaeger?"

"Would you press against the upper hinge there while I try to lift this catch? I think the casement is bent."

I sensed her raise her arms, golden in the late light, and I turned. She considered me calmly over the hunch of her shoulder, her lips slightly parted, her eyes deep and green and inscrutable. I kissed her lips, and they were cool and tranquil, unmoving, and I could sense the slow astonishment in them. Then they quickened, and I knew I had her.

But it wouldn't work.

I pushed her away.

"I'm sorry," I said, sick.

She stood there, eyes large and serious, arms still raised. "Sorry?"

I gazed at her directly and felt a sadness.

"What is the matter?" she was asking. "Why do you look like that?"

"I was going to seduce you."

"I know."

"I couldn't do it."

"Why?"

"I can't tell you."

She examined me solemnly for a time. Still calm, she reached out and touched my shoulder. "Is it because you're an American and I'm a German?"

Jesus. Holy, tenderhearted Jesus.

She said in her grave tone, "I know about you, you see."

214

"How?"

She smiled guardedly, a small parting of those smooth lips. "I suppose I've known from the moment you stepped in my door that first evening. It's not just that you're different—you're, well, especially different. From the first you've been half sick with worry over something, I could see that, and yet you always were kind or had a smile or did some little thing to cheer me. Even when I was the rudest you'd always be sweet, in your way. But more than that, you're the first person ever to accept me for what I am and the only one never to tell me what I should be. My whole life has been that, you know: 'Chris, do this; Chris, be that; Chris, don't do this, don't do that.' You've never instructed me. You've assumed I'm a woman. And I found myself trying to live up to your assumption. You started me thinking, and I've not stopped thinking. And I decided, finally, that I love you . . ."

I grabbed her wrist. "But how did all that make me American?"

"It didn't, of course," she said gently. "I just knew you weren't a German. There is no German alive who treats women with that strange kind of deference you show, that's all."

"But American. You just now said American. How did you know for sure?"

She dropped her gaze, and the golden twilight caught in her hair. "I knew," she said, "because I've been asked to spy on you."

"Spy on me? For whom?"

"I don't know. The Russians, I believe."

"*Russians?*" I caught her shoulders with both hands. "What are you talking about?"

"That night you arrived and fell asleep on Herr Klottner's couch —a man called Hartmann came here and said that if I'd let him get a good look at you without your knowing he'd give me a piece of news. I had nothing to lose, so when I was sure you had fallen asleep I took him to your room. Downstairs again, as his piece of news he told me he'd heard my husband was still alive."

"Go on. What else did this Hartmann say?"

"He said that if I did what he wanted he'd arrange to have my husband come home. I didn't owe you anything then, and I was bewildered by the thought of Franz being alive, and—"

"And you did owe something to your husband."

215

"Yes. I've told you that," she said tonelessly.

"Where is your husband supposed to be?"

"In a Russian prison camp."

"I see," I said, my mind very busy. "And Hartmann proved this?"

"Eventually. With a picture of Franz in his prison garb. And a letter from Franz telling me how much he wanted to come home and how I should do anything Hartmann asked."

"So what have you told Hartmann?"

"Just what he's asked: when you come in, when you go out, who comes to see you, what you say at supper. Those things. And he taught me to operate recorders, too. . . ."

"Did he tell you who I am or what I'm up to?"

"I've never wanted to know. You can believe that."

Not sure why, I did believe it. "Did he say why he was interested in me?"

"No. He said only that you are an Ami spy and that you must be watched."

I reached out and took a cigarette from the pack on the desk. In the flare of the lighter, her eyes shone and the ivory of her face was soft.

"You realize you've been tricked, I suppose," I said sourly.

"Tricked? How?"

"Your husband is dead, just as the casualty lists said."

"But the picture, the—"

"A snapshot found on him, maybe, or his ID picture, either one superimposed on a prison outfit. A letter drafted by an expert forger from samples of his writing in a letter found on him or something. The Soviets have many cute tricks. Did the letter say anything personal, for instance? Something only your husband would know about or be likely to say?"

She stood motionless for a long time, and the silence became unnatural and oppressive.

"Well, did it?"

"No. I guess not—"

"Well, then."

She fell silent again, and I was half through with the cigarette when she turned from her study of the sunset. "It was a monstrous thing for them to do, wasn't it?" she asked in a cloudy voice.

"People who engage in espionage are monsters. Monsters do monstrous things."

"But to prey on widows . . ."

"To prey on widows is not very nice. I just tried it."

"You think me a fool, don't you? A treacherous fool."

"I don't know what to think about anything any more. I can't count on anything being the way it looks. I can't expect anything to be the way it should be."

"Well, there's one thing you can count on," she said awkwardly.

"And what's that?"

"I love you. That's what."

I turned and stared at her silhouette. "You love me so much you sold me down the river. Romantic as hell, isn't it?"

She stiffened, and there was something new in her tone. "Now, just a minute. I did what I did primarily because I owed Franz something. A trip home was little enough to give him."

The anger heating up, I asked, "What would you have done if your husband *had* been alive?"

She gave me a long glance through the dusk. When she spoke, it was with a kind of subdued dignity. "I would have brought him home. My love for you doesn't keep me from paying my bills."

I sank onto the chaise, weary beyond tolerance. "This love you say you feel—isn't this also a—bill?"

"Yes. And I'm trying at last to pay it."

"By telling me about the Russians?"

"And by offering to do anything you want me to do. About that. About anything."

"You've fallen for a fraud, you know that, don't you?"

"Fraud? A decent man like you? Nonsense."

"I'm not decent. I have nothing decent to give you."

She laughed then, a pleasant sound in the dusk. "You've already given me the greatest gift I could want—your honest, unqualified respect."

"I tried to seduce you."

"That's what I mean," she said, smiling with a curious inward relish. "You tried. But you didn't. Besides, how could you seduce a woman who's already yours?"

217

TWENTY-THREE

"Let's have the picture, Nikki."

"You know my price."

"Your price is too high."

"Then no picture, sweetie."

"Give me the picture. Or I'll tell Behncke about your little deal with Oswald Linck that time."

She laughed sharply. "Silly. I told Otto about that a long time ago. I've found it's often better to admit things before they come out some other way. Otto thought it was funny. He said he'd suspected it all along."

I saw pinwheels, and was a little sick when I realized I'd punched her in the ribs, hard.

She was doubled over, gasping, tears forming. "Are you crazy? What's the matter with you? Wait—"

"The picture, Nikki. Right now."

"Don't you dare hit me! I'll—"

"The picture. Or the next one will be on the end of your lovely little nose."

"Wait. Don't—"

"The picture?"

"All right. All *right!* Here's your filthy picture! Now get out of here! Get out, get out, get *out!*"

It was a good picture, for a chest camera.

How long ago that seemed.

It was remarkable that a chest camera could pick up so much detail: my worried eyes; the set, strained look; the half slump, half crouch, as I huddled in the rear seat of the Opel; the strange bagginess of the mountain trooper's uniform; the birch-laced woods on the ridge beyond the highway.

Herr Hartmann was a very proficient fellow indeed.

It's very difficult, after all, to pretend to be a busy motorcycle trooper, warning motorists of air raids to come, and snap a quality photograph in the process. . . .

The stairwell leading down from Nikki's top-floor suite was even more dank and chill than usual. I pulled my jacket closer, then paused to check the time by the niggardly glow of the solitary lamp. Eleven-thirty already. God.

I'd lowered my watch arm and taken two steps toward the stairs when I saw the wink of light in the darkened corridor beyond, felt the loud, dry-stick breaking of the air beside my cheek, and sensed the concrete shrieking behind me. I was aware of blinking and hearing the hollow *ka-choong* of the silencer.

I went down, gasping and kicking my legs. I sighed once, then made myself lie still.

It was impossible for the man with the gun not to hear my heart. Like a great ram, it was, bashing the lining of my jacket, and the fear was an incredible physical force. A year later a sound came—a ghostly clicking of heels on asphalt block. I concentrated on not screaming.

Just out of the range of my eyes, which I willed into a stare at the ceiling, a darker dark moved against the dark, then a shoe nudged my ear and set my head to rolling—sideways, up, sideways, up. The man stooped and clutched my hair as if to turn my face to the light.

I grabbed the gun with one hand and, with the fingertips of the other hand bunched into a pointed knot, swung a furious short arc that slammed the man just under the nose.

He went down, yipping soft little sounds.

Covering him with the gun, I flicked on my lighter, then clacked it out.

It was Pfennig.

"All right. Up. Get *up*."

"I can't," Pfennig gurgled. "I think you broke all my teeth."

I hauled him erect and propped him against the wall. "God," he groaned. "You hurt me. Bad. You're going to kill me?" The question sounded like porridge seeping through wet bread.

"Why should I? I need your help."

"Help? What kind of help?"

A door down the corridor opened and a man's voice, sleepy and cross, demanded, "What's going on down there?"

I called back, "My friend. He's drunk, and I'm trying to take him home."

The disembodied voice grumbled, "Well, hurry up about it, will you? You're waking up the whole damned building."

"All right. Sorry."

"Bah." The door slammed.

Pfennig leaned against the wall in the gloom, dabbing his face with a handkerchief. "Jesus. You hurt me bad."

"Are you going to help me?"

"What do you want me to do?"

"You killed Schultzi, didn't you?"

Pfennig remained silent.

"Well?"

"If I did you don't think I'd tell you, do you?"

"I checked Blatz's trip tickets for that day. You told Schultzi you were going to Harlaching to pick up a part. But you forgot to cover yourself with a trip ticket. Blatz didn't have a ticket for any Harlaching trip, let alone one for you. You took Number One VW and went out and took up station in the rubble and waited for me to come along in Number Three. But you didn't figure on Schultzi riding along and you knocked him off instead."

"Prove it."

"You shot at me just a minute ago, didn't you?"

"That's different."

"Why?"

"I'm not telling you anything, pal."

"Maybe not," I said, clicking the revolver's hammer and pressing the silencer's big barrel against his Adam's apple. "Maybe not."

Pfennig moved away, flattening against the wall. "What if I do admit it?"

"Then I'll know I can trust you."

"Trust me with what?"

"I want you to help me get Behncke. Even though you *are* a usy shot."

"How come?"

"He just made me second in command. I want to be top dog."

"What's in it for me?"

"Second in command."

Pfennig dabbed at his lips again, thinking about this. Then he ;ked, "Why me?"

Remembering an old gangster movie, I said, "I like your style."

"Well, I don't know. . . . What do you want me to do?"

"First I want proof of your honesty. Did you shoot Schultzi?"

Pfennig humphed. "I meant to get you. But your being late, me a hurry . . . I made my try but got only Schultzi. Too bad, too. liked Schultzi."

"Who gave you the order to knock me off?"

"Behncke."

"Why?"

"He didn't say."

I pressed the silencer deeper into the flesh under his chin.

"Honest to God," he hissed, "Behncke just gave the order. He idn't explain it. He just said, 'Take Number One, hide down the :reet, and when Number Three comes along, blast it open.' That's ll. Honest."

The door opened again, and the man's voice boomed with out- ige. "Will you goddamned drunks shut up and go *home?*"

"Sorry," I answered. "We're leaving right now."

"And watch out for those stairs. They've just been waxed. I on't want ambulances howling around here on top of everything lse."

"Yes, sir. We'll watch it. Good night."

"Pigs."

To Pfennig I whispered: "Let's go to my place and talk things ver. Go ahead. I'll hold your arm."

As we approached the landing, my mind, a knot of heat, tried) weigh this abominable complication against the many things emaining to be done. I'd have to get Pfennig to a safe lockup)mewhere, of course. But where? The house on Freudestrasse

was out, because there was a major piece of business to transa
there yet tonight. CIC headquarters would call for time-consur
ing red tape. And—

When it came, it was like a series excerpted from a badly
stop-action sound film.

Pfennig's erratic stumbling ceased. An arm, fist clubbed, hurtl
around in a swishing curve, a wristwatch winking in some vagra
drift of light. A soft grunt, a hushed eruption of tobacco-staine
breath, the insane clatter of the fallen pistol—all of these a mute
accompaniment for the jerky, wild attack.

Out of reflex alone I had thrown my head to one side, but th
rock-like arm, wrapped in its sleeve of rough cloth, was a da
horror that nearly tore off my ear and set my brain to singing
marbled yellow tune. Through the hot tears and the freeze
fright, I sensed the arm's withdrawal, a new cocking, an
Pfennig's clenched-teeth staccato malevolence: "You-scared-m
Jaeger-but-Behncke-scares-me-more." I tried to hide behind n
arms, and my feet slid clear of the floor and I was down, th
yellow turning to purple.

But the wax surprised Pfennig, too.

His piston-like jab met empty air, and his shoes scraped. H
lurched, arms waving.

I raised a foot and gave him an almost gentle push, and h
went out neatly through the large pane between two steel fram
of the great window. The glass formed a tinkling, diamond-lik
cascade in the light from the street lamps below, and Pfenni
turned twice, slowly, as he went through the night. There was
single abrupt bleating before the far-off, wet explosion.

On the way to Bogenhausen I stopped the Opel twice so
could throw up.

But I hadn't had much to eat for several days, and even th
didn't work the way it should. . . .

TWENTY-FOUR

Taking her hand and pulling the receiver close so we both could hear, I waited, listening. The phone at the other end lifted and the man said, "Yes?"

"Herr Hartmann?" she asked, her voice small and worried.

"Ah—good evening, my dear."

"He's gone out, and he said something I think you ought to know right away."

"Well?"

"He telephoned the man called Champion."

"Ah-hah. And what did he say?"

"He asked Champion to come here. He said he wanted a conference." She paused. Then: "At two o'clock, he said."

"That's about twenty minutes from now. They will be in Jaeger's usual rooms?"

"I believe so. He thinks I'm asleep."

"Very well. I'll be there in fifteen minutes. Leave the library window unlatched and the foyer light on. I want a picture of our mysterious Champion as he enters. Right?"

"As you wish. Anything else?"

"Yes. Go to bed and stay there."

"You there, Champion?"

"We's heah, Bawss."

I moved through the shrubbery into the alley, where the jeep, idling restively, made a lump in the dark. "Move the jeep down the alley and park it in the turntable. And hurry up. He'll be here in a few minutes. You men in back get out here."

I waited, my back against the garage wall, my eyes half closed

223

with burning. The two Ops men from Region Four eased through the gloom and took up station beside me.

"Who are you guys?"

"I'm Mr. Kruger. That's Mr. Ecke there."

"O.K. We're making a pinch. Kruger, you move up to the front of the house and cover everything on the street side. Ecke, you take a post in those shrubs by the French windows at the back of the house. Champion and I will be in the library. I suspect our man will arrive alone, but if he brings pals, cancel them out."

The shape called Ecke whispered, "Any gun games expected?"

"No, because I want you to cancel the Opposition before they even think of guns. Just put them to sleep. The man I want likes to enter the library way. You see somebody going in through the French doors, Ecke, you let him go, hear? We'll take him inside. If he's able to break away from us and make it outside, nail him. O.K.?"

"What do we do with the sleeping beauties?" Kruger wanted to know.

"We'll take them in, too. But I don't think we'll have any more than our single target to worry about. I hope not. The Opposition can swallow a single pinch. Three or four can be a real dicey thing."

"Why?"

"Tonight's Opposition is Russian."

"Ouch."

"Yeah."

"Our Soviet allies are great ones for tit for tat," Kruger observed mildly. "Things could get quite hairy around the old intelligence campus if we start picking off their people like this."

I yawned an honest yawn, hoping absurdly that Kruger wouldn't think I was pretending nonchalance. "That's what we're paid for."

"Oh, I'm not complaining," Kruger assured me. "But our relations with the Russki spooks have been altogether manageable up to now. I just hate to see a rat race start, that's all. I'm the lazy type."

"And I'm the nosy type. I want to know what this bird's up to."

"Thy will be done."

Champion came through the hedge and gave a springy, British-type salute.

"Fourth for bridge?" he asked blandly.

It was dark, very dark, in the library, and I could hear the branches of the old chestnut outside clacking together and the leaves whispering fretfully in the quickening breeze. It was a hot wind that promised rain, and it made the house creak, and some of it crept through the rattling, loosely latched doors to agitate the plants in their pots on the long, low table.

There was a sound, different from the others.

I tensed, glancing across the darkness to where Champion made a smudge against the faint traceries of the bookshelves.

The pistol was heavy in my hand, and slick with sweat.

Gently the latch turned, and one of the doors swung open. A gust sent the plants into a frenzied rustling, and there was the smell of cigars. Then the room was quiet again, except for a soft shuffling and the movement of a shadow among shadows.

I flicked on the lights and said, "Good evening, Herr Hartmann. Sit down, won't you?"

The man was big, but not very, and even in his surprise there was a genial air about him. He stood frozen in mid-stride, the camera and its long, snouted cyclops eye swinging easily on its strap. He blinked several times and smiled. "Aha. A reception, eh?"

"Welcome to my landlady's home."

"Thank you." Hartmann chuckled, turning his amiable eyes to Champion, who stood by the French doors, pistol at the ready, and trying to look like Humphrey Bogart. "And this, I presume, is Herr Champion, is it not?"

"How do you do, Herr Hartmann?" Champion acknowledged in his Ivy League German.

"Sit down," I repeated, frisking Hartmann and finding not even a wallet. "You must be tired from all this sneaking around."

"Oh, I'm used to it."

"I dare say. Where's your motorcycle?"

Hartmann smiled his appreciation of the little joke. "That was a long time ago, eh? You seem to have grown much older since then, Herr Jaeger. Or is it Schaue? It's so difficult keeping up with all your names."

"Who are you?"

Hartmann sank into the easy chair. "Do you mind if I light cigar?"

"Smoking in the outer lobby only. Who are you, and what d you want?"

"I'm just a tired, middle-aged man trying to make a living."

"Doing what?"

"Traveling, selling, writing reports. A dreary life, really."

"Who are you on the road for?"

"No matter."

I hit him with a bunched fist, making the blow a twisting thing that made a dull thump and created a red mustache. Hartmann sighed, a sucking sound that ran, tiny and hurt, around the roor and down the darkened hall.

"Who? Who are you traveling for? What are you selling?"

Hartmann held his coat sleeve to the dripping below his nose blinking away the tears that had formed. He murmured: "Yo need lessons, Herr Jaeger. One never strikes a prisoner in a man ner that brings blood. It's not tidy, for one thing; it's amateurish for another."

"I'm appearing on Major Bowes' program tomorrow. Mean while, shall we make more mess?"

"Do I have a choice?"

"Certainly: get chatty or get bloody."

"I'm a terrible conversationalist . . ."

I hit Hartmann's nose again, and now the flow was a fountai whose spurting turned his shirt and necktie into a dark red bib His head rocked backward, then snapped forward again, shaking

"For Christ's sake—" Champion murmured.

"Shut up, Champion. Who are you traveling for, Hartmann?"

"So this is the American Gestapo at work, eh?" the wavy-haired man gurgled.

Another punch, and this time Hartmann could not contain a liquid groan.

"Who?"

"For Christ's sake," Champion spat, "you trying to kill him?"

"Who? Who, you son of a bitch? *Who?*"

226

Far away I heard a ringing—a recurrent, arbitrary jangling somewhere just behind my eyes, and it came louder each time, reaching across a great void to insist on recognition. I listened. After a long time it occurred to me that something held my arm, and a voice like—Whose? Champion's?—was saying: "Telephone. The telephone's ringing. . . ."

"Get it."

"You all right?"

"You're speaking English, Champion. . . ."

"Why not? This fellow knows we're Americans."

"How? That's what I want to know. How?"

"Are you all right? Jesus, you look awful."

"I'm all right. Get the goddamned phone."

I sat on the divan, aching, and watched Hartmann's attempts to collect himself. The ringing stopped, and Champion came to the archway and said: "You'd better take this call. I think it's important."

"Keep an eye on this guy," I said.

"He isn't going anywhere. His ankles are like wet spaghetti."

It was Smith.

The nasal superiority of his voice was amplified by the phone, and it worked an astringent effect on the heavy lump resting on my brain pan. I blinked my eyes, opened them wide several times, then rubbed them with thumb and forefinger.

"What's on your mind, Smith?"

"Can we talk on this phone?"

"Just a minute." I stooped, lifted the umbrella urn's false bottom, jerked out Hartmann's recorder, and threw it on the floor. "O.K.," I said into the mouthpiece, "I got Sis off the extension."

"I had to chance this call," Smith said. "Time's important."

"Why?"

"We're foreclosing on Behncke." From Smith's tone the very idea was akin to abolishing sex.

"Are you out of your goddamned *mind?* We're just getting started."

"That will do. We're foreclosing. Do you understand?"

"Oh, come on, now. You must be joking. . . ."

"Don't argue. Those are my orders."

"Well, you stupid bastard, how—"

"Now, just a minute, you young smart aleck. I'm your superior officer, and this is still the military service, you know—"

"So put me on KP."

Smith made a small sound, then said through his teeth, "Who do you think you are?"

"I'm your penetration on the Scab case, remember? Your onliest penetration. Treat me sweet and gentle." The unreasoning rage made the phone slippery in my hand. "Now, are you going to explain this insanity or are we going along this way? If so, I'd like to run upstairs and get my insult thesaurus."

"Don't bother. You're no longer working."

"I'm what?"

"You're fired."

"Don't make me laugh. You're going to fire me just before you close out the case? Not very ding-dong likely."

"The orders have been cut and are en route to Region Four."

"Now I know you're insane. I'm holding all the loose ends. There's the Eric Hammer thing to follow, for one thing. And there's to be a big meeting tomorrow at the General's place. We're trucking a piano down there and then—"

Smith broke in: "You needn't worry about Hammer. British MI-5 reports that Eric Hammer was picked up in Lübeck three days after the German surrender and has been held in Hamburg for war-crimes prosecution ever since. Behncke has been feeding you a line about Hammer wanting a cut in the business."

"You *sure?*"

"Oh, stop it, Jaeger. Of course I'm sure. Now listen to me: the case is no longer any concern of yours. I'm taking over down there Sunday at noon. Meanwhile, you report to the Ops Chief at Region and await further assignment. Your orders will arrive there by tomorrow morning."

"Listen to me now, Smith: this is my case. I've worked my behind off on it and I plan to be in on the finish." I realized I was trembling.

"One more word like that and I'll have you court-martialed. Do you understand?"

Through pinwheels of color, I spat out the only trump I had. "Here's something for *you* to understand, Major Manley Smith:

228

he Russians have muscled into the act. How do you like them
·pples? We've got Russians for company. Russians. *Russians.*"

There was a full half minute of silence at the other end of the
ine, and I leaned against the wall, doing what I suppose you'd
:all relishing every second of it. When Smith spoke again his voice
ounded like its own echo.

"What did you say?"

"I said we have company from the East."

"How do you know?"

"I'm playing host to one right now. He's in the library, bleeding
all over his cheap necktie. Russians sure dress lousy, don't they?"

Smith asked hollowly, "Who is he?"

"Calls himself Hartmann."

There was another silence, broken only by the sound of Smith's
breathing.

"You say he's bleeding?" Smith asked eventually. "What have
you done to him?"

"Just caught his attention. He's a poor listener, a worse conversationalist."

"What do you plan to do with him?"

"Take him to Region and sweat him, that's what."

This pause was even longer than the others, and I thought I
could hear Smith's mind grinding. He said finally: "Now, I want
you to listen very closely. Just hold him at Region. No questioning.
Understand? Don't ask him a thing. Keep him on ice until I get
there, that's all. I'll handle this thing."

"Now, wait a minute—"

Smith exploded, and his undisguised venom surprised me. It
surprised me to learn he could explode.

"I said leave the Russian *alone!* Keep him entirely—absolutely
—incommunicado. That's a direct order, Jaeger. Understand? A
direct order. If anyone—the Region commander included—so
much as asks Hartmann the time of day it's a court-martial for
you. Do you *hear* me?"

"But—"

"Just follow that order if you want to stay out of Leavenworth.
Hartmann is, as of now, under my direct control. He will not be
moved, consulted, or discussed without my personal approval."

"All right. All *right.*"

I hung up and went, stiff-legged, to the library.

Champion looked around at me, and I was distantly aware of a thing in his eyes. Was it disenchantment? Disgust?

Probably both.

"What now?" Champion wanted to know.

"Call in Kruger and Ecke, will you? Tell one of them to bring the jeep around front. I want you and the others to hold Hartmann in solitary at Region. Nobody is to see him. He's to be kept safe, quiet, and alone until a man from USFET gets down here to interrogate him."

"When will that be?"

"The day after tomorrow—Sunday."

Champion asked, "What about you? Aren't you going to Region with us?"

"I plan to avoid Region like the VD. I expect something in the mail there, and I don't want to be around to read it." I hesitated, remembering. "And something else, Champion: take Chris with you. It won't be long before the Russians miss Hartmann and come looking for him. She'd be the first they'd hit. I suggest you cool Hartmann, then put Chris in the CIC safe house until I can take over. Got me?"

Champion shrugged. "Yea, verily. Don't worry about the girl. I'll protect her with your life."

After they'd gone, I sank into the easy chair.

Through the weariness I felt a sullen satisfaction of sorts.

Of all the orders, all the direct orders, Smith had handed out on the phone, there had been one he had failed to give.

Not once had Smith given me a direct order, formally stated, to withdraw from the Scab case. . . .

PART 3 *FORECLOSURE*

TWENTY-FIVE

Our start for Fliegerfreude had been considerably delayed. For one thing, Nikki and Behncke had undergone five hours' interrogation by the Staats- und Landes-polizei. A week ago, Schultzi's shooting had stirred only mild interest among the civilian police, who were already up to their chins in a soldier-civilian crime wave and a rash of suicides—half of these among Germans hopelessly despondent over having to remain in Germany and half among displaced persons hopelessly despondent over having to leave Germany. But now, with a second Behncke employee turning up dead, even the most jaded police official would have to admit that there might be more than coincidence involved. So out had come the notebooks and off to headquarters had gone Nikki and Behncke, Nikki as a fellow Kaufmann employee whose dwelling had been besmirched by Pfennig's blood, and Behncke as the employer who could establish the victim's background. But the scores of souls who occupied Nikki's apartment building had been similarly questioned, and when the police coupled Nikki's honest-to-God innocence with the indignant Bürger's complaint over drunks falling down in waxed hallways and going through windows, they chalked up one more coincidence in a profession ridden with coincidence and got everybody the hell out of the office.

For another thing, Behncke, after his release, had been compelled to scour Saturday-preoccupied Munich for an off-duty driver to replace Pfennig on the piano-moving detail. This, combined with Military Government's failure to deliver the properly revised moving permit, had served to push Behncke into a blue-faced fit. His mood hadn't sweetened, either, when by four o'clock in the afternoon the mess had finally been untangled and we headed for City Hall to pick up the corrected papers Major Sneed had good-naturedly arranged by telephone from the bedroom of his paramour in Schwabing.

"I tell you," Behncke was saying to no one in particular, "it's a bloody shame that things can't go the way they're supposed to. You work and slave to organize your affairs, and what happens? Some silly corporal in some asinine branch of the great fiasco of the American army gets too busy staring at some sow's backside and fouls you up to chaos and back. It's a bloody shame, that's what it is."

Nikki, who was in no better mood, shifted in her place next to Behncke in the back seat and said, "Please watch your language. I'm not one of your truck drivers."

"Oh, excuse me," Behncke snapped. "I forgot you're a clergyman's wife."

Busy at the wheel and fighting to keep awake, I said nothing.

"What I'd like to know," Nikki said irritably, "is just what Pfennig was *really* doing in my apartment building this morning."

I waited to see if Behncke would say something, but when the back seat became notable for its silence I decided to build a little defense of my own. I yawned. "What time did all that mess happen, anyhow? I never did get it all straight."

Nikki, because she had no choice, played the game. "It was almost midnight. I'd been in bed for hours. I went to bed right after Herr Behncke stopped by to drop off the spare-parts inventories," she lied.

"Where were you last night, Jaeger?" Behncke put in.

"Why? Do you suspect me of doing in good old Pfennig?"

"Of course not. I merely wondered where you were, that's all."

"I was working on the gasoline deal for the Augsburg branch. I thought you knew that."

"Well, I knew you were involved, yes."

"So that's where I was." I nudged him right back. "Where were you last night, incidentally?"

"That's none of your business."

"True. But you and Pfennig were pretty good pals. I thought you might have heard him say something that could give us some ideas. After all, Behncke, there've been two violent deaths on the payroll in little more than a week. If somebody's working on us—

paring us down to size, say—we ought to start some counter-planning."

"Frightened, Jaeger?"

"Murders always frighten me. Especially when I'm a murderee, as I apparently was when SS Scharführer Schultzi passed on to that Big Gas Oven in the Sky."

Behncke remained silent, so I swung into full offensive. "Do you accept my theory that Eric Hammer and Associates are trying to give us a message?"

"Like what?"

"Like: 'Play our game, or this is what happens to all of you.'"

Behncke did not answer, and I could feel him staring at the back of my neck.

"You know," Behncke said finally, "I think you might have something there. I do, by God. That *must* be it."

"Have you heard any more from Hammer since we last discussed him?" I drawled.

"Why, yes. Yes. As a matter of fact, I have. Yes."

"What did he say?"

"He—he called me on the phone. He said the northern group was getting impatient. That we'd better make a decision soon or there'd be real trouble."

"Like what?"

"Like—raids. Raids on us. Raids on the General's place. That sort of thing . . ."

(Raids on the General's place?)

"When did he call you?"

"Several days ago. Last Tuesday. While you were in Augsburg."

"Why didn't you tell me about it before this?"

"I—I didn't want to concern you. The work you've been doing —it's delicate, and I didn't want to make it more difficult—"

I turned left at the imperious motion of a traffic cop's white glove and eased into the mainstream of the Prinzregentenstrasse. In line and cruising, I fished out a cigarette and lit it. I said: "Tell you what, Behncke. Set up a meeting. Tell Hammer I want to talk to him."

The silence in the back seat was a palpable thing. I found myself enjoying it. "Well?"

"I'd better think about that. After all—"

"After all, what? Set up the meeting."

"Well—why? I mean, what good would that do?"

"Hammer's two up on us. Let's start making the score more even."

"How?"

"Well, as a first step, I give Hammer two or three more navels, for instance."

Behncke cleared his throat. "You'd shoot him?"

"Why not? It's only politics."

Nikki sputtered, "Why, that's a horrible idea. You men—"

"Shut up, Nikki. Well, Behncke?"

"No. No—I won't—I can't permit that. It would start an open war between Hammer's people and us; that is obvious."

"You forget. War's already been declared."

"No. Let's think some more about it. Just get that kind of thing out of your mind, Jaeger. No killings. Not yet."

The attack was shaping up well and, as I congratulated myself, I pulled the Mercedes to a halt before the great pile of gingerbread that made up City Hall. And, at last, I saw the route I'd been feeling for all along. In a split moment of insight it had arrived; I'd been groping, and then I'd found it.

Behncke opened the back door and, with a jerk of his head toward the building, told Nikki: "Run in and get the papers, will you? Major Sneed said they'd be at the Officer of the Day's desk."

When she'd gone, I said, "I've been thinking."

"So?"

"Yes. I think we'd better ready our defenses for Herr Hammer's little war against us."

"What do you mean?" Behncke's tone was tentative.

I gritted my teeth and took the plunge. "The big money. It isn't safe where it is."

I could hear Behncke's soft intake of breath. "The General has told you about Bormann's boxes of gold?"

"Sure. Why wouldn't he? I'm his buddy." I yawned to cover my astonishment over the jackpot I'd hit with my wild-swinging guess.

"Well, I must admit I'm surprised. Did he tell you where it is?" Behncke asked guardedly.

"No. But I've guessed. Just like you have."

"What do you propose, Jaeger?"

236

"I think you and I had better convince the General that the gold's hiding place should be changed. If Hammer's getting ready to fight, one of his first moves will be to descend on Kolb and sweat him for the location."

In the rearview mirror I could see Behncke's pale pout ease off. Slowly, a faint smile formed on the cupid's lips, and Behncke smoothed his mustache with the delicate motion he used whenever he was pleased.

"Well, I follow your reasoning," Behncke said casually, "but just moving it from Fliegerfreude is not going to do it. The General could still be sweated for the new location. . . ."

"He can't be sweated if he doesn't know where it is."

"Now I *don't* follow you."

"How about this: you and I persuade the General to let us move the gold to, say, his father's hotel at Südberg. I've checked the hotel, incidentally, and somebody—it must have been Hammer—has been there already, looking for the loot. He didn't find it, of course, so he won't think of looking there again. So we claim we're going to move the stuff there, but we actually hide it someplace else. All along, then, Kolb will think the money's safe in the hotel cellar and that we're continuing to finance our Kaufmann operations with operating income and liquid assets. But really he's got nothing but boxes full of sand in the cellar, while Otto Behncke and Heinz Jaeger are up to their sweet little rumps in gold which they use to diversify and expand Kaufmann—and, in the process, keep a ton or so for themselves, eh? And, if Hammer sweats the General and raids the hotel, all he gets is a sandbox to play in."

(God. Could Behncke *really* swallow anything so crude?)

Behncke could.

"By God, Jaeger," he exploded, "you're a genius!"

"Yes."

"That's a wonderful idea!"

"Oh, I wouldn't say it's wonderful. It's only stupendous, sort of."

"I've certainly underrated you. I didn't realize when you came on the scene last March what a perfect gem you'd turn out to be. . . ."

"We ought to try to set it up as soon as possible."

"Certainly. Certainly. When?"

"What's the matter with tonight? We've got a truck big enough

237

to handle most of the load. We've got the men to do the loading. What's wrong with tonight?"

Behncke slapped his knee and laughed outright. "What's wrong indeed? Tonight would be perfect!"

I yawned again and stretched. Resting back in the seat and flipping the cigarette butt out of the window, I continued to feed out the line. "We move the piano to Fliegerfreude, see, and then you spring the Hammer threat to begin raids. Between the two of us, we convince the old man that the gold should be loaded and moved immediately. I've got Kolb pretty well under my thumb, and I think I can sell him on the idea."

"What if he wants to ride with us? I mean, we tell him we're taking the gold to his father's hotel. Won't he suggest that he go along with us to make the storage arrangements?"

I shook my head. "I don't think so. He and his old man are very dear enemies, so it wouldn't do any good to have him along. In fact, it would be better to keep his father in the dark about whose stuff it is."

"Well, hell. Then how do we get Kolb's father's permission to store the boxes?"

"Simple. We drive to your place with the gold. We empty the boxes, fill them with crap, then put the boxes on the truck again. Then I arrange to have my black-market contact—a Yankee lieutenant named Champion—take the phony load to Südberg, where he tells Kolb's daddy that the boxes contain secret U.S. Army goods that must be stored for troops planning maneuvers in the Südberg area. The old man won't dare touch the boxes, won't dare let anybody else touch the boxes, and won't dare to open his mouth about them."

"Ha! Delightful! *Delightful!*"

"Not bad."

"It'll work beautifully!"

"It should. All we have to do is pull a real sales job on Kolb."

"Well," Behncke chortled, "we have two murders to show Hammer means business. Kolb shouldn't be too tough to convince."

Now I knew why I had been shot at. Behncke had been trying to set up this little caper from the very first.

I slumped further into the seat, but not before I'd caught one more glimpse of Behncke stroking his mustache, and beaming.

I closed my eyes then, and dozed. I came to the surface with a nervous little jump when the clack of heels announced Nikki's return.

"Well, here they are," she grumped, "and if anybody ever tells me the U.S. Army is capable of blitz warfare I'll just laugh and laugh. Honestly, I've never seen such rigmarole over a few silly papers in my life. I hate to think of what a bunch of oafs there must have been in the Wehrmacht if those oafs in there were able to defeat it. Honestly!"

She was standing there, fussing with the door handle, when a set of spotless, faultlessly pressed OD's and an MP's brassard moved up to fill the window at my left shoulder. The creased uniform buckled painfully and a face appeared, set and pompous under a glistening service-cap visor.

"Du willst have to moven das car, mein Froond. Parken verboten."

It was—of all the people in the great, double-damned, sighing world—Lieutenant Haley, Princeton boy first class.

"Well," Haley said, his haughty gaze reflecting recognition. "I see you're still out of uniform, Lieutenant Klaussen."

✠ ✠ ✠

TOP SECRET

From: Technical Aids Section, MISC, Oberursel
    Our File No.: QF WR-731
VIA COURIER—RUSH

To: Maj M. Smith, c/o 970th CIC Det., USFET
    Pursuant to your request, we have made the rush-order excerpt of the telephone conversation recorded by your hqs and forwarded to this section hqs this morning. The spool is mounted on the machine delivered to you herewith. To play, simply press start button. To replay, press rewind button, then start button. Call me if you have any questions.

                        Burton Collins, 1st Lt, MIS

You're fired.

Don't (word lost) me laugh. You're going to fire me just before you close out the case? Not very (garble) likely.
The orders have been cut and are en route to Region Four.
Now I know you're insane. I'm holding all the loose ends. There's the Eric Hammer thing to follow, for one thing. And there's to be a big meeting tomorrow at the General's place. We're trucking a piano down there and then—

And there's to be a big meeting tomorrow at the General's place. We're trucking a piano down there and then—

We're trucking a piano down there and then—

We're trucking a piano down there and then—

We're trucking a piano down there and then—

TOP SECRET

TWX: TOP PRIORITY URGENT
CIC REGION IV, MUNICH, VIA ALPHA CHANNEL. ATTN: OPS CHECK MIL GOVT MUNICH FOR SIZE OF TRUCK AUTHORIZED OTTO BEHNCKE FOR MOVEMENT OF PIANO MUNICH-ABENDSEE. ADVS SOONEST.

SMITH, G-2, USFET

TWX: TOP PRIORITY URGENT
AC OF S, G-2, USFET, VIA ALPHA CHANNEL. ATTN: SMITH TRUCK 10-WHEEL, DIESEL-POWERED CONVERTED WEHRMACHT HEAVY TRANSPORT. SER. NO. WH 273340. CIV. NO. H 14473. CAPACITY, 10 TONS. LOAD: 1 PIANO, GRAND. CREW: 1 DRIVER, 6 LABORERS, LITHUANIAN, ON DAY LOAN FROM DP CAMP VIC. STADELHEIM.

OPS CHIEF, REGION IV

Most Urgent via WOLF Radio

Spike:

Hartmann's instructions to us were that should anything happen to him we were to use this method to inform you. Therefore we now advise you that Hartmann has been arrested by US agents. Do you have any instructions?

Padushkov
Soviet Fine Arts Cultural Mission

Most Urgent via WOLF Radio

Spike:

Please acknowledge. Any instructions?

Padushkov

Most Urgent via WOLF Radio

Spike:

Are you there?

Padushkov

Most Urgent via WOLF Radio

Spike:

Are you there?

Padushkov

TWENTY-SIX

The weariness was now a sort of three-dimensional shadow that formed an overlapping phantom image of myself. When I moved an arm, it was as if another arm followed in sluggish mimicry; if I shifted my body, I'd be moving two weights; as I struggled to think, one mind would roll over and yawn while its companion slept on, deep, heavy, and immobile. Even the close call with Haley had failed to return me to my natural state of clear-eyed, keen-witted, alert-postured ineptitude.

Some one of my instincts still up and about had shown Haley to be one of those atrocious coincidences Smith had always warned against, and it let me see that the unshaded truth was the key to the management of this situation. Behncke, being a charter-member Nazi, could accept coincidence as one of the more melancholy facts of life, I felt, so as we'd driven away from City Hall I said indifferently, "Odd thing—the American said he thought he knew me. Coincidence, I guess."

Behncke had reacted as I'd expected, only more so. He had said nothing at all. And this had served to sharpen the continuing, indefinable uneasiness. Behncke should have said something—should, to be in character, perhaps have made some acid comment about the Ami busybodies or whatever. But outright silence? I wondered. . . .

We made rendezvous with the truck at Harlaching. The piano was an enormous concert grand scrounged from a movie-studio warehouse by a friend of Major Sneed's mistress's mother-in-law and had been loaded that morning by a six-man crew of Lithuanian DP's. These wraiths—slab-faced, disconsolate, and mute—had swung aboard the big van and taken up station, three to each side of the piano, to stare at nothing while Wolff, the relief driver, had worried the monster out of the warehouse dock and into the alleyway. The truck was a former Luftwaffe vehicle of indeterminate make—a diesel-powered, ten-wheeled brute that snorted and thundered and threw up great clouds of sooty exhaust. Wolff assured us that he'd handled such a truck many times in France, and it had been quickly obvious that there was no disputing his claim. I had climbed into the cab to brief him on the back-roads route we would follow, and watched in fatigued approval as he'd slid the gear into reverse and backed unswervingly down the alley to make a tidy turn south on the Grunwald road.

The grotesque convoy formed, we had headed out for the storm that flickered along the distant Alpine waves.

And now we were in the gut of it—the crashing and moaning and hissing made almost dreamy by the sturdy house, the General's playing, the wine and lamplight. Leo's buffet had settled heavily. I'd only nibbled, but even that had been too much.

Slumped in my chair, falling asleep around the edges, I rummaged again for the string that dangled so elusively. Things were moving beyond my control somehow, somewhere; I felt this with a creeping certainty. There was a key, a link in a chain, a nut-and-bolt combination that I'd missed somewhere along the line. I knew that all I was required to do, actually, was to sit and watch Behncke play his cards. It was quite apparent that Behncke had known all along that Bormann's gold was hidden here at Fliegerfreude. It was easy, too, to see that Behncke, with his little Hammer-Lübeck fiction, his silly machinations involving the piano, his frantic efforts to locate a big truck, his too large moving crew, had planned to leave Fliegerfreude with the gold tonight. And all I really must do was to help the plan along, truck the loot to Behncke's place, then have the Ops Chief arrest Behncke on charges of sedition and possession of contraband Nazi funds. Seize the gold in Behncke's pockets, and the die-hard Nazis in the provinces would wither on the vine for lack of supervision and nourishment. Seize the gold, and the foreclosure so cherished by Smith would be a fait accompli before Smith could get out of his swivel chair. . . .

But—

But what?

What was I missing?

I thought of Hartmann.

No. Hartmann was one of those asinine quirks. Hartmann obviously was a manifestation of that national propensity for snooping which made spying and counterspying the Soviet way of life. Somehow Hartmann, as a Soviet agent, must have learned of the Bormann-Kolb-Behncke plot at about the same time G-2 had—last winter, about. Somehow he had been tipped to the parachute landing at Obermühlhausen and had been there to see what it was all about. I told myself that Hartmann's awareness of all this was not so difficult to understand when the Rote Kapelle was considered; if the highest German echelons could have been penetrated by the Rote Kapelle at the peak of Nazi power and vigilance it was no miraculous thing for a Hartmann to learn of a Kolb or a Behncke or a Jaeger, or of a Bormann gold cache, and to attempt a penetration of a ragged, war's-end plot. And, most significantly, Hartmann's heavy-handed exploitation of Christl Werner, his frantic digging at Obermenzing and Südberg, showed pretty clearly that he'd been just outside it all, waiting to find a route by which to climb in.

No, Hartmann was not the string. He was another coincidence. Another coincidence safely in jail.

Nikki?

Nikki was as transparent as Behncke, actually. Money was her motivation in life. She was thoroughly in league with Behncke, of course. That had been obvious from the moment she'd refused a cash fee for snitching on Behncke. The only time Nikki Meier would choose a lover in lieu of cash would be when she had so much cash it could make no difference. An upcoming share—even, say, of one-tenth—in the Fliegerfreude gold would readily put her in such a position. No, I had Nikki's number, all right. . . .

What, then?

General Kolb completed a delicate arpeggio, then arose from the piano bench to stretch his arms. Glancing at his watch, he showed mild surprise. "Well, I guess I've bored you all enough for one evening. I've been playing for two hours. . . ."

"Nonsense," Behncke gushed from his place on the great sofa.

"I could listen to you all night. You're really excellent, you know. Isn't he, Nikki?"

"Oh, I should say."

"Don't you think so, Jaeger?"

"He's damned good."

The General shook his head and waved a hand in dissenting little arcs. I could see that he was genuinely embarrassed. "Oh, come now," he said, "that's enough. But I do thank you, Behncke. It was a nice thing for you to do."

"My pleasure, General. After all, we have to keep our leadership happy, don't we? Ha-ha."

I rested my head on the back of the easy chair and closed my eyes, not daring to keep them shut for too long for honest fear that they might grow together. Above Behncke's effusive chatter and the sounds of the storm I could hear the radio and the muted voices of the Lithuanians; their alien intonations were lonely sounding, and I felt a twinge of depression.

The DP's, working silently under Behncke's red-faced, arm-waving supervision, had unloaded the piano and moved it to its place by the big window. Afterward, the General had led the DP's to the kitchen and seen personally to their supper, since his man Leo had gone to bed with a raging fever. Once fed, the Lithuanians had followed Kolb into the big garage and service quarters at the rear of the house, where they squatted on blankets and listened dully to Behncke's instructions to await his word to reboard the trucks. Before hitting the sack, Leo, obviously depressed himself by these Banquos of Germany's past, had suggested to Kolb that perhaps the DP's would pass the time better if they could play cards and listen to the radio on the workbench. The radio was playing now, quite loudly, and the Lithuanians were apparently in listless debate over trumps or something. They had been at it for several hours now.

I opened my eyes and turned them painfully to the sofa when I heard Behncke call my name.

"Jaeger? We're about to talk business. *Jaeger?*"

"Go ahead. I'm with you."

Behncke cleared his throat, adjusted his glasses, and leaned forward over the brief case he'd opened on the coffee table. Nikki sat primly, a steno book on her knee, her pencil poised. The General stood by the window, peering out at the nervous night.

"Before we get down to regular business," Behncke said, fussing with some papers, "we have a rather bothersome development that should take precedence, General. I think it would be best to have Jaeger tell you about it, since he's most familiar with the details and has authored what I think to be an excellent corrective measure."

The General turned. "What's the matter? Trouble?"

"Well, yes. It's more troublesome than trouble, I'd say. Why don't you fill in things for General Kolb, Jaeger? Take as long as you like. This is very important in its way, and I think the General will agree once he's heard the story."

I bent forward to place my glass on a table. The grip of the pistol in my shoulder holster dug harshly into my chest as I did so, and I shifted slightly to ease the pressure. Something shifted in my mind, too—right at that very moment. Like a trapdoor crashing open, a section of my brain broke loose from the gumbo and I saw what I had been failing to see all along.

"Come, Jaeger. Tell the General," Behncke urged.

I traded stares with Kolb, and Nikki's pencil made polite little noises as it wriggled along the pad.

"Well," I said, yawning despite the alarm and my anger with myself, "it's important, as Behncke says, and it's trouble—as you say, General."

"So? What is it, then?" the General demanded.

"Behncke is about to steal the gold."

There was a loud pop as Nikki's pencil point broke.

Even the storm seemed to pause in awe of the screaming silence that followed. It was the General who snapped the weird spell of suspended time, motion, and sound.

"Behncke's *what?*"

"He plans to steal the gold Bormann ordered you to hide here," I said through the cotton mat in my mouth.

Behncke stood up, his fat knees jarring the table, his jowls shaking whitely. "Jaeger," he thundered, "have you gone completely out of your *mind?*"

"Well, aren't you? Isn't that your plan?"

"You know very well what my plan is." The plums behind
ehncke's spectacles glowered. "I should say *your* plan. After all,
's the plan you came up with—"

I shook my head, and the motion sent a flash of pain across my
noulders. "No, Behncke," I said dully, "it's been your plan all
long. I merely gave it words."

"Will somebody," the General snapped, "please tell me what
his is all about?"

"Sit down, Behncke," I sighed.

"Who do you think you're—"

"I mean it. Sit down."

Behncke sank to the sofa, his lips quivering. Nikki, her eyes
aring unseeingly into her lap, sat redly silent and motionless.

"Well, Jaeger, out with it. What's this all about?"

"It's simple, General. Obviously, Bormann must have told
ehncke about the gold hidden here, and since very early in the
ame Behncke has been laying the groundwork for a fictional situ-
tion by which he hoped to persuade you that the loot should be
noved to a new hiding place."

"Situation?"

"Mm. Although he played it straight at the outset, he gradually
ot a hankering for the big money. And the bigger the hankering,
ne more aggressive his planning. With help from Nikki and
fennig, he finally contrived a little drama in which a group in
übeck, led by a character named Hammer, was to propose a
nerger with our forces here in the south. Behncke is supposed to
ave scorned the suggestion, and Hammer is supposed to have
nreatened open warfare for the gold."

"But it's true!" Behncke barked. "Damn it—"

"Behncke has even engineered two killings to give credibility
o his little fable. Because I was expendable, I was to have been
ne victim both times. (There was a third time, incidentally, when
was shot at while at my own front door, but that didn't come off,
ither.) However, Behncke decided that Schultzi's and Pfennig's
eaths would suffice to impress you with the basic point: i.e.,
Iammer meant business. Well, tonight Behncke planned to pre-
ent us with this fiction and convince us that the gold should be
noved to a safer place—a place where he could subsequently

247

plunder it at his leisure. But being a brilliant and imaginative defender of the Moral Law, I saw through the plan and, drawing myself up in righteous sneakiness, I suggested the very plan Behncke had in mind. As an extra touch, I pointed out that the safest place to hide the stuff—because of its very unlikeliness—would be your father's hotel. I also suggested that while in transit the gold be unloaded at Behncke's house in Munich and sand substituted for the loot, with only the boxes and their phony contents ultimately stored at the hotel. Behncke agreed to this very fast, naturally, because, for one thing, it was a fine improvement on his own plan, and, for another, instead of having to plead the case, I, your trusted lieutenant, was to do it for him."

The General, leaning against the piano, nodded thoughtfully "I see. Very interesting indeed. Is this true, Behncke?"

The fat man puffed his cheeks in and out and ran a finger along his mustache. "Jaeger," he rasped, "is a filthy goddamned liar. Are you going to believe me or a lying, sneaky American gangster?"

"Where is this Hammer fellow now, Behncke?" Kolb asked darkly.

"How should I know? He might be right outside the door at this very moment, for all I know."

"No, he isn't," I murmured. "He's been in a British jail since last May. You should be more careful in selecting characters for your plots, Behncke. Hammer's being 'way up north in another occupation zone didn't mean there were no ways for us sneaky American gangsters to check on him."

Emitting a sucking sigh, Behncke fell back among the sofa cushions. He swallowed twice. The General took a cigarette from a brass tray on the piano and studied it.

"Well, Behncke?" Kolb asked.

In a blur of motion, astonishingly rapid for a man of his girth Behncke bent forward, reached into the brief case, and produced a flat automatic pistol. The click of its safety catch going off was a twig-snap in the storm's C-minor strumming.

"Well, what?" Behncke snarled.

TWENTY-SEVEN

)h, God," I groaned. "No melodrama, Behncke, please."

"Put the gun down, Behncke," the General said.

"Raise your hands, both of you," Behncke grated. "Nikki—
earch Jaeger for a gun. And get his keys to the Mercedes."

"Nikki, too, eh?" I said, pretending elaborate surprise.

"Keep your hands up, I said."

I noted that Kolb seemed remarkably unperturbed by the
evelopments, and this gave me the irrelevant urge to laugh.
'ikki's trembling, scented hand fumbled at my shoulder holster,
nd then the pistol was gone. She took my key chain next, lean-
1g across the chair and brushing my face with her filmy hair.

The General said thoughtfully, "You knew all along about the
old, then, eh, Behncke?"

"That's right. I've known a lot of things all along. Now both of
ou get up against that wall over there. Quickly, now!"

General Kolb, suddenly angry, turned his head and shouted,
Leo!"

"Never mind, General," I sighed. "That's what I've been over-
ooking. Leo. How else could Behncke have planned all this? He
eeded inside help, and Leo was it. And how else could Behncke
ave learned that I'm an American?"

From the balcony came Leo's serene tones: "As they say in
he thrillers, brilliant deduction, Herr Jaeger. A bit late, but bril-
ant nonetheless. Shall I shoot them now, Herr Behncke?" He
'as covering me with a hunting rifle whose barrel probably was
o larger than the Washington Monument.

"No, don't shoot them, Leo. We'll walk them off the sundeck."

I said, "You've already loaded the gold then, eh, Behncke?"

249

"That's right, you smart-aleck American bastard. You don't think for a moment that the DP's have been listening to the radio do you?"

"Quite a job, loading all that gold."

"Quite a long dinner hour. Quite a long musicale. Quite a good straw boss, Leo."

"Pretty slick, Behncke. I didn't think you had it in you."

"I have a lot of hidden talents."

"Academically: what are you going to do about Wolff and the six Lithuanians out back?"

"After they've unloaded the gold, Wolff will drive the DP's back to their camp. There will be a very impressive truck wreck en route. Wolff will be the sole survivor. Ingenious, eh?"

"Hollywood invented that years ago."

"Good things improve with age."

"Wolff, too, hm?" I stalled. My tired eyes regarded Nikki, who stood with a flushed, confused look on her face, my pistol dangling gingerly from her fingertips. If I could only get close enough to her. . . .

"You don't really believe Behncke will let you share in the gold do you, Nikki?"

"Shut up, Jaeger!" Behncke shouted.

"He'll walk you off the sundeck, too. If not that, something equally final."

"Shut up, or I'll shoot you on the spot!"

Nikki stammered, "Yes. Shut up. Shut up, Heinz. . . ."

"You nutty dame," I sneered. "Do you really trust that fat little peacock? Enough to gamble your life on him?"

Behncke raised the automatic. "I mean it, Jaeger. You're asking for a bullet."

I started to answer, but General Kolb, eyes fixed on the balcony said, "You surprise me, Leo."

"Yes, I suppose I do," came the answer from above. "But—that's life, as they say."

"Haven't I treated you well?"

"Of course you have, General. But I need money. Real money."

I snorted. "Oh, for Christ's sake! Do any of you, really, honest to God, believe Behncke will cut you in?"

Behncke raised the pistol and aimed, his spectacles twin circles of opaque reflection.

I knew then that I had pressed the man too far. Involuntarily I shut my eyes against the shock to come, aware somehow that I was too tired even to feel fear. . . .

The sound of the shots was a total thing. It filled the room, floor to ceiling, corner to corner—twin concussions so complete and tangible they were like gelatin in a mold. Entirely on their own, my eyes opened wide, and in the caroming echo and Nikki's thin, animal keening, they registered vignettes of seemingly frozen action, each an entity, standing apart, yet interwoven with the others so as to comprise a kind of mobile tapestry:

Behncke, his spectacles askew, sinking to his haunches, contemplating the red fountain pumping from the center of his starched shirt front; Nikki, her eyes wide over the hands she'd clapped to her mouth, shrilling and weaving from side to side; the General, white-faced, standing flat against the wall; the creaking, the swishing, the crash, as Leo came over the balcony railing to shatter the reading table and roll to a still, broken-doll heap.

At the door, two pistol-swinging men, their dripping rain gear making blackish blots on the carpet.

In the center of the room, big and smiling faintly under his bandaged nose, Herr Hartmann.

"You've had a busy day, my friends," Hartmann was saying, "and I dislike compounding your weariness. But please stand over there against the wall, will you?"

"Hartmann?" I heard myself asking.

"Yes, my boy: Hartmann. Quickly now, over by the wall with your hands up. We've much to do tonight."

I moved woodenly to the wall to take up position beside the whimpering Nikki. On her other flank was the General, again looking thoughtful. Hartmann hummed a little tune as his hands moved expertly over each of us in turn.

"Now then," Hartmann said softly, "all in order. Sergei, tell Vassily to warm up the truck, will you, please?"

One of the men by the door returned his pistol to his raincoat pocket and turned to leave. He paused, then asked in atrocious German: "Excuse me, Comrade, but will you be riding in the car or the truck?"

"The car, the car. Hurry, lad. We've little time to spare."

The man went out the door, and a whorl of cold, damp air stirred the draperies.

"Beastly night," Hartmann suggested, winking at me. "But perfect for sneaking up on a place, eh?"

"Who are these people, Jaeger?" the General blurted testily.

"Soviet agents. They're taking the gold."

"Tut-tut," Hartmann cautioned, "no discussions, please."

Outside, exploding above the sounds of sleet at the windows, the truck engine burst into a full-throated roar, then dropped off to a series of barkings before taking up its deep-bellied idle.

"What are you going to do with us?" Nikki's voice was querulous.

"You'll see. In a few moments, as a matter of fact. Now, no more chitchat, please." Hartmann glanced at his watch, and even in my numbness I thought I could discern nervousness in the gesture. Nikki began to weep noisily.

Behncke, on his back now, turned his head, started to say something, seemed to think better of it, and died.

The man called Sergei came through the door again, holding out his arms and shaking them free of water. "All set, Comrade," he said.

Hartmann nodded and smiled his faint smile. He groped in the pocket of his parka and withdrew an enormous Colt .45 automatic pistol. Holding it in one hand, he used the other to operate its slide, and the machinery clacked in well-lubricated snaps.

"Some weapon, eh?" Hartmann said, regarding me amiably. "My favorite American invention. Reliability. Good heft. Big enough to be fitted with wheels, actually."

"I rather thought it was a Russian invention," I parried inanely, struggling against the lethargy, probing for a way out. "You fellows are the greatest little inventors there are."

252

"We've done quite well tonight, don't you think?" Hartmann laughed pleasantly.

"I'll say."

Hartmann winked once again, then raised the pistol. Pointing it at Nikki, he said, "Ladies first, eh?"

"No," Nikki whispered liquidly. "I'm only a woman. I don't know anything. You've no reason to shoot a mere woman—"

"It's a shame, of course," Hartmann agreed. "But the ways of politics and gold are cruel and uncompromising, Fräulein Meier. Good-bye."

The gun roared, and Nikki bounced off the wall and was halfway to the piano before she stopped rolling for good.

Beside me, the General clucked his tongue and shook his head, pondering the sprawled bundle that had been a beautiful blonde who loved money and tiger rugs and sex and thought Ike was adorable and lied and schemed and took pictures and winked cornflower-blue eyes over a typewriter and smelled good all the time.

I would have thrown up if I hadn't been so busy pondering the .45 Hartmann was now leveling at the General's stomach.

"Wait a minute, Hartmann," I said. "May I ask a question, please?"

The bandaged nose turned toward me. "Question, Herr Jaeger?"

"Yes."

"Well, what is it, man? Can't you see I'm busy shooting people?"

"I hate to interrupt, but it's only one question."

"And what is it? Hurry, please."

"Only this: if I'm going to be killed, would you mind awfully much if it's while I'm fighting?"

Hartmann was thinking this over when I hit him in the belly. It was a good one, because I was very frightened, and he went down, bent in a horizontal, fingers-to-toes U. I went down with him, using his bulk as a shield and his pistol for a blast over his shoulder at the man called Sergei, who stood by the door looking foolish. The General had become a pinwheel of motion, and the goon who had been leaning on the piano caught his whole mo-

mentum. They waltzed briefly, then collapsed against the key
board to sound an imperious lost chord. By the time I had the .4
untangled again, Sergei had disappeared into the night, hollerin
all sorts of things in Russian, so I merely clobbered Hartman
across the eyebrows with the flat of the gun. Then I clobbere
him again, because by now I was very peevish.

"How are you doing, General?" I panted.

"I'd-be-doing-better-if-this-fellow-weren't-so-tough."

"Stand back and I'll shoot him."

"No—I have him now."

He did, too. The man's gun hand was jammed under the key
board lid, and Kolb was sitting on the lid and squeezing th
fellow's throat. I could see that the Russian was already uncor
scious.

"Come on, General, we've got to get out of here."

"No, Jaeger. You try for a car and get some help. I'll cover yo
from upstairs with a hunting rifle. And I can keep the Com
munists here, too, because they won't want to leave without th
gold. But they won't get near that truck because I'm even bette
with a rifle than I was in a Fokker D-7."

Deadpan, I said, "Anything I can't stand is a braggart."

"Get going, lad."

"Well, have fun," I said. "I'll try to come back for you."

I ran out the door into a hell of flickering lightning and slee
that whirred along in weaving, wind-lashed trajectories. I wa
drenched immediately, and as I flattened against the hous
squinting into the mountain spume, there was a wink of ligh
from beyond the big truck. The wooden siding next to my elbov
hummed and threw out a confetti of splinters. I had no idea ho
many of them were out there, but to keep their respect I squeeze
off a round from the .45.

They respected me so much they did nothing but fire some fiv
hundred thousand shots my way.

I dropped to my hands and knees in the ivy bed bordering th
house, my heart thumping and my mouth dry. From what I'
been able to see, most of the fire had come from behind the hedg
that marked the border between the parking area and the su

deck. That meant that if I was to grab a car I'd have to run across the open area to their front, thereby becoming exposed to at least a half-dozen pistols for, say, ten seconds. This didn't appeal to me very much, so I went into conference with myself on what to do.

Another spattering of bullets along the clapboards above my head closed the meeting. I scrabbled along through the ivy until could round the corner of the garage. There I stood up and ran like hell for the deep shadows of the great mountain, praying I could find a hiding place. I was outnumbered, outgunned, and out of nerve, and all I wanted was out.

The small door at the right of the main garage door swung open, and in the oblong of light it made I saw a man in a peaked Wehrmacht-style hat come running out, all elbows and knees and winging a Schmeisser. I worked the .45 again, and he went back through the door, only this time skidding along on his back and howling. I was past the door when I thought of something, so I turned back and went in. Wolff and the Lithuanians were lined up against the wall, hands high, eyes white dots of fright. I made a threatening motion and showed my teeth, and the hands went higher and the dots grew bigger. Then I stooped, swept up the dead man's peaked cap, and pulled it on. I picked up the Schmeisser, too, and, after presenting the group with another snarl, I scurried out, locked the door, and made for the hills.

But it was no good. The mountain was glass-smooth, and the single route open to me was a narrow alley-like corridor made by the house on one side and the mountain base on the other. And the only place this could possibly lead was the cliff that went straight down to the lake. I had a choice: either to go back the way I'd come and chance the guns of Hartmann's hoods or to go down the corridor and try to find a place to hide until 1985.

I skittered down the narrow space and, at the end of the house, stopped to consider the black void at my feet, an enormous blackness in the black where even the lightning dared not go. The lake and I. I and the lake. Me up here. It down there. Beautiful, gorgeous, faraway lake. Come see the lake. Take a step and see the lake.

On the other side of the house there was a lot of shooting, and

255

I thought I heard the General's voice shouting some dirty word There was more shooting, and I guessed that the Hartmann boy were making a try for the truck and its gold.

Here we go gathering gold in May, gold in May, gold in Ma I didn't know whether I was actually singing or—

The Schmeisser had a carrying sling, so I hung it across n shoulders and shoved the pistol into my belt. Then—dizzy, fair sick—I lay on the stone and dangled my head in space. In th next lightning I could see them: the beams that came out from th cliff in a diagonal to support the sundeck floor. About eight of them, there were, and, at the other end, a ledge of the parkin area's foundation.

I slid over the cliff and caught the first beam in the crook of n arms, legs swinging and clothes whipping in the wind that howle in the venturi formed by the deck and its supports. The beam wa jacketed in ice, and it was all I could do to pull myself up an rest in the V it made with the cliff side

Eight times I went through the ritual: a witless kind of praye a deep breath, a launching, a clutching, a swinging, a heaving then a numb, fleeting rest period. There wasn't one time in ai eight when I really thought I'd make it.

But I did. And Hartmann had been flanked.

While I sucked air on the final ledge, with the parking are inches over my head, I decided I'd risk all on a variation of n Mountain Road Theme.

I clambered up to the gravel, stood erect, and, squinting int the sleet, called out in what I hoped sounded like German wit a Russian accent. "Hey, everybody! Come here! I've got an idea

I stood there in the lightning with my peaked cap an Schmeisser.

"Come here—quick! I've got a plan!"

Four shadows detached themselves from the hedgeline ar came running. I waited until they were very close and then la the Schmeisser make some lightning of its own.

They went down like dominoes.

I broke into a run, yelling, "Don't shoot, General—it's n Jaeger!"

A gun went off in my ear, and I was nearly blinded by its flash. The big charcoal-hued Mercedes was at my elbow, and Hartmann was in the back seat, holding a hanky to his head and shouting orders at his driver, who was trying again to pot me. I ducked and scrambled for the truck, bobbing and weaving as I cleared the front of Hartmann's car. I skidded around Behncke's car and, puffing hard, made it the length of the truck. I seized the handgrip next to the truck cab and pulled myself into the driver's seat.

It was warm in the cab, surprisingly warm, and the big engine —still idling—grumbled and shook. I released the emergency brake and set the hand throttle high to avoid a stall.

Behind me I heard Hartmann's Mercedes kick into life and its tires whining and spinning against the ice-lacquered gravel.

Double-clutching as I'd seen Wolff do, I shoved the gearshift lever into reverse, slammed down on the accelerator pedal, let out the clutch, and felt the sick pain in my head as the titanic vehicle lurched backward.

It had been my plan to back the truck crosswise to the road, thus bottling Hartmann in the parking apron, but the steering wheel had been cocked and the initial rearward leap—spurred by my inexperienced jab at the gas pedal—tore the wheel from my grasp. Bobbing around like a one-man band, I fought to regain control, but the ponderous weight, the racing motor, and the glaze ice had fixed things but good.

I felt a crash, a squeal of rubber, a shriek of ruptured metal— a great sliding and turning. Flinging open the door, I tumbled into the night, scraping my hands on gravel and rolling over and over to clear the runaway wheels.

There was a gigantic, suspended flash of lightning, and from my prone position I watched the truck slue toward the lake, Behncke's Mercedes bucking and jouncing before it. The weird train then jammed hard into Hartmann's car, swinging it sideways, and in a crazy action like those Dodge-'em rides at a carnival, all three vehicles ground through the hedge with a great slamming and banging. The sundeck, of course, had not been designed for such compound loads, and with a stupendous crackling and roaring— the sound of a dinosaur in a thicket—the deck separated from

257

the house. In the fading glare, truck and cars seemed to hang fo
a moment as if in indecision, and then, rolling over in massiv
laziness, they disappeared over the ledge.

After a long time I felt the monstrous concussion in the lak
two hundred feet below.

TWENTY-EIGHT

The day was bright and blue and yellow and green, and th
valley was dappled in sun and shadow. I was standing by the bed
room window, wrapped in a towel and inhaling the rain-washe
air, when a jeep came bouncing up the road to make a high
school-hotshot stop beside the house.

Champion swung out from behind the wheel and stood for
time, surveying the remains of the sundeck. I heard him sa
admiringly, "My, my. The General must throw one hell of a part
Saturday nights." Then he turned and helped Chris from the jeep
She was wearing a soft summer-kind of dress, and she seeme
hypnotized by the shambles.

"Hullo," I said from the window.

They looked up, and Champion said, "Ah. Jack von Armstrong
the all-American German."

She asked in gentle agitation, "Are you all right?"

"I'm all right."

"My father—"

"He's fine."

"Come on down," Champion said. "I've got some bad news fo
you. Your pal Hartmann's been sprung. When I found out th
morning, I asked Chris to show me the way here. I just want yo
to know it isn't my fault—"

"I know. It doesn't make any difference now, I guess."

General Kolb sat at the piano, one hand forming soft little chords, the other holding a delicately steaming china cup. His hair was combed and brushed to a luster, and the hunting jacket and jodhpurs were crisp and correct. It occurred to me that I'd never seen the General look quite so well set up.

"Ah," Kolb said, waving the cup and smiling easily, "you hardly seem to have had such a busy night, Herr Jaeger."

"The bath and bed helped. And so do the fresh clothes. Thanks for the loan. They fit quite well."

"So I see. Coffee?"

"In a moment. Where is everyone?"

"Well, now: Hartmann and his driver are at the bottom of the lake; Behncke, Nikki, Leo, and Hartmann's assorted hirelings lie in the cold-storage bin. Our friend Champion is in the cellar, checking on Wolff and the two surviving Communists, who've been locked in the tool room. The Lithuanians are playing skat in the garage, my daughter is in the kitchen where a woman belongs, and I am here, contemplating the verities. What are your plans, Jaeger?"

I felt a wave of depression with Kolb's macabre inventory. "To be in Munich by noon. I have an unpleasant duty to perform here."

"What do you want us to do?"

I shrugged. "Stay here until my headquarters can work out a disposition. Keep watch on the prisoners and the DP's until the police arrive. That sort of thing."

"Police?"

"Landespolizei, CIC, CID, District Constabulary, MP's, MG— the works. In case you didn't notice, there was trouble here last night and there will be a lot of explaining to do. Since the truck accident took out the phone line, I'll have to file a report in person when I arrive in the city."

The General gazed at the ceiling and made a little joke: "I wonder if someone in the vast array of officialdom will fix my sundeck."

"Don't count on it."

"You mean I'll have to fix it myself?"

"Don't count on that, either. You're automatic-arrest material now that you're—sane—again."

"Arrest, hm? Well," he sighed, "perhaps. But I don't think it in the cards."

"That's what you think."

The General smiled again, this time with a curious superiorit "I think that you and I will be associated for some time to com Jaeger, or whatever your name is. I think you will prevent m arrest. Why? Because I will pay you to."

I humphed. "There isn't enough money for that."

The General winked. "Not even a third of more than fou millions in your dollars?"

I stared at him as if he'd just turned into a petunia. "What d you mean?"

"I'll let you in on something, Jaeger," he purred, studying th end of his cigarette. "As the war was coming to an end, Marti Bormann took charge of hiding the Reich's cash assets. A po tion of these—one hundred tons of gold bullion and I don't kno how much in currency—was to be placed in the salt mines nea Merkers, and it was. Except for nearly ten troy tons of bullio that is. These tons Bormann diverted to his personal use. He a ranged to have roughly half of it hidden in some fifty two-hur dred-pound crates under the false floor in the garage here—th understanding being that I would have a share in it once he' made his exit from Berlin and joined me. The other half ha been spotted around the country—where, I don't know.

"Well, as you probably know, the cache at Merkers was seize by Patton's troops after a pair of housewives gossiped too mucl And, as your intelligence people probably have discovered b now, Bormann never made it out of Berlin. (Kurt Bednar—on of Behncke's Werewolf chieftains, you'll recall—was among th last to leave Berlin, and he told me he'd seen Bormann as dead a a kipper under a culvert near the command bunker there.) So, yo see, at least half of Bormann's private fortune is now mine."

I nodded. "Sure. But you're going to have to go some to pull i out of a truck that's now under three hundred feet of mountai lake water. Salvage parties would get nowhere at that depth an in those currents."

Kolb laughed easily. "Oh, that. Decoy, Jaeger. Decoy. Boxe of sand topped with a layer of stage-prop bullion. The bulk o what Bormann liked to call the Fliegerfreude gold is high and dry. Or low and dry, depending on how you look at it. You see, I expected someone might learn of Bormann's gold some day, and so Klottner and I took precautions. Secret precautions. Now, with Klottner gone, only I know where it is."

If I looked incredulous it was because I was. "You mean we went through all that crap last night to keep first Benhcke, then Hartmann, from running off with fifty boxes of sand?"

"That may be what you went through all that, ah, crap for, Jaeger. But I went through all that crap to save my life. I did not want to be assassinated for fifty boxes of sand."

"Well, where is the gold, then?" I asked stupidly.

Kolb waggled a finger. "Ah-ah-ah. Ask me no questions and I'll tell you no lies."

I tried to hide my annoyance, but it was like trying to hide a Zeppelin in a cookie jar. "So where does all this leave us?"

"We'll simply continue the way we've been going. You take charge of Kaufmann and eventually turn in all those nasty Nazis; I'll play the undercover mastermind and try to make up a few things to Christl."

"But the gold: what are your plans for that?"

The General stubbed out his cigarette. "Let's put it this way: you and I—and Christl, of course—are now very well-to-do."

"And in return I keep you out of jail, eh?"

"Precisely."

I sat thinking for a time, partly trying to digest the fact that I'd been offered the kind of bribe a speed-trap cop dreams of, partly trying to understand something else. To stifle the rising anger, I asked about the something else. "You weren't a bit surprised when Behncke made his play for the gold. Why?"

Kolb arose, went to the shattered window, and stood there, rocking gently on his heels and gazing out at the lake. He said, "Oh, he did surprise me, in a way. Of all the potential gold thieves of my acquaintance, he was among the last I suspected, because he took his Party assignments most seriously—when it came to following orders Behncke was usually an automaton. I simply underestimated his piggy-bank mentality, that's all."

"Piggy-bank?"

"Mm. Behncke was a strange, unfortunate man. I had never liked him, myself. He was primarily a sycophant, a type I despise. I honestly believe that he could have had a spectacular career in the Third Reich if it hadn't been for this trait of his. Behncke was a self-made man and, underneath all the obsequiousness, was really quite expert in business administration. But those foppish, fawning mannerisms of his irritated many of the Nazi crown princes, too—and they were a bunch rarely noted for their rejection of the yes-man, believe me. So Behncke, who had been a Nazi before the Beer Hall Putsch, climbed through a series of important but obscure fiscal and administrative positions in the SA and RJF without ever breaking out of that special kind of limbo prescribed for men of much talent and little taste who, in the effort to please the boss, only annoy him the more. You know the type, I'm sure.

"Behncke had another weakness which might well have been the basis of the first. He seemed to be morbidly preoccupied with security—personal security, I mean. He was no physical coward, God knows—I'd seen that in the Purge of '34 when he stood toe-to-toe with two SA fairies who had decided to resist. Shot it out with them, he did. Point-blank. But he was a son of a ragtag Ruhrland steelworker, and he'd grown up in abject poverty, and I think he never got over it. One of the favorite stories among middle-management wags in Berlin was Behncke's strongbox. He'd sit in a plush office roughly the size of a soccer field, issuing orders over three phones to some one hundred lackeys, and at his feet in the deskwell would be a padlocked tin box. Once, when his boss asked him what was in it, Behncke said that it held cash. 'I never again want to be without cash,' he said. He was known from then on as the 'million-Mark executive with the piggy-bank mind.'

"Well, yesterday, when I looked out the window and saw the size of the truck he was bringing to move a mere piano, I decided that the truck would make a hell of a piggy-bank. So I told Leo to play sick and cover us from upstairs, just in case Behncke had something silly on his mind. Only, I didn't know, of course, that Behncke had bought Leo with a promise of a share in the sand pile."

I looked around at him. "Leo was your confidant—had been with you for years. How come he didn't know the boxes in the garage were phonies?"

"Klottner, with the help of some Russian prisoners of war, had moved the real gold elsewhere while Leo and I were setting up house in Obermenzing before your arrival. I say again: only Klottner and I have shared the secret."

"What about the Russian PW's? The moving crew? They will know...."

The General sighed. "Klottner told me that they had been foolish enough to try to escape after the movement had been completed. Klottner said he was forced to shoot them."

I stood up and joined the General at the window, sicker now, and angrier. "Well," I said, "it's all very interesting. But I'm afraid you're still out of luck."

"How so?"

"I've had orders to stand by for reassignment. And you and the others are to be rounded up."

Kolb sat silent for a time, and I thought this was due to shocked surprise. But, as usual, I'd figured it wrong.

"Oh, well"—he smiled—"the offer still stands. They won't keep me in jail forever. And you'll be out of your army one day. And then you and Christl and I will get together and have a marvelous time spending our money. Eh?"

I gave him a narrow look. "That money's contraband, you know. It's illegal Nazi stuff, automatically impoundable."

"Only if it's found, Jaeger. Only if it's found."

I decided to come to the point. "Tell me straight out, General: why are you cutting me in on this? Why give me a share, when all you have to do is serve your time, then take all of it for yourself?"

Joachim Kolb nodded wry approval of my directness. He returned the favor: "Oh, believe me, Jaeger, I'd love to leave you out of the gold picture. I'd have been very happy to let you go on thinking, along with the rest of the world, that the gold was really at the bottom of the lake. But as I've told you—probably to the point of distraction—I want only to make my daughter happy. She will not be happy without you. I'm simply offering you the greatest inducement in my power to keep you near her."

"Does Chris know about this?"

"Of course not. She'd be mortified at the very thought—"

The words came in individual little bursts: "So what this means is that you're trying to buy me as a playmate for your daughter. Is that it?"

"Let's say I'm offering a kind of dowry. Do you accept?"

The kitchen door swung open, and Champion came through it, whistling "Rum and Coca-Cola." He paused. Clasping his hands under his chin and batting his eyelashes, he said mincingly, "Breakfast is ready, Your Majesties."

I did not look at the General on our way to the kitchen.

Champion took Kolb's elbow and asked with mock adulation, "Is it true, General, that you conquered a Communist agent *singlehanded?*"

"Why? Is there a law against it?"

"Probably. But you're a little young for that kind of thing, aren't you?"

"As a matter of fact," Kolb chuckled, "I've never felt younger."

From the corner of my eye I caught the gentle curve of her primly crossed legs, the fold of her hands in her lap. She was wearing the spectator pumps—brown and white and proper— that her father had withdrawn from an old Wehrmacht map carton. The General, awkward and clumsy-tongued, had confessed that he'd been saving the shoes for her since his last trip to Paris in '43, trying in a deprecatory way to minimize the gesture's significance and making it clear that he knew nothing of women's styles and preferences and perhaps they wouldn't do at all. She had thanked him stiltedly, her large eyes a pensive green, and had said very little after that. Apparently to cover his discomfort, her father had gone for a cigar. When he'd returned, she was wearing the shoes, and I noted the silent exchange of glances and the General's pink, embarrassed pleasure.

We were alone now, seated in the kitchen alcove and gazing out at the exuberant Sunday.

I was weighing the General's earlier speech again when she broke the silence. "I'm very sad," she said. "I sense that everything is over now and I'll not see you again."

"Probably not."

She unfolded her hands to brush her skirt. "I'll miss you terribly."

I considered her averted eyes, the soft down-turn of her lips. I said, "Don't worry. You won't be missing much."

She looked up, and her gaze was direct. "Why do you run yourself down so? Is this the way of American men? To disparage themselves? To discount their value?"

"I don't know about American men. I don't know anything about anything or anybody any more. The whole world is nothing but a great big stinking fraud."

"What has hurt you, Heinz?"

I humphed. "There. How's that for fraud? You don't even know my name."

"Heinz will suffice until you give me another."

"Don't be long-suffering and understanding, please. I can't stand female forebearance."

She laughed, and it surprised me. It had been a long time since I'd heard honest laughter. "Oh, I'm not long-suffering, I assure you," she said. "It's just that I can't be insensitive to a little boy who's been hurt, that's all."

"Little boy? Oh, you *are* in a female mood, aren't you?"

"I mean it. You've always been like a little boy."

"What in hell do you know about it?" I decided to get it over with. "You'd better forget about me. I'm not for you."

"Why not let me make such decisions?"

Something inside me stood up and began to pace. "Look," I said, "what kind of man would you be getting in me, for God's sake? I'm a man who isn't even sure himself any longer of what's real and what isn't. You'd never know when I went out the door if I was actually going where I said I was going, if I was saying yes and meaning no, if I laughed and meant to scream—you wouldn't know because I wouldn't even know myself. How could you settle for a man whose most highly developed skill—beyond lying, theft, murder, fornication, and duplicity—is his own confusion?"

She shifted in her chair and gave me a long green stare. Then she said in a small voice: "You're missing the point: a woman loves, and that's that. I don't care what you are or what you aren't.

265

Whoever you are, wherever you go, you'll need someone—some one to love you and care what happens to you and be glad when ever you might come by. Then you'll know that wherever you go or whatever you do in the world there's someone who thinks you're important and good. You'll no longer have to feel alone trapped in that horrid, solitary prison we build around ourselves when there's no one to share with. And I don't ask anything in return, believe me. I want only to be there if and when, by being there, I can help you. I love you, you see. And that's the way of love. You may learn that some day. . . ."

"Please don't love me."

"I have no choice."

"Find yourself another man. A man who knows who he is and where he's going."

"You couldn't say that if you loved me. You know that much, don't you?"

I pounded the table and heard myself shouting, "I say that *because* I love you!"

"Then that," she said serenely, "is all there is. Rationalize all you like, but you have no choice, either."

We fell silent and avoided each other's eyes.

At one point in the stillness she asked, "More coffee, Heinz?"

"Peter. Peter Klaussen."

"You see, Peter Klaussen? You love me, and already you've told me a truth."

TWENTY-NINE

For months I'd been living among traitors, and in all that time, I knew now, I had never really seen the true face of treason. Even at this very moment, when staring into the eyes of a traitor, I found it impossible to read beyond a man's façade for the inner sign of the turncoat. Behind the face was a face, but even now I could not see this second image—even with the proof assembled I could not see it.

Smith leaned forward across the Ops Chief's desk, his eyes widening. "You're *what?*"

"I'm arresting you on charges of collaboration with foreign agents, obstructing a U.S. officer in the discharge of his duties, conspiracy to steal contraband funds, and whatever else a good military lawyer can come up with."

Smith blinked, his face taking on a faint color. "You look awful, of course. But I had no idea you were really so ill—"

"I'm not ill. I'm charging you as an enemy of the United States."

Placing his hands flat on the desktop, Smith sank back in his chair. He seemed what they call very tired and drawn, and it occurred to me irrelevantly that Smith could probably be classified as a handsome man.

"Why did you do it, Smith? Why did you spring Hartmann? Didn't you *remember* that I knew you were the only one who could release him? Didn't you *realize* I'd see your connection with him? Didn't you *consider* the possibility that I might survive Hartmann's little shoot-'em-up? Why did you pull the rug on me, for God's sake?"

Seeming to be deep in thought, Smith did not answer.

"I'll tell you why," I said. "You're a Soviet agent. You're a thieving, murdering traitor, that's what you are."

The gray man smiled wanly. "You're a great one for melodrama, aren't you, Klaussen?"

"Cut out the crap. I'm serious. You're in trouble."

"Oh, shut up and sit down, will you?" Smith barked in sudden anger. "I'm sick and tired of this horse manure. Sit down, I said; I'm going to give you a little lesson in what trouble can really be."

"Don't try anything cute, Smith. . . ."

The major emitted a groan of frustration. "Oh, God. Sit down, will you, please: And stop looking like the goody in a Grade-C oater. Against my better judgment I'm going to explain some things to you."

Despite myself, I sat.

"You're right," Smith sighed resignedly. "I'm in trouble. But not in the way you think."

"So how, then?"

"Hartmann was known as 'Peppermint.' Hartmann was an American agent. When you killed him last night, you destroyed an operation I've been building—ever so delicately—since the summer of '44."

"Hartmann was an American agent?"

"Yes. A German, of course. But an agent working for us."

"You're joking."

"No joke."

"But he was going to kill me."

"I couldn't help that."

"But you'd *let* him kill me?"

"As I've often said, you're incredibly naïve, Klaussen. The truth is that Hartmann's success was of much greater importance to the United States than your survival was. When I learned the size of the truck Piggy-Bank Behncke was using to move the General's piano, I knew he must have found the gold. The only chance I had to save it for its proper purpose was to release Hartmann. If you died in the process, too bad."

I felt myself nodding, as if hearing the voice of sweetest reason. "You can prove all this, of course."

268

"I don't have to prove it. The rationale for your—expenditure—is on file at USFET."

"How does it go?"

"It goes like this: Heinrich Mueller, Gestapo chief, had been a Russophile for years and, as such, he became a member of the Rote Kapelle. But by last summer, after our landings in Normandy, he had become disillusioned with the Soviets and decided to switch allegiance to the Americans. As his go-between with our OSS people he used Hartmann, a Gestapo officer and fellow Kapelle member. I was made case officer in charge, and code names were assigned: 'Spike' for Mueller, 'Peppermint' for Hartmann, and 'Putzi' for me. It became apparent that Mueller's single greatest value was the possibility he offered for penetration of Soviet intelligence. We told Hartmann—'Peppermint,' that is—to tell Mueller, or 'Spike,' to stand by for such an assignment."

"You mean," I managed, "that all the time he was the arch-Nazi Mueller was really a Russian agent? An agent working against Hitler?"

"Essentially. But when he offered to double—that is, to become an ostensible Nazi chieftain thought by the Soviets to be working for them but actually working for us—we decided that we should hold him on ice until the war was over. We suspected that if he survived the war he would be taken in by Soviet Intelligence as a full-fledged member. If so, we'd have made a significant penetration. So we ordered Mueller, through Hartmann, to do whatever the Russians wanted him to do—to build Russian confidence in him in every possible way.

"Mueller's first postwar assignment from the Soviets was to develop an espionage ring in southern and western Germany—a ring that could be put to work on American, British, and French activities when the occupation ensued.

"Last winter Mueller learned of Martin Bormann's talk with Kolb and Behncke. It seemed to him that the Behncke Werewolf operation would offer a tailor-made apparatus for the Soviet purpose. All Mueller would have to do would be to penetrate the Behncke organization and, once Bormann had brought his gold out of hiding, assassinate Bormann, Kolb, and Behncke, take custody of the gold, and assume leadership of the Behncke group.

With Mueller in command, Behncke's so-called Werewolves would automatically become a Soviet apparatus financed with Nazi gold. Very tidy.

"Mueller's penetration of the Behncke group was made possible when Behncke decided that he needed a black-market specialist. Behncke asked Eugen Klottner, Kolb's confidant, to set it up. Klottner contacted Heinz Jaeger, an old Gestapo friend, and asked him to connive a transfer to Munich. What Klottner didn't know, of course, was that Jaeger was also one of Mueller's fellow Soviet agents. Jaeger told Mueller of Klottner's request, and Mueller saw he now had his working penetration of the Behncke group. 'Go down there,' Mueller told Jaeger, 'and keep me posted on things through Hartmann.' But, lo and behold, Kolb arranges the paradrop of one Peter Klaussen, and, lo and goddamned behold, when Klottner and Jaeger are killed in an air raid, said Peter Klaussen assumes the identity of said Heinz Jaeger. Hartmann told me that Mueller just about had a nervous breakdown. However, Mueller and Hartmann had no choice but to attempt repenetration, and they selected Christl Werner as their patsy."

"And," I grumbled, "when Behncke asked Berlin for confirmation of me as Jaeger, Mueller intercepted the request and sent Behncke the picture Hartmann had taken, is that it?"

"Yes, Bormann's secretary was a Mueller agent and it was easy for Mueller to read Bormann's mail." Smith paused for a moment, then went on. "Well, Klottner told Jaeger of the plan to collaborate with the Americans, since Klottner mistakenly believed Jaeger would be in sympathy with the idea. They drove down to Obermühlhausen to meet you and take you to Kolb. Before they left, though, Jaeger tipped Hartmann. Hartmann hopped on his cycle and ran down behind them to sneak a picture of you for Mueller's information. (It's SOP in the Soviet Intelligence to do such: whenever a new spook shows up, get him mugged fast—you might never get another chance.) But when he could find no trace of you after the bombing, Hartmann went to Frau Werner's place to see if anybody had survived. He found only you, of course."

"So you knew from the moment of my touchdown, practically, where I was and what I was doing."

"And when Hartmann asked me what to do about you, I told him to keep you fat and happy."

"Unless I got in the way, eh?"

"Unless you got in the way."

I closed my eyes, trying to swallow all this. Today was becoming a hell of a day. I said, "I sure got in the way last night, didn't I?"

"By knocking off Hartmann, you cut off my only contact with Mueller, now hiding God knows where. By running Bormann's gold beyond salvage into three hundred feet of water, you've made it necessary for the United States to use its own funds to finance Mueller's phony little apparatus—provided we ever find him again. You've screwed up a gorgeous chance to penetrate Soviet Intelligence, and you've cost your nation a fortune. In the *way*? Jesus to *Jesus!*"

Anger convening at the base of my neck, I snapped: "You could have avoided all of that if you'd filled me in. Don't give me all the blame."

Smith sighed through his nose, his thin nostrils flaring. He said, "You are naïve, aren't you? The first rule of espionage is to tell as few people as little as you can. If you think you can change that rule, Klaussen, you are a very silly fellow indeed."

"I'm very few people."

"But you knew a lot of the wrong people. How could I be sure you wouldn't bull your way into a jam and spill everything? Hm?"

"Tell me something," I said stiffly. "If I was such a peanut in your chewing gum, why didn't you withdraw me from the case as soon as I returned to Allied control?"

Smith's fingers drummed the desk top. "Hartmann and Mueller, at my direction, had been searching for months for the precise location of Bormann's gold. Reason: we wanted to keep it under absolute surveillance so that some bandit like Behncke wouldn't run off with it. We felt that you and the Werner woman might—by your very close association with Kolb—unwittingly pass along in your regular reports some clues as to where we should look. Furthermore—"

"It was you who kicked the MP's out of Kolb's Obermenzing house?"

"That's right. Hartmann wanted a close look at that place. He'd always had a hunch about it. Of the scores of places we examined, that and Kolb's father's hotel at Südberg were the last on our list."

"How about Fliegerfreude?"

"Ironically, that was one of the first we hit. Hartmann simply didn't look hard enough, I guess. Where was it, by the way?"

"Under the garage floor."

Smith blinked, and an odd expression came to his face. "So? Interesting." He paused, then: "Hartmann said he'd examined the garage very carefully."

"Then Hartmann was a liar. Either he didn't look carefully, as he told you, or he found the cache and didn't tell you."

Smith thought that over for what seemed to be a long time. I did, too.

"You mean," Smith said, as if to himself, "Hartmann could have known all along that the gold was at Fliegerfreude? And he didn't tell me because he might have had other plans?"

I sighed. "Did it ever occur to you that Mueller and Hartmann might have been playing the U.S. of A. for a patsy?"

"Like how?"

"Like this, for instance: they see the war is lost; they know Bormann is hiding gold; they ingratiate themselves with U.S. and Soviet intelligence sufficiently to be entrusted by both to track down the gold. When they find it, they kiss everybody good-bye and take off for parts unknown. With the loot."

Smith shook his head. "It doesn't hold up. If that were the case, why didn't they steal the gold as soon as Hartmann found it?"

"It takes some doing to make off with a load that big. Look at the trouble Behncke went to. Maybe Hartmann and Mueller were waiting for the right time; maybe their plans weren't complete; maybe a lot of things."

Smith did some more thinking, his eyes narrowed, staring unwaveringly at me. Then he spread his hands and said: "Well, it's all academic anyhow. The gold is now beyond recovery, and Hartmann's death cuts us off from all contact with Mueller. Besides, even if we were to find Mueller again, we could never really rely on him. If he had indeed been playing us for suckers, he'd do it again."

"No," I said evenly. "Not so. He could be made to play our game very straight and proper—regardless of what his intentions had been or would be."

"How so?"

"Blackmail. We simply could tell him to play the game our way or we'll betray him to the Soviets. The Reds would make short work of Mueller if they learned he'd been in dalliance with us good guys."

There was a period of silence, and I watched Smith's face go through a series of subtle changes. I was wondering about these when he laughed. He actually laughed. Aloud. And I noted with genuine interest that he had very good-looking teeth and he was indeed a handsome man. But I noticed something else, too: the laughter had a creepy sound to it. Something like, well, hysteria.

"Klaussen," he managed, "that's a delightfully dirty way of thinking. What a shame you haven't developed it." He took a deep breath, and added, "We thought of all that a long time ago, of course, and that's another one of the reasons you were kept on the case. By your very presence, you tended to keep Mueller and Hartmann honest. But how interesting it is to find that *you* can think in such a way. Remarkable."

I peered at him, instinct telling me that he had been sucking me in right along. "What's so damned funny?"

Smith withdrew a brief case from the deskwell and, after rummaging a bit, produced an envelope. "I have here," he said, shaking his head in sad amusement, "G-2's orders assigning you to my job."

I manufactured a cough to hide my surprise. "*Your* job?"

"Yes," he said, his eyes overly bright and strange, "I'm being transferred to Washington at the end of the month, and G-2 thinks you're the man to salvage Appleseed—code name, by the way, for our little Mueller ploy. Can you imagine? You, in my job? Ha-ha."

"And just what is this job?" I asked, trying to ignore the alarming redness that had come to his cheeks.

"First: Find Mueller, wherever he may be in this sorry old world, and set him up as chief of a Soviet espionage net here in West Germany. Second: Help him succeed so well in his work that he's promoted to a key post—somewhere, anywhere—in the Soviet intelligence policy-making chain. Ha-ha."

"That could take years and years."

"Of course. But no matter. You won't take the job. You'll wait out your service points and go home and become a Sunday-school teacher. You're a natural-born Sunday-school teacher."

"You mean I have a choice?"

"G-2 said you must volunteer for Appleseed. If you decline, home you go. But this, too, is all academic. Even if you took the job you wouldn't succeed."

"Think so?"

"Know so."

"How can you be sure?"

"Money. There's never enough money. The only chance we had of making Appleseed work in the first place was the Bormann gold. But that's gone now, and you'd have to connive, bootlick, sweat, beg, plead, argue, and prostitute yourself to get enough U.S. funds to pay your own hotel bills, let alone support a Soviet spy ring. Appleseed is doomed to starve to death, my boy, no matter who takes it over now. It's doomed in spades if a Sunday-school teacher like you takes it over."

I found I had no trouble keeping my voice calm, because now I could see it all. Just like that I could see it. "You know what? I think I've got your number, Smith. You're brokenhearted over your failure at this thing. You're brokenhearted, by God. . . ."

"I really don't care what you think, Klaussen. Nor do I care about Appleseed, one way or the other. It's no longer my concern."

"On the contrary," I said, feeling a melancholy, "I think you care very much."

"Here are your assignment orders," Smith smoldered. "If you accept, clear out of here and get to work. If you don't, say so, and I'll take over until the foreclosure is finished and my successor has been selected. But either way, just leave me alone. . . ."

I shifted in my chair and watched a high-flying plane etch a chalky contrail across the blue that filled the upper window. Suddenly I had become very drowsy.

"Smith?"

"Well, what is it?"

"May I have a couple of days to think it over? I want to talk money with a guy."

"One day—no more."

Blinking away the gathering torpor, I stood up and went to the

274

door. Then, not sure why, I turned, looked Smith straight in the eye, and gave him my best OCS salute.

Caught off balance, he nevertheless managed to touch his brow. He cleared his throat and drew himself up.

"The United States needs people like me," he murmured. "It's a very sad thing, but the United States needs people like me."

What could I say to that?

PART 4 PENETRATION

THIRTY

From the Philadelphia *Inquirer*, January 8, 1964:

Ex-Gestapo Chief Reported Alive

HAMBURG, Germany, Jan. 7 (AP).—The West German magazine Der Stern said Tuesday the last chief of the Nazi Gestapo, SS. Lt. Gen. Heinrich Mueller, holds an influential intelligence post in Communist Albania.

Mueller was the immediate superior of Adolf Eichmann, hanged in Israel in 1962 for his part in the massacres of the Jews. The West German Central War Crimes Investigation Agency lists Mueller as killed in the battle of Berlin.

Sources close to the agency expressed skepticism about Der Stern's report.